Traces of Magic
in a Harsh and Bloody Land

Book I
Magic in the Valley

Rev. Patrick J. Dolan, PhD, SThD

Traces of Magic in a Dark and Bloody Land
Book I: Magic in the Valley

For information contact:
Rev. Pat Dolan
903 Fairdale Rd, Fairdale KY 40118, USA
MUCL@hotmail.com

Cover Art: Pat Dolan

Book Layout: Tim Schoenbachler

First Printing: October 2018

TABLE OF CONTENTS

CLUES TO TRACES OF MAGIC

Many visitors to Kentucky each year enjoy the excitement of the Derby Festival and smile at the combination of backwoods charm and traditional elegance that makes up the mystique of the Bluegrass State. Those who know the history of Kentucky, however, wince at its nearly three centuries of conflict and bloodshed. From the kidnap raids and scalpings of the late 1700s through the brother-against-brother battles of the Civil War to the mountain and mining violence of the Hatfield-McCoy feud, blood has continued to stain the rocks and soil of the Bluegrass, the Knobs, the Pennyroyal, and the Cumberland Plateau. It seems appropriate, therefore, that the very name Kentucky, in at least one Native American woodland dialect, means "harsh and bloodied land."

But Kentucky's dark name actually came long before its checkered history. Was it merely prophetic, or did the name really refer to a pre-history even more tragic?

Hints at that pre-history come to us from a variety of sources. First is the unexplained fact that the whole Bluegrass area was strangely uninhabited when European explorers in the 1600s and 1700s visited the North American continent and ran into significantly advanced native societies all around the Bluegrass. Second is the clear archeological evidence that the Norse were in North America both in 998-1000 AD at l'Anse aux Meadow, Newfoundland, and in 1362 in Canada and Minnesota, as documented both in Norwegian chronicles and the Kensington Stone they left behind. That stone and those chronicles show that the explorers were looking for a lost colony large enough to warrant searching for. Similarly, many Irish swear to the veracity of the account of St. Brendan the Navigator's visit to North America at the same time early Irish Monks went every other direction. There is even strong evidence that the Carthaginians were in South America centuries earlier, for their coins depict a clear map of the world that specifically includes Brazil.

The third hint is linguistic. The Mandan language (from tribes dwelling along the Missouri River) is remarkably similar to medieval Welsh; and there are countless tales of ancient Welsh prayer books and bibles among them. Moreover, there is more than just a lingering legend of the extermination of a group of blond, welsh-speaking settlers on Corn Island in the Ohio River about a century or two before the arrival of French Explorers in the 1600s. These Welsh were said to be the remnants of a much larger colony that came with Prince Madoc in the 1100s in two trips of his 11 vessel fleet – bringing groups from northern Wales (and very likely Ireland where they would have stopped on their way west) as well as the druidic culture mingled with Christian belief and discipline. The city of New Albany, Indiana, actually traces families back to those who bear a family curse for having mercilessly exterminated this last group of Celts.

The fourth hint is a piece of physical evidence. At the top of some ridges or "knobs" in Marion County, Kentucky, sit a series of unusual stone walls. They are on private property primarily on the hilltop at 37 degrees, 28 minutes, 35 seconds north, and 85 degrees, 14 minutes, 39 seconds west. Some observers have said that they look like Inca-style constructions. Chemist that I am, I thought they looked like they had been crystallized there – much like some of the rock formations in Yellowstone National Park, but with no nearby volcanic activity to produce such formations in Kentucky. The blocks averaged about two feet by four feet by a foot deep. Some were perfectly squared; others were precisely angled. They appear to have been shaped without the use of tools. Some had tumbled from an original position. I could not move any of them. They have been there since before anyone can remember – certainly before any settlers came to Kentucky in the 1700's.

No Indian legends account for these stones, which are more like European castle foundations than Inca handiwork. Could the early Celts or Prince Madoc's colony have come here in the twelfth century up from Mobile Bay just as the legend claims, following in the heritage of the Irish monks who traveled all over Europe to re-educate and re-evangelize it in the seventh and eighth centuries?

Few people pay any attention to the legends of Celtic voyages, but just as few gave any credence to the Norse claims until archeology verified them. It is intriguing to wonder if there ever were Celtic colonists here. I know of no records in Rome of their clergy, even though there are just a few open records of Norse clergy in Greenland around that same time. Could the periodic church feuds between the Welsh and the English hierarchy at the time explain the absence of such documents? Who knows what communication the renegade Irish pirates raiding the west coast of all the British Iles at that time may have stopped? (Are there records in Rome we don't know about?) Could early Celts indeed have been here and be responsible for those stones on the hilltop? If not them, who else?

Wherever they may have come from, it is entertaining to wonder what a Celtic-Norse settlement in early North America might have been like. Were the North American Celts small and jovial like many Irish-Americans today – with a bit of leprechaun in their heritage; or were they as reclusive as elves compared to the more-native Indians? Were their religious prayers and European-style healings and extensive learning interpreted as magic by the Northern Indians, just as the Spanish armor and gunpowder were viewed by the Aztecs of Mexico and the Incas of Peru a few centuries later? Similarly, would most of our ordinary modern devices like microwave ovens or antibiotic medicines or artificial joints or limbs or cell phones or even flashlights be viewed as magic back then no matter how we would try to explain them?

Parallel to how clergy progress from being seminarians to deacons to priests to bishops with increasing sacramental abilities, users of magic in medieval times would start with some particular skill and "grow in wisdom and age and grace" with time and practice. Do not skills in music or medicine develop and increase that same way even today? Though we do not know whether spells of any kind were ever real or simply imagined, we do know that brain waves do exist and are detectable, and that even today we use only a small portion of our brains. Was medieval Celtic magic simply rudimentary science or was it artful deception or was it diabolical assistance or was it parapsychology or an older form of "new age" practices – or some combination of all of these influences on human belief and behavior? Whatever it was, some grew in their ability to use it (from just a few simple spells as beginners to many and powerful spells as masters) and paved the way for modern science, medicine and engineering in the process.

Military skills also developed in Western and Eastern cultures over time. In this frontier land, did knighthood continue to flourish here among the Bluegrass Celts as it did among their cousins in England and France and other "Faithful" in Germany or Italy? Did they continue the sacred healing orders like the ones that spawned the Templars or the Knights of Malta? How sure are we that they did not?

A number of other questions spring up naturally. Did the Norsemen seem like barbarians by comparison? Did Druidic lore survive and help develop groups of forest-dwelling Rangers to protect outlying districts, much like the Texas Rangers did for the Southwestern Frontier in the late 1800's? And, other than the Celtic dialect spoken by the Mandan tribe or the medieval European style of house-building and farming of the Lumbee and other "civilized tribes" in the Carolinas and Georgia, were there any lingering traces of the Celts when other Europeans finally reached the interior of the continent? Besides the various coins and pieces of Celtic armor referenced in the New Albany, Indiana, records, are there any traces that still linger even today, like those strange stone walls, waiting only for us to look carefully enough to notice them?

We don't know what happened to these Celtic and Norse colonists who might have been here but who left little trace in these areas of Kentucky strangely uninhabited by any of the nearby Indian tribes when Europeans came again over the Appalachians. Perhaps the following (purely fictional) story from those same mountains and the "knobs" in the area between the Ohio and Cumberland Rivers comes as close to the truth as any explanation found so far. You be the judge.

Fr. Patrick J. Dolan, PhD, SThD
Teresa of Calcutta Parish, Fairdale KY
CH (BG-R) Army National Guard

Coming Soon...

Book II: The Curse of the Spell Book
Book III: Completing the Circle
Book IV: Healing Down to the Roots

Cast of Characters

(in partial order of appearance)
Characters may be listed in more than one category,
even if not active in the story.

Paladins

Mike Stilwater
Ray Hillman
Clement Horssemaster (Ambrosian)
Ron King
Sam Whitetail
Andrew Javin [Croatoan]
Thomas Osborne (Vincentian)
John-Baptist (Laurentine)
Nathan Eaglet
Peter Hawkwing
Herman Saddleman
Eddie Windlass
Isaac Hacker
Joshua Plowman
Roger Plowman (infirmarian)
Templar (unnamed)

Clergy

Fr. Patrick Elfkind
Bishops (unnamed)
Msgr. James Beaumont
Msgr. Kieley
Fr. Gregory Oxentrail
Fr. Caleb
Fr. Klaus Rainard
Fr. Peter Dwarfkind
Fr. Lawrence [Croatoan]
Br. Ansgar
Ben Hillman (seminarian)

Druids

Heather Prairiedove
Mildred
Lucas Greyfox
Forest
Daniel Redleaf
Woody
Dusty
Jimmy
Eric Branchwalker
2 young scribes

Magic Users

Patrick Elfkind
William Magus (dec.)
James Meaderer (dec.)
Kresov Wilson
Edgar Adcautelam
Philip Treebark
Leo Ridgewalker
Appr. Lawrence Gmellin
Paul Jugler
Rod Hayfield
Edmund Paramenter
Roy Oysterman
Peter Dubious
Joseph Warden
Henry Ralston
Nick Earthenglow
Dean Whitcomb
Gus Fideles
Apprentice Freddie Cooper

Assassins Guild
Nadine Wilson
Eddie Banker
George Paddlefoot
several others unnamed....

Thieves & Bards
William Wheatfield (Weed)
Nick Earthenglow
Benedict Prowler
Gilbert Vixenbrood
Colt (William Coltan)
Kevin Robinsong

Rangers & Barbarians
Kilian Eagleclaw (and family)
Alex Runningbear (and family)
Rosalie Hillman
Rueben Playbear

Animals
Jake & Sir Wolf
Whitewind
Blue Cloud
Starfield
Sunbridge

Bauers & Innkeepers & Lawmen
Cutter & Sky & kids
Adam Greyhorse (and family)
Jonathan Greyhorse
Tall Paul
Mary Lou
CPL Mark Cobbler
CPL Johnny Adamson
Don Ironfist (Field Sheriff)

Herbert Crowman (Constable)
Bobby Foxcub (Deputy)

Royal Council
Duke Nathanial
Count Robert Fielder, Cpt of Royal Guard
Edward Fuller of the Textile Guilds
Albert Baker of the Food Guilds
Joseph Runner of the Transport Guilds
Paul Cutter of the Forest and Fuel Guilds
John Mason of the Construction Guilds
Ben Coppersmith of the Fine Crafts Guilds
Louis Banks of the Commerce Guilds and the exchequer
Edgar Adcautelam of the Magic Users Guild
Judge Hugh Adamson of the Legal Guild
Madam Nadine Wilson of the Arts Council
Paladin Clement Horsemaster, the Holy Cross Ambrosian
Monsignor James Beaumont, Rector of the Cathedral

Map of the Valley

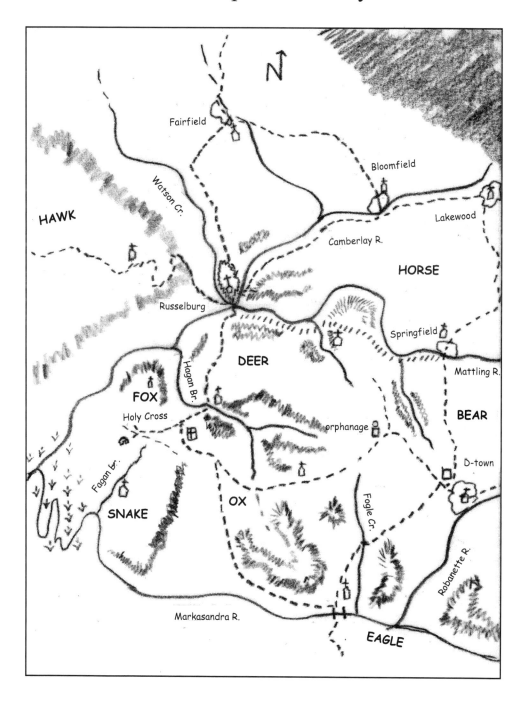

Chapter 1
THE HOLLY GATHERING

Dwarven Proverb:
There is a reason that GIFT is the
ancient barbarian (anti-magic) word for poison.

The winter had been suddenly cold. Sub-zero weather had struck with its icy sword on Christmas Eve with almost no snow cover to protect the sleeping plants. On some of the cold, still nights one could even hear the branches crack – like bones breaking. Cold wounds cut deep. The dryness of January and February didn't heal those wounds. Many of the trees, especially the younger ones, would not wake up this spring.

But time waits neither for man nor for nature. Lent began with more ashes than usual: one thing after another broke down, there was no trapping season to speak of, and our valley had several unexpected deaths. There was more howling than usual in the hills, and more "lost" animals. Yet Lent trudged on and holy week was upon us – which meant gathering the dead holly branches for the paschal fire. So Patrick Elfkind, the youngest of the clerics here, asked his friend and blood-brother Kilian Eagle-claw if he would like to help gather wood for that fire. Because he would need to take off half a day from this week's job of manure shoveling and spreading, Patrick had to ask Kilian's parents. Reluctantly they let him go with him to the far side of Gunner Mountain with Jake, their wolf-dog, to gather the winter-killed wood from the tops of living trees. Kilian's fiancée, Heather Prairie-dove, a slender young druidess with long dark hair and deep blue, almost violet eyes, had not been feeling well all winter and hadn't been out much. So since the day promised to be unseasonably warm, her druidic family group allowed her to go with them for the walk and the fresh air.

The morning had dawned bright but somehow not cheerful: the sun rose pale and tarnished in the empty sky. Its unfiltered light made even the repaired portions of the town's wooden and waddle & daub houses look faded and brittle. The dirt streets and split-rail fences felt barren, almost withered, and the early-flowering trees like the greybark and wild crabapple were still just blossomless shadows. Since Patrick was also a journeyman magic user, he had intended to stop at the orphanage on the way back from gathering wood to entertain the young-uns there with some songs, dance and a little magic. He brought props and had memorized some entertainment spells like ventriloquism and create images as well as the more typical outdoor spells like spider web and magic dart burst and cure. He had also grabbed a few small toys as well as his one-wheeled wood sledge which collapsed so completely that folks considered it a magic device. But the temper of the day felt ominous enough, the hills and forest strangely "out of tune," that he used an augury-like prayer right away to see if he and Heather had indeed chosen the best spells for that day. A favorable answer came to him: a prayerful serenity.

While Kilian finished sharpening his dagger and double-headed (woodcutter-stonecutter) axe as he sat on the cracked oak steps outside the rectory back door, Patrick bundled those few little toys into his rucksack along with his collapsed wood sledge there, and Heather packed some bread and cheese and carrots and fruit for lunch. The air began to grow sultry as Kilian and Heather followed Patrick and Jake through his back yard, between two of the stores near the red stained church, across an alley and down a few streets out into the fields south of town. Though all three of them had begun to sweat heavily even before they reached the woodlot at the northern foot of the mountain, Heather still felt cold. Kilian insisted that she wear his green leaf-patterned ranger's cloak and made her rest a few minutes while he swapped stories with his buddy Alex Running-bear, known by everyone around as "the barbarian" since he had been a little boy. His relatives in the Bear Clan, the only one of the eight valley clans that really came from Viking stock, considered the name a compliment.

Though very skilled for an apprentice wood-carver, Alex or "Lex" to his friends wasn't experienced enough yet to work in the shop in town with his father and older brother. But the hard labor in the wood lot kept his tall broad-shouldered frame tanned and well-muscled; and he kept his straw-colored hair short (and cool). Kilian was a hand's-breadth shorter than Alex, with dark wiry hair and just the beginnings of a beard. They both had finished school and had been confirmed in church, and only a few weeks ago they had dragged Patrick along with them to undergo the trial to become braves in their respective clans. Wearing only a loin cloth and with no weapons, they had "braved" the elements individually for three days and three nights and had not only survived but found the medicinal herbs and special items required to achieve that status in their clans. Each got a special tattoo-like marking in the ceremony, and like all the young braves would find any excuse to not wear a shirt so as to show off that status. Indeed, all summer and whenever there was a warm day, it was normal for males in the Markasandra valley to wear a sweat-band or a buckskin vest or apron perhaps, but no shirt.

Though Kilian's buckskin leggings and vest and forest-green flannel shirt fit him well enough, his body looked awk-ward. With long pointed ears like Patrick's, but with a mischievous twist to the shape of his mouth, he looked more like an elongated dwarf than human or half-elf. Yet his knife sheath and quiver and bow fit him well enough, and his body was coordinated and strong. Both he and Lex could hold their own in a fight in the woods, or in town, and had – often. In fact, in the 2 years since they had finished schooling and had done their months of military training before going into "range farming" and wood apprenticeship respectively, they had cracked more than their share of bones (their own and others') in the usual tavern brawls – and in accidents from taking risks to help others. Don Ironfist, the field sheriff, and even Herb Crowman, the Dennistown constable, had gotten to know them both very well, but couldn't help but like them anyway.

When Patrick asked politely if he could leave the sack of props and toys there to pick up on his way back, Alex grumped about having to work and not being able to come along; but the sparkle in Lex's eyes betrayed just as strong an interest in the toys. His promise to safeguard the toys did not mean that they would go un-played with. In return he made them promise:

"If y'all happen t' spot the scraggy pack o' wolves's been carryin' off our ranch stock, you whistle for me right away!"

"Me and Jake can handle 'em easy," replied Kilian, smiling confidently, as he balanced his dagger on his finger, "if Heather don't try 'n' stop me."

Heather pretended to throw him an angry glance, but the hint of a smile on her lips betrayed her. She then turned and looked questioningly at Alex. Though Alex had hunted several times with Kilian and knew his ranger skills were formidable, Heather could see by the hint of his eyebrows knitting together that he was genuinely concerned about their being out that far south of town. Lex felt a little reassured when Heather told him that they knew (though they weren't supposed to know) that their friend Michael Still-water, the paladin whose family had lived next door to hers when they were both toddlers, was doing his isolation training (the final portion of his third year's duties in preparation for his yearly vows) somewhere nearby there. As they left, they agreed with Alex to whistle twice if they needed him.

Kilian, in addition to his weapons, carried on his equipment belt their common canteen and the folded up wood carrier. Patrick insisted on carrying his bow-saw, the tree balm and his medicine pouch with the components he needed for his good magic. Heather, sick as she was, carried their lunch – since Kilian couldn't be trusted with it.

They had to approach the holly grove over the summit of Gunner Mountain, since its southern, wild side drops off rapidly. On the southeast flank were the Yellow Cliffs of starkly beautiful sandstone; on the southwest, the limestone Gray Cliffs shone like a half-buried skeleton when looked at from the ancient temple across Fogle Creek or from the valley of the Markasandra into which it flows just south of the cliffs. Between the two sets of cliffs a thorny tangle of greenbrier and dense cedar made the whole southern face of the mountain virtually inaccessible from the road running along both rivers. On a small knoll atop the Gray Cliffs, in direct sight of the temple far to the northwest, grew the holly trees. Patrick's heart sank when he saw them, for one could build a paschal fire the size of St. Stephen's church with all the dead wood still in the trees. At the sight of so much tree destruction Heather was appalled: the shock to her forest-sensitized spirit left her body rigid and her eyes glassy. Kilian had to shake her out of it. But they'd have to leave most of the wood there till later; for, besides the planned orphanage visit, holy week, with confessions and all, was too short for this much outside work.

Patrick had just begun the ritual prayers and had removed his tan leather armor-vest and badly worn green shirt so that it wouldn't catch in the holly trees. He rubbed a glob of tree-balm on his left shoulder (so he could easily reach it to put it on the parts of the holly trees he'd cut or break) when a very distant whimper seemed to waft its way toward them over the mountain. Immediately each stopped and looked at the others, not really sure they even heard it. Kilian went back to practicing his knife throwing in the nearby winter-dry grass where Jake would actually leap and catch them in the air and bring them back to him. Heather continued slicing the apple and pear, and the cheese and brown bread for lunch, while Patrick finished the ritual prayers, put his left arm through the bow-saw, and braced himself for the 300 or so tiny cuts he'd get as he climbed the holly tree. Ancient legends claim that elf-blood is the sacrificial price one pays to the forest for that hallowed wood. It's a reasonable price, but it still hurts.

The second cry reached them when Patrick was in the top of the tree and had dropped only two of the tree branches he needed. It sounded almost like the pain cry a horse gives when stung by hornets – only more desperate and getting closer. By the time Patrick got down they could hear growling and thrashing in the distance. He was bleeding in several places, including from one large gash above his left eye from which blood kept dripping down his nose. Kilian would have teased him about it, but was more intent on the unusual movement nearby in the forest, and ran to get his bow. Patrick grabbed a carrot (and got blood all over it), asked Heather to cast her Speak with Animals spell on him, and ran toward the disturbance.

Chapter 2
THE UNICORN AND THE SHADOW BEARS

He must have looked rather strange to the unicorn, walking slowly toward him wearing only his boots and tan deerskin leggings, bleeding in several places, smeared with amber colored tree balm, and holding out both hands – one with a carrot in it, the other holding up a cross, his holy symbol. Whitewind stood very still for a moment as his gaze pierced through the half-elf. By now the druidess's spell started to take effect; so Patrick's greeting of "Peace and health to you," as well as his obviously good alignment, allowed him to approach the badly wounded unicorn.

"I thank thee for thine gr-greeting" he replied, "but thou and thine art in danger. Behind me commeth a dark wah-wizard wha-with assa-a-assins and-d mha-many drog-he-e-eda..."

All three of them shuddered involuntarily at that terror word: drogheda, the legendary black-shadow bears, part animal and part ghost. They barely heard the unicorn continue: "Rha-run! Lha-leave me and-d they mighest ha-halt at me-e. Rha-run quickly! Nha-now!"

"No, we will not leave you like this; we..."

"Nho-no time, flee whilst thou canst...they be too strong for ye..."

"We'll fight anyone," interrupted Kilian, dropping his bow and swinging his axe around his head. "Let them try to..."

"Nho-no time!"

"You're right," Patrick interjected, "so don't interrupt. Just enjoy your carrot," he ordered as he practically shoved it in his mouth. Whitewind was too surprised to react. Patrick continued in a clear, straightforward tone of voice that lacked his usual lilt:

"Heather, cast your Entangle Spell to protect us. Kil', bring Jake over so he can help us."

"Oh, he'll fight automatically," said Kilian confidently.

"But I don't want him to fight; we need him to lead them away," explained Patrick.

"He won't go without me," Kilian replied firmly, "so don't even think about it!"

"Look, the unicorn's right," Patrick argued. "If he couldn't handle them, how can we? A sorcerer? Droghedae? Assassins? We don't have a chance! Think of Heather."

"There's no way I'm gonna' run and leave him ..." They were interrupted by shouts and curses coming from the northeast: a sign that the entangle spell had taken effect, but would only slow down the hunting party.

"You hear that?" whispered Patrick emphatically. "They want this unicorn – who knows what for. We can't fight them and I don't want to leave him either; so let's steal him to get him home safe. Use the thief part of you!"

"Now you're talking," Kilian whispered back as he pulled out his black-handled dagger. "What do you want us to do?"

"Tell Jake I'm going to put a spell on him – which will hurt a bit."

"Are you crazy?" shouted Kilian.

"Quiet!" cautioned Heather.

"Are you crazy?" Kilian whispered, "do you think ..." but by now Patrick had cut off a lock of his own short brown hair, a piece from two of his fingernails and dipped both in his own blood from the holly wounds, which was just starting to congeal. So Kilian held Jake calmly as Patrick made a small cut on Jake's back and put the bloodied hair and nails in it all while muttering something. Immediately the pieces disappeared and the wound closed up; and while Patrick, still muttering, gazed intently at Whitewind while pointing at Jake, the wolf-dog grew taller, leaner, and bright white. When the horn began to grow from Jake's now horse-like (or elk-like) forehead, Kilian began to get the idea.

As Patrick finished the spell and pulled a tiny vial of an oily yellow potion from his medicine pouch, he explained to Kilian in hushed tones, "You and Jake are going to lead them away from here all the way out of the forest. Try to confuse and tire them while we try to cure the unicorn. Let Jake run his usual wide circles further and further from here. When you've lost them, use your ranger sense to reach Mike without being discovered. We'll try to alert Alex and meet you there. Maybe you can even lead them into one of your traps. Get your cloak back from Heather so you can stay hidden, but let Jake be seen now and then. I'll start them your way with my Ventriloquism Spell." Kilian nodded slightly. Patrick grasped his left arm firmly with his own, looked him in the eye for a split second, and then said with more fear than hope, "May the Lord of the Rangers guide you both."

They both let go slowly. Then as Patrick put the vial of yellow oil on a flat rock and picked up another to crush it, he called softly over his shoulder, "Heather would you please prepare your invisibility-to-animals spell for you and me while I finish this?" Watching his brother stand there indecisively for the moment he pleaded, "Kil, get moving, now – or the stench will catch you!"

Again Patrick began muttering the ventriloquism spell as Kilian walked up to Heather, took her slender chin gently in his right hand and kissed her once on her forehead. She hugged him tightly, and then he was gone. Jake, following him in the image of a unicorn, was all that she or the half-elf could see.

By now the sounds of growling, hoof-slashing and twigs snapping that Patrick had conjured had started drifting away from the area where he had broken open the skunk musk. Patrick used his wood sledge as a carrycart under Whitewind, who had now just about passed out from the two poisoned arrows in him; and Heather cast her untrack spell on them. As she led the way, they moved around behind the knoll with the holly trees and out onto a ledge in the gray cliffs just barely wide enough for the three of them as the first of the droghedae, the dreaded black-shadow bears, broke through the entangled brush. Claws bared and forepaws whipping about, it stood there upright, its midnight-hued fur shimmering as it pulsed in and out of phase. Almost twice the size of the unicorn, its huge body swayed from side to side as if ready to spring into a fight. Saliva dripped from its snout as it flung its head back, recoiling from the skunk smell. It was then that Heather remembered their packs and tools. Patrick saw her turn to go back and grabbed her arm.

"Our equipment," she whispered plaintively, "it'll give us away."

"You're still too weak to carry it all," he reminded her, "and we can't risk two trips. I'm going."

"But you can't get by the unicorn. The ledge is too narrow."

"Watch me."

As a second drogheda lumbered into the clearing, the half-elf leaped up, grabbed an overhanging branch, and swung clear over Whitewind. Heather crouched down to avoid him as the cedar whose limb Patrick hung on started to come loose. He almost lost his balance as he touched down, scattering bits of dirt on Heather. She bent over even further and cradled the unicorn's head in her lap. Patrick then snuck out of the hiding place as a third and fourth beast joined the others. Quickly he grabbed the two packs and stuffed the cleric equipment and their lunch in them. These disappeared from the conjured animals' view as he touched them. Then he noticed his green shirt, vest and bow-saw just as he heard some humans cursing the forest in words that only assassins would use. He threw the saw over his shoulder and held his clothing in his teeth as he raced to the cliff ledge with both arms full of equipment. The two city assassins, who didn't like being in the woods and hated the entanglement, didn't notice the slight rustle the other

24

side of some big holly trees – so distracted were they by the skunk smell – and Patrick's trail disappeared in the "untrack spell" dweomer.

The animal sounds had drifted off in the direction Jake had taken due to the Ventriloquism Spell: so when the final two droghedae arrived, followed by the sorcerer and the other assassins, they smelt and saw "evidence" of a chance encounter between the first Drogheda and what must have been at least one skunk. A glimpse or two of Jake was all they needed to lure them in his direction and away from the smell that was so bad that they didn't feel like investigating the area too closely.

When it sounded as if they had all chased Jake, Patrick risked a glance – hoping that no humans remained behind. One of the assassins, a bounty hunter, dressed in dingy brown and gray and moldy green rather than in black, lingered a while, studying the ground doubtfully. He noticed the broken vial and picked it up, then discarded it very quickly because of the smell. He looked around just a bit further, then, instead of following Jake, he went off in the direction Kilian had taken. When everything looked safe, Patrick pulled out the two arrows, dripping their crimson blood mixed with the swirls of a blue-black oil. He wiped the oil off the wounds and tried a curative spell. It didn't work.

Whitewind opened his eyes a bit and tried to speak but couldn't. He moved his horn slightly and rolled his eyes back as if to say that even his horn couldn't work on this poison. As Heather stroked his mane to soothe him she got the feeling that her hands could almost touch his thoughts, that he was trying to send them: his regret at trying to toy with these hunters, thinking he could outrun them; his fear of teleporting so close to the unicorn herd, wanting to lead them further away before teleporting back; his surprise that the arrows followed him even when he did teleport; and his despair at feeling the poison – made from parts of another unicorn, his friend Starfield – slowly take over his body.

As Heather related these thoughts, almost in a trance, Patrick who had been cleaning out the two deep wounds, finished it slowly and deliberately and looked through the still barren dogwood branches up at the hazy, tornado season sky. Then he looked at Heather and said with an almost disquieting calmness:

"We have only one chance. Like most magic, what you call your un-poison spell and we call neutralization won't work on him; but it might on me. Get ready to cast it when I take in his poisoned blood. If it works, I'll transfer my blood back to him to undo the damage."

"But what if it doesn't work?" Heather asked hesitantly.

"Then remember me to your grandchildren."

As she started to argue he said firmly, "Look, nothing else is working. It's our only chance: his only chance."

Patrick picked up one of the two razor-sharp arrows and held it in both hands in front of him. He said softly, just once, "Help me, Lord" and cut two short, shallow gashes inside his left arm on the veins just above and below the elbow. He tried to put that blood stream on the wounds on Whitewind's side, but it wouldn't reach right, so he cut a couple of gashes on his own shoulder as well. He laid his shoulder against the unicorn's wounds and felt the blood mix. He put his right hand on the unicorn's horn and touched Whitewind's jugular vein with his left, causing more poisoned blood to spurt into him. He felt Heather's hands on his head, reaching through his short brown hair, touching his skin, and heard her whisper some strange words tinged with plaintive desperation into his pointed ears. But he felt himself getting weaker and weaker, going under as pain slowly but resolutely moved through him.

Chapter 3
The Ranger and the Huntsman

Troy, the bounty hunter who had lingered in the clearing, scratched the back of his neck beneath his greasy black hair and went over the "evidence" in his mind as he followed the boot trail rather than the unicorn as the others had done. Things didn't seem to fit. The noise as they approached sounded like a skunk but there were no skunk tracks – and no blood. "At least I know where the smell came from…" he mused as he remembered the broken vial. "When we got there the droghedae had been confused: as if they knew something and didn't know it. Then there was the unicorn that still looked wounded but ran and jumped more like a deer, jumped differently than it did before. And of course there was the Entangle Spell – which almost shouted 'druid' – or ranger. Perhaps that guy and his dog who made these tracks is a ranger – or an ex-ranger like me. Competition! Whoever it is, they're not going to steal my kill. Let them try to outsmart me, they've met their match. They may get something away from me for a while, but I'll get even with them or 'more than even' when they least expect me. Maybe I'll even get all three of them together; the whole group would be fun to kill – more challenge than the other unicorn we trapped with that wimpy "animal holding" spell on our ropes. I'll immobilize them first, perhaps with a paralyzing poison, and gloat as I make them watch me tear out the unicorn's heart. Then I'll kill them: with something slow and satisfying – like feeding parts of them to the droghedae. I can just see the shadow bears standing up, begging for them. Ha! Let them bleat for help that doesn't come – like the fawn whose mother I frightened away did when I tightened my hands around its neck just before I snapped it." As these remembered images crossed his mind he let out his icy laugh –

till a greenbrier snagged his sleeve. He continued tracking in angry silence.

At the edge of one of the gray cliffs Troy was stopped by the disappearance of the trail. It should have gone down, but obviously didn't. "The ranger couldn't have flown away, could he?" he wondered. For about five minutes he searched till he noticed that a few of the boot prints further back seemed to be blurred impressions. Could they be double? Finally he found the brushed-over rocky area and the half print about twenty feet further beyond it, so he knew to keep looking. When he finally noticed the scuffs on the side of one of the larger oak trees and the rope burn mark on one of its branches, he guessed how the ranger had escaped the cliffs.

"This character is clever," Troy thought, "but not clever enough to escape me." Then the word hit him: "Escape! This guy isn't hunting the unicorn, he's trying to get away from something else. From what, and why?" he wondered, "why isn't he going after the unicorn? The money's worth it. Money means power, and friends." Troy admitted that he bought the "friendship" of his gang, but he thought they were too dumb to know it.

"They're useful, especially for giving me the advantage," he thought, as he picked a flea out of his dark scraggly beard, "but they're also expendable. I can get new friends with new money" he thought. Then darker memories came back to him. "I want it more than anyone else in the county, so I'll never again have to beg anyone for a stale crust of bread – like I did when I ran away from the orphanage." Then he drove out that old memory with newer interests: "Money also keeps the Assassins' guild and the town authorities off my back," he remembered. "And if a woman is foolish enough to ignore my interest in her, money can help her change her mind, too. It always does – or makes her wish she had."

By now he had lowered himself down the cliff face the same way Kilian had – but with more damage to the trees.

Troy didn't care; he wanted the money – any way he could get it. Even if it meant stealing sheep and cattle like he did last winter while imitating wolf-howls and making fake wolf-prints in the ground – he wanted the money.

....

The other hunters followed Jake down the easier slope on the west side of the mountain, just north of the gray cliffs. As Jake ran back and forth between several of Kilian's traps with the six droghedae close behind him, one of them snagged its hind leg in a snare and whined for help while another tumbled into a concealed pit and was impaled by the spikes in the bottom. Its struggle against the spikes only drove them deeper, tearing open its paws and stomach, spattering the sides and bottom of the pit with blood. The humans who very reluctantly approached the first shadow bear to cut it loose didn't even try to rescue the second. Its howling haunted the area over the pit long after its body could no longer even twitch.

Jake seemed to stay within sight, able to lure the hunters along, but kept just out of bow shot. Kilian miraculously remained undetected even though Jake would return to him periodically and then start on another wide circle. He asked himself how he got into this mess. Fighting an ordinary bear was bad enough, but one that had the spirits of dead animals diabolically added to it to disrupt its location and enhance its size and ferocity was more than he bargained for. Nor would he admit that the thought of a sorcerer, a magic user turned evil and thus with diabolical connections like shadow bears, daunted him. His usual cockiness was fading fast as he concentrated on leading the hunters out of the forest. As he neared the edge Jake ran out – then ran back in again. Now he had no choice but to try to reach Mike and find another method of escape before the Hunters caught them all. Though he usually left the "cleric stuff" to Patrick, as he tried to find Mike's isolation camp he started to pray.

Even though his cloak snagged in the greenbrier once and pulled off him as one edge of it shredded, only the bounty hunter noticed his tracks; and neither Troy nor the sorcerer nor the other assassins actually saw him. He and Jake seemed to stay just one step ahead of their pursuers. It was more than just luck or magic, it was almost as if someone unseen were helping them.

Dwarven Proverb:
We do not always notice the help we are receiving.

....

Mike had been practicing his swordsmanship that morning after his usual meditation on God's holy words. All his food had been rationed and assigned to each of the four days he was to be outside the Paladins' Fortress of the Holy Cross. Though on his own, he was permitted to eat only cheese and bread and dried fruit, and only the amount he was issued – so he wouldn't be tempted to waste his isolation time by hunting. He was allowed to bring with him only his sword and armor, and that was only because part of his training was to integrate his strength and spiritual self-control. Because the afternoon was so hot and muggy, he had taken off his chain mail and even his tunic. Sweat dripped from the edges of his short-cropped reddish hair down his square cut face, ran over the muscles in his chest and arms and soaked into his black leather sword belt and black leggings as he continued training with just his shield and "Trail-healer," his blue-tinged holy sword. He had to keep blinking his steel-gray eyes to keep out the salty sting as he thrust and slashed at the air again and again.

Though he heard the noise of something approaching, he was still startled to see a unicorn leaping into his camp. It smelled like a skunk, but acted like his friend Kilian's dog Jake, especially as it jumped all around him – trying to nip at his nose. Mike didn't even notice Kilian come in, even though he had removed his battered ranger cloak and his shirt. As he wiped his face with his shirt, he shouted anxiously at Mike: "Don't touch Jake yet!" then whistled Jake back to himself. As he explained to Mike, between deep breaths, the happenings of the last hour and the plan they had, an arrow whisked right through Jake – or what would have been him had the unicorn shape really been his own. Before they could react, a bright orange ball of flame like a small sun came rolling toward them from the direction of the arrow shot. It got bigger and bigger each second and started to engulf them in its blinding light and searing heat. Mike's shelter and wood pile and royal blue cloak hanging nearby burst into flame. Without thinking, Kilian instinctively ducked and hid his eyes as it approached. The last thing he saw was Michael standing there resolutely facing the blast, ready to protect his friends with sword and shield – and with his life if necessary.

Chapter 4
THE SORCERER AND THE ASSASSINS

Slowly Patrick became conscious of the battle going on inside him. Not just his own defenses, but some outside power was attacking that poison. He entered it, and began to feel a friend trapped in him – a friend whose healing didn't want to be changed, whose horn rebelled at being realigned to kill. In his dream or delirium Patrick felt himself saying:

"Starfield, I know you, I feel you in me. In the name of the one God I release you. Be free to die in peace – and be at rest in His presence."

Joint by joint he felt the poison ebb away and the now re-formed antidote throb in his veins and flow back into Whitewind. He switched his pressure from Whitewind's jugular vein to his main artery and felt the strength return to him as the blood trickled back into him. His horn grew warm instead of clammy.

Slowly Patrick stood up and bandaged his shoulder and arm as Heather did the same to the unicorn. Since they both still felt woefully weak, Patrick used his last curative spell on himself since Whitewind claimed he didn't need it and felt well enough to travel. Heather threw a glance at the half-elf that showed she didn't believe it.

Hearing sounds of fighting below them, they all knew there was no time to lose. Whitewind convinced Heather to carry their packs and climb on his back as Patrick grabbed his saw and ran ahead to get Alex. Patrick hadn't taken the time to put his shirt or leather vest back on, so since he had thrown the saw over his shoulder as usual, the blade gnawed into his back while he ran. By the time Heather and Whitewind caught up with him, the red splotches on his bandages showed that his shoulder was bleeding again too, but he didn't notice it.

They met Alex at the summit – for he had heard the entangled hunting party's shouts and knew something strange was afoot. He got there as quickly as he could. Since it was clear that Patrick and Heather knew him, Whitewind wasn't startled at seeing the tall barbarian come toward them. The same could not be said for Alex, who had never yet seen a unicorn, much less one of his friends on one. Twenty seconds of explanation was all they needed for him to become enraged that someone was attacking people he cared about. Patrick and Heather could see his shoulder muscles enlarge with each seething in-breath, and couldn't help but notice his fingers tighten around his sword hilt as their story continued. Then this huge flash of light and flame shone over the cliff edge. That glow was reflected in the anger glistening in Lex's red-brown eyes as he imagined what had happened. The forest seemed to actually get out of his way as he blazed a path down that mountainside. Halfway down, the other three lost sight of him; but a few minutes later they could hear the battle intensify as different-pitched shouts rang out below them. Fearing the worst, Patrick prepared his silencing spell.

When they got near Mike's camp they could see pieces of one drogheda on the charred grass and the mutilated body of one black-leather-clad evil looking human – a sign that Lex had come through and caught the unicorn hunters by surprise. From her vantage point on Whitewind, Heather could see off to the other side of the camp two other assassins in black leather with bows drawn protecting a gray-robed figure. She felt something else there too, but it was too small for her to see it clearly. Outside of about a ten foot radius around Mike, everything – plants, rocks, equipment – was scorched horribly and the fire on the periphery was spreading. Footprints in the ash showed where Alex had rushed in after this attempted fireball blast had been shielded by "Trail-healer." He had taken one of the assassins and bears by surprise and vented his anger on both, as Kilian and Michael recovered from the blast; but this also gave the hunters, human and ghost-animal, time to regroup.

Within minutes the four remaining droghedae had them backed against the rock face. The animals stayed out of weapon reach by lunging to swipe at them with their claws and then backing away all in one move. With his rage subsided, Alex was slower now and an easy target. His right shoulder had been ripped raw and yet no drogheda had any wounds to show for it. Mike fared better, cutting off a forepaw each from the two beasts on him, and making them less eager to continue to attack; but Kilian's axe and dagger were too short to be very effective. As Mike slashed at one of the bears he hit its head, cutting through its jaw and into its eye. But while his shield kept at bay the other, the two assassins shot at him again – this time hitting him in the left side. It was just a flesh wound, and the arrow went all the way through him and out – but it had done its work. The blue-black oil mingled with his blood; and, with the other shadow bear still attacking him, he had no chance to wipe it off. He felt the pain creep through him and start to sap his strength. He finished off the wounded, one-eyed bear and made one last lunge at the other one, then dropped his sword. Patrick threw his spell.

....

Kresov, the middle-aged sorcerer, had wondered why his fire-ball spell hadn't worked, nor the two powerful magic dart blasts he had thrown. He looked at his pale, claw-like hands in frustration. He shook them, blew on them and they seemed all right; yet the spells seemed to "die out" or dissipate away. Something was wrong, and he couldn't have the assassins thinking the problem was in him. Then, as he stroked his graying but elegant goatee, his slate gray eyes noticed the holy symbol branded on Mike's chest. Infuriated, he ordered his assassins to hit that interfering paladin, and get his sword out of the way, while he waited with his Cloud of Poison spell ready.

He despised paladins. They were the only fighters who could stop his dark magic – and only when holding rare, spell-absorbing, "Holy" swords. They were also the only group, other than these accursed unicorns, that the assassins' guild hadn't been able to burn out or disperse. It was getting frustrating: each time he and the guild would try to control the weather – for power and profit – a group of "beasts" would oppose them: first the pegasi, then the glow dogs, now these unicorns . . ." But we'll get them (or at least disperse them and break their power) like we did the others," he thought as a twisted smile crept over his corpulent face. "It was a struggle six months ago when the assassins' guild sent me to the plains north of the city to wipe out the pegasi there," he mused to himself while he had waited for the sword to drop. "Fortunately no one knew how upsetting it was getting right up close to those big winged-horse brutes to touch-charm them and then kill them. And how they stank! The combination of horse stench and bird odor smelled worse than either. Yet worse than that was being so uncouth as to actually sleep out in the open while waiting for them." He shuddered a bit as his thoughts continued: "There was nothing to do after dark: no one to harass or intimidate, no excitement, no intrigue. Everything was dull and dirty, thoroughly disgusting!"

He couldn't wait to get back to the stone streets and narrow alleys and sewers and inside plumbing and crowds of "normal people" in the city. The memory of the burning of the glow dog glen a few weeks later was almost as bad.

"At least there I had the pleasure of frying them with distant spells like Lightning or Fireball – and I didn't have to get near the 'vermin.' And of course there was the ridiculously funny sight of the puppies trying to blink away from the fire on their tails and backs, only to whine in pain as the fire stayed with them. Oh, and when the older dogs would try to save the puppies, only to catch their own whiskers and ears on fire it was just too much fun!" he chuckled to himself.

"But this time the guild lied more than usual," he thought. "'Only a quick trip,' they said. Liars! Not only do I have to live unknown and unfeared in this dumpy little town for days, but even be civil to these bumpkins who stink like the animals they work with. Their trees, their flowers, their smiles make me want to vomit. Their clerics are so naive they'd be chewed up in a minute in the city, and their grubby little magic users aren't even worth talking to. What can a hick possibly know that could be of use to me, a real crafter of magic?!" He remembered when he had been at their level, in his early days of guild training, and he despised them. How feeble the bright magic had been – slowly understanding nature and gently coaxing it into cooperation until it could be played almost like an instrument. Much easier was it to force it into slavery with a little diabolical terror. He recalled his "conversion" from magic to sorcery. The hours of study and the practice of techniques and little tricks had been so slow – till he met a "friend" who showed him how fireballs really work and where their source came from.

"As soon as I can get rid of this unicorn herd so we can collect the weather control protection money from the dumb farmers throughout this dukedom," he thought, "I'll be out of this disgustingly dull town and away from the fools who live in it. And I'll be especially glad to dispel back to normal these flea-bitten overgrown bears! The sooner I can get cleansed from their necromantic taint, the better," he resolved, and put his left hand to his mouth. He mumbled something through his hand and the droghedae started retreating. Then he stepped forward, raised both hands, and started chanting his Poisoned Cloud spell. He stopped suddenly in mid-syllable – astounded that he could mouth the words but that no sound would come out. By the time he or the assassins knew what was happening, Patrick had hit them with the Spider Web spell that he had started preparing just as soon as he had cast the circle of silence. Both assassins were caught, but the sorcerer seemed to have some resistance to the magic. Jakc alone saw what it was, raced forward and pounced on the rodent-like demon. The quarterghost squirmed and struggled, but couldn't quite reach Jake with its claws or fangs; yet neither could Jake harm it. The sorcerer felt the attack on his "pet" and drew his dagger, lunged down, and jabbed Jake in the haunch, hoping to make him yelp and drop it. Alex and Kilian were both furiously battling the three slowly retreating droghedae to get to Jake, but couldn't quite reach him.

Patrick raced across the scorched area toward them while Heather dismounted to try to stop the fires from spreading beyond the cliff area. Jake, as usual, bolted away with the quarterghost and ran in a big circle, limping this time and leaving a trail of blood. When Kresov pulled out a wand to aim at Jake, Patrick was close enough to slash at him with the only weapon he had, his saw. He caught the sorcerer on the wrist, and nicked the wand but didn't knock it out of his hand. The backstrokc raked the saw directly up across the wand, cutting an angled groove more than halfway through it. Patrick pushed his bow-saw forward, cutting the wand so thoroughly that one half merely dangled from the other. Kresov tossed it away lest it backfire on him. As the two magic users sliced at each other, dagger versus saw, both could feel the stone wand's energy draining into the ground, petrifying the scorched stubble around it.

Jake's circle now took him past Mike who had raised himself on one arm and was leaning on Trail-healer. Overcoming the agonizing pain, he raised his sword and sliced completely through the quarterghost – destroying it without sending it back to hell. This stunned Kresov, but the lust for revenge snapped him out of it. Patrick was close enough to almost feel the hate. Mike sank back down in his own blood, happy to have neutralized a demon before dying himself. Whitewind tried to get up to go over and help him, but couldn't. With no antidote to the poison they would die together.

Chapter 5
BATTLES

Heather had just put out the peripheral fires and was heading toward the assassins when Troy snuck up behind her. He grabbed her wrists and easily knocked away the kitchen knife she went for. Then he forced her to the ground outside the circle of silence as she started coughing again.

"What's a pretty little thing like you doing out here?" he taunted. Then in a lower, mock-sweet voice: "And so sick! You should be home in bed – with me."

Something snapped inside Kilian when he heard that insult. His axe blazed a trail right through the Drogheda unfortunate enough to be on him as he stormed over to Troy. He was so mad he threw his thief's dagger at Troy's back, but it only grazed the back of his head as he bent over Heather. Troy straightened up quickly and placed the tip of his sword on her throat.

"Close, but not good enough," Troy smirked. "Drop your axe or I'll lean forward."

Kilian froze.

"Do it!" Troy shouted, "and tell your friends to drop theirs too."

"The bears will tear them apart!" Kilian replied.

"That's right," sneered Troy as he leaned forward just enough for a trickle of blood to sprout from Heather's neck. "It's just a matter of which of you gets it first. I'm sure you don't really want to see what I do to her, do you?" he taunted.

Jake let out a sharp bark and jumped at him. It was just enough movement to distract Troy as Heather hit the razor sharp edge of the sword blade with both hands and pushed it to the side. It sliced deeply into the palms of her hands and took a little piece out of her neck and even almost pulled Troy off balance. Kilian was on him like a falcon on a rat. An axe blow knocked Troy back but did little damage. With the agility of a master thief Troy recovered his balance and started back toward Heather, swinging his sword down at her; but Jake was there first to protect her, with just his body if necessary.

....

Despite his strength and rage, Alex was having one horrible time with the two droghedae, even though one of them had lost its right paw by now. He constantly kept turning, trying to keep both at bay. While he concentrated on one bear, the other would claw his back and legs. Sections of his leather armor had been ripped to shreds, and his shoulders and back looked like they had been dragged two miles over cactus and rock. Fortunately Lex was smarter than they were, so since they kept up this tactic he played their game too. He started to strike at one that tried to draw him toward it, then wheeled around quickly and caught the other unexpectedly in the throat. Its long, curved claws tore through his leather armor vest and raked down his chest as he drove his sword into its flesh up to the hilt. He wrenched his sword up over his head between its huge jaw and ear and out the side of its face, severing its main artery and spinal chord. Its front paws tried to close on his arms, but fell limp and helpless at its sides as dark blood gushed from its neck all over them both. Now Alex turned and glared at the other creature. The fiery look in his eyes kept saying that despite the damage to his shoulders and back, and the claw lacerations causing his chest to drip blood and even a broken rib or two, he was still an opponent to fear. The fight would be to the death.

....

Time was running out for Patrick, and he knew it. Kresov kept maneuvering his way toward the edge of the circle of silence as they swung at each other. As neither of them were

40

fighters by nature, their awkward combat looked clumsy and childish. Since his "weapon" had a longer reach, Patrick could keep pushing Kresov back; but he knew his silence spell would last only a few more moments. Both had spells prepared for when the silence would give way: Kresov had his slow-enemies or "stall" spell, which would effectively kill his opponents by forcing only them to fight at half speed. Patrick had only a one-person/one-word spell of command. He usually chose the word "surrender", but he knew Kresov would probably be able to block that with will power. His only real hope was to keep the melee continuing so that the sorcerer couldn't have a chance to cast his spells.

When Patrick heard Alex roar in pain as the last shadow bear bit into his left leg just as he shoved his sword into its back, he knew he had to attack furiously. He hit the sorcerer once across the face, cutting his lip, but not enough to stop a spell. He hit again, but snagged the saw on the left shoulder of Kresov's gray robe. With Patrick stuck, Kresov jabbed at his right arm, easily piercing all the way through to the bone. Patrick jerked the saw loose, careful to say nothing even though the pain in his upper right arm made him want to scream in agony. As he used his left hand to stop the blood, Patrick swung once more with his right, weakly. The sorcerer easily knocked the saw out of his hand and backed Patrick into a scorched tree where he crumpled at its base. With dagger raised high and the lust of destruction radiating from him as he towered over Patrick, Kresov closed in for the kill. Despite the command spell waiting to be released, all Patrick could utter was a plaintive cry for "help!"

Neither of them realized at first what was happening, even though Patrick felt power pass through him. The dormant command spell produced an unhoped-for effect because the word "help", though expressed as a noun, was understood by the magic of the spell itself as a verb. Such a turn of events caught Kresov off guard. As he towered over Patrick he suddenly felt the urge to "help" rather than attack him. Instead of an enemy, here was a fellow magician: a youngster, perhaps a protégée. He was hurt, he was surrounded by danger, he was calling to his master for assistance. Kresov let the dagger fall into Patrick's lap and stood there trying to figure out how best to help. He started to bend down. Then, just as suddenly as it came, the spell wore off.

Abruptly Kresov regained his original attitude. He again saw Patrick as a dirty, unworthy enemy to be crushed like the other vermin around them. Unfortunately, now that enemy was armed with his own magic weapon. Kresov lunged forward for the dagger as Patrick looked up, dumbfounded. Kresov knocked him backward onto the ground and threw his whole weight on top of him, reaching in, trying to get to his dagger. They grappled and struggled there – blood spurting from Patrick's arm leaving bright red streaks on both Kresov's robe and Patrick's bandages. Each had one hand on the dagger as they tumbled over the tree roots and through the dirt and ash, which turned their bloodied clothing black. As they rolled once more the dagger again found a mark; neither of them moved.

Patrick felt the pain in his shoulder and arms as he came to. He was afraid to open his eyes. He felt helpless and waited for the inevitable. He knew playing dead wouldn't work; the sorcerer was probably just toying with him till he would beg to be put out of his misery. He knew his Magic dart burst was weaker than the sorcerer's and wouldn't kill him, but it was all he could prepare, and it might buy some time. At least he'd go down fighting. He raised his head and looked around cautiously, ready to fire a spell one last time, and saw the sorcerer's body near him, and beyond it the ranger and ex-ranger fighting against the charred gray cliff.

....

After knocking Troy away from Heather, Kilian swung again and again wildly as his neck and shoulders bristled with rage. Troy side-stepped these delicately, trying to wear him out. When Kilian's breathing slowed a bit, Troy began to parry Kil's axe with his longsword. Careful not to let his sword get damaged, Troy first nicked Kilian's right hand, then laid a little cut on his left arm. A few swings later, Troy sliced a sliver of skin off Kilian's right shoulder with the point of his sword. Slowly, craftily, Troy with his longer weapon forced him toward the rock wall. Kilian's right foot turned on a loose stone there as Troy hit him hard on the left shoulder, cutting his skin and fracturing the shoulder bone. But Troy had finally overreached himself. This move made him lean over Kilian, whose axe reached up and sliced through Troy's leather armor: into the flesh on the left side of his chest outside the rib cage.

The blow shook him enough that he dropped his sword, which tumbled behind Kilian. As Kilian tried to swing again his fractured shoulder kept him off balance. Troy grabbed both his wrists and shouldered him into the honeycombed rock face, scraping the skin off Kilian's bare right shoulder and banging Kilian's head so hard that he tore his ear on the jagged edges of rock. By the time Kilian recovered his balance and senses, Troy had picked up his sword and had swung one handed full circle up, while his left hand staunched his own side wound. As he came down heavily to cut through Kilian's skull, Kilian flattened himself against the cliff face, rather than jumping away from it as Troy had expected. Troy only caught him on his lower left side, cutting through his belt just above his hip – still doing only surface damage.

Thinking his own left side was protected from Kilian by a pock-marked and paper-thin out-cropping of the eroded limestone beside them, which acted like a natural shield, Troy slowly backed Kilian into the tall crevice behind it. Though Troy's sword point darted in and out easily, Kilian had less and less room to swing his axe as the bounty hunter inched him back. Each time he tried to swing at Troy's wounded left side, he was blocked by portions of the rock curtain. It and the long-sword kept him at bay; and he couldn't fight with his left hand because of his fractured left shoulder. The smile broadened on Troy's face as he forced Kilian back against the cliff wall, finally pinning him there; his sword point just inches from Kilian's chest. Kilian turned his axe around and swung once more.

The axe head sliced right through the rock as if it were worm-eaten paneling and grazed Troy's neck as it swung past it onto his raised left hand. But since what magically slices stone only bruises flesh, it only broke two bones in the back of Troy's hand. The follow-through spun Kilian around into the crevice as the axe embedded itself in the rock wall, allowing Troy the chance to backstab. But the blow to Troy's own neck had jarred the nerves extending out his arm and weakened him enough that even though he hit Kilian's back he couldn't push the sword in at all. Troy's weakened blow did, however, make Kilian let go of his axe handle and slump to the ground. Frustrated, Troy started kicking Kilian's crumpled figure, bruising a kidney and dislocating his left kneecap. As Kilian struggled to get up, Troy kicked that left knee, sending him to the ground again in pain. Troy regained his composure and raised his sword, this time to drive it through Kilian. He paused deliberately in mid strike – savoring the moment. Patrick fired his spell, and then collapsed from loss of blood.

The three bolts of energy, combined with the sight of a barbarian limping toward him with blood lust in his eyes made Troy forget about Kilian – who grabbed his foot as he turned to run. Troy fell on his broken hand, letting out a whelp of pain as the two fractured bones pushed their pale white jagged ends up through his skin. He struggled to his feet just a few steps ahead of Lex and disappeared into the woods.

Alex took out his frustration and anger on the two webbed assassins. They were dead long before he stopped scattering pieces of them around the camp with his sword strokes.

Kilian put a smooth stick in his mouth and took a deep breath; then he pushed his kneecap back into place. He got up slowly, pulled his axe out of the cliff face and wiped the blood and dirt off it. He found his dagger on the way over to Heather. She had just finished bandaging her neck and hands, using up her curative spell powers in the process. After finishing off the assassins, Alex sliced up the magic user – just to make sure he really was dead. Then he forced a drink from his own wine skin into Patrick to revive him, and applied a tourniquet to his right arm. In exchange, after Lex had removed his shredded leather vest and torn and bloodied gray tunic, Patrick cleansed his badly lacerated body and gnawed leg with some water he had magically located to wash off most of the dirt and tingling "spectral hair" before applying the healing agents he always carried in his medicine pouch. It would be weeks before Lex would be able to run again.

Chapter 6
THE GIFT OF DEATH

Michael was just barely breathing and was writhing fitfully when the others reached him: he was sinking fast under the poison. Patrick tried cleaning the wound and sucking out the poison, but the wound was too big, and the poison from a magical beast. He tried hypnosis to slow its spread, and it seemed to help calm Mike a little, but only a little. Feeling helpless, he went over to Whitewind and spoke to him what little comfort he could give. He asked forgiveness for not listening to him in the first place, and thereby not only not preventing his death, but causing the wounding and death of his own friends.

"Nho-no need for mha-my fha-forgiveness. Thou didst try thy bestest," Whitewind interrupted. "Berate not thyself. Thou couldst nha-not prevent mha-my death-the; but thou hast fha-freed mha-me and-d Starfield fha-from an undead slavery. Tendest thou to thy fha-friend. Thy blood wilt still the antipoison containeth."

Before Whitewind could finish the sentence Patrick had jumped up and was hobbling as fast as he could back over to Mike. He reopened Mike's side wound and then quickly loosened the tourniquet on his own right arm to allow his blood to drip into Mike's wound. When the cut was filled with his blood, Patrick retightened his pressure bandage and massaged Mike's side to let the blood in the wound be drawn into his veins as the poison had been. Slowly it started to take effect: the convulsions stopped. His muscles all tightened once and then relaxed. His eyes opened and seemed blood-shot, but seemed also to be clearing up. While Kilian and Heather patched up Jake, Lex and Patrick helped Mike to his feet. When he seemed to feel well enough, Mike's concern turned again to others' welfare. Because of the deep cut on Patrick's arm and its continued bleeding, Mike used his paladin's holy ability of laying healing hands on him there; but he could not help the other wounds on his shoulder.

Eventually the whole group gathered around Whitewind. It was obvious that the poison was still in him. Its effects had been slowed but not neutralized. It was as if all the pain they had gone through – and the killing they had done – would make no difference: they had failed to save him. Whitewind looked peaceful, however, as he breathed slowly, weakly. He asked Heather to plead with the first bird to come by and ask it to take a message for his herd. A tiny green and yellow wild finch agreed and came over to the unicorn. Whitewind whistled and nodded to it in what must have been "common finch," and it flew off southeast past the yellow cliffs and across the broad Markasandra river valley.

....

With nothing else urgent, Kilian's thoughts turned to treasure; but he found only a few small red gems and some silver pieces on the assassins and sorcerer. As they stripped the bodies to burn them (and scatter the ashes), Patrick decided to concentrate hard and use his ability to detect magic auras – just in case. Besides Kilian's and Mike's magic axe and sword, an aura shone around the sorcerer's dagger, several white enamel-like arrowheads and a small leather-like band around the sorcerer's left thumb. When Mike had determined that none of these were inherently evil and Kilian had found no other treasure, they collected a large pile of dead wood and placed the bodies (and pieces thereof) on it to allow the flames to purify the area. In that fire, five strange, weird-colored flashes appeared at random intervals. Even though it was mid-afternoon, the stagnant day actually seemed to grow fresher, freer. As the smoke carried away the remnants of the evil ones, the first traces of springtime color finally began to return to the forest.

....

A slight rustle or two in the nearby trees clued Alex and Kilian to the approaching unicorn herd. Slowly they emerged from the forest and gathered around Whitewind. Patrick was still scattering the ashes while reciting the absolution chant – which he suspected was probably useless here. Heather was continuing to do what she could for Whitewind, while the three fighters cleaned what little was left of the drogheda hides. With the death of the sorcerer, the enchantment from the restless animal spirits had been dispelled and they had returned to their normal Appalachian black bear size. The unicorn herd circled the group warily, and lowered their heads menacingly at Jake who darted about playfully. Kilian called him off, and Whitewind let out a series of rapid snorts and whinnies and whistles that seemed to soften the unicorns' attitude toward them.

Blue Cloud, a large gray colored unicorn with blue-white splotches on her neck and a bright white billowy mane stepped into the center of the circle next to Whitewind and Heather.

"Mha-my husband-d hath told us of thy sacrifices-es," she began. "We likewise thank ye-e fha-for his fha-freedom, and fha-for thy peace to Starfield. Each of ye-e choose thyself a comapa-a-anion fha-from amongst ourselves so that ye-e mha-mightest come us-with. Fha-for he desireth to gift ye-e within his death passage. Yet quickly must we move."

Mike very respectfully approached a bright blue-streaked unicorn with a shimmering silver mane and beard that reminded him of clear spring water. Its touch was cool and reassuring. Lex found a fiery golden-red stallion with energy enough to challenge him and spirit enough to intrigue him. Heather stayed with Blue Cloud herself, which pleased and honored both Blue Cloud and Whitewind. Kilian noticed the midnight black unicorn standing just outside the circle. Sleek and strong, she looked dangerous – yet alluring. She let him approach her only because she chose to. Jake and her baby brother became fast friends, chasing each other and rubbing noses.

Patrick, as usual, liked them all and didn't know what to do. While he just stood there looking stupid, a colt wandered over and licked him on the side of the face. Its soft curly hair was a chestnut brown with swirls of a golden tan, which coalesced in its mane and beard. Its coat seemed to change hue, as a wheat field does when the breeze ripples it in the sunlight. Yet it was the bright green sparkle in Sunbridge's eyes that let Patrick sense a touch of the lifegiver in him, and realize that his unicorn guide had found him.

While each of the characters were being "adopted" by a unicorn, four large stallions approached Whitewind and nuzzled him gently. As the remainder of the herd closed tightly around them all, suddenly the sky seemed to go out of focus and the breeze seemed to pick up a bit. Patrick became so dizzy that he clung tightly to Sunbridge's neck as he stood next to him. When he regained his sense of balance a few moments later, the whole herd looked the same; but now he could see the ancient temple, and in place of the rock cliff-face behind them there was the holly grove! Several unicorns were gathering branches and piling them under Whitewind, but how they did it neither Kilian nor Mike nor Patrick could figure out, and Lex didn't care.

....

Dwarven Proverb:
Even free gifts sometimes come with a cost.

While Patrick watched the holly gathering, Sunbridge confided to Mike: "A unicorn darst only here die, fha-for the rhoroadway through thy Lord's temple into His stars can we only fha-from this holy ground discern. Thus explaineth Whitewind's arrival this morning-g. Thy kindness-es then doth allow us to be with him nha-now. But nha-now the passage time approacheth. Come, receivest thy gifts."

"What gifts?" asked Patrick, as his attention came back into focus. "We deserve no..." He choked on the sentence as Kilian grabbed him from behind and held his mouth shut.

"You idiot!" he "whispered" into Patrick's long ears. "If they wan'a give us somethin' don't turn it down! If you don't want it that don't mean the rest of us don't. What kind o' fool do you think I am anyway?"

"Well, you..."

"Don't answer that!" Kilian interjected, "Just thank them politely and let's get our tails home before you get us into more trouble."

Patrick backed away from him, saluted him casually once with his left hand (he still couldn't use his right arm much) and very slowly and formally walked over to Whitewind and addressed him solemnly:

"I am Patrick, from St. Stephen's Church in Dennistown, cleric and magic user. My friends and I beseech our God's blessing on you as you undergo your death passage. May He..."

"Wha-withhold thy prayer, mha-my fha-friend," said Whitewind haltingly, and the other unicorns flinched involuntarily at the word "friend." "Please let each of thy brave ones ta-touch me erst they lha-leave. Since wha-we cannot nha-now mha-my death sta-stop, lha-let mha-me tra-a-ansfer what I mah-may of mha-my powers to thee and thine compa-a-anions, that ye mightest protect wha-what I nha-now cannot. Wha-we nha-need thy help still."

"As you wish, my 'friend'" replied Patrick as he bowed slowly and backed away; but his last word came out awkward too.

Kilian came forward first, with an expectant yet wary smile on his face. He glanced for reassurance at Lex who was right behind him. Whitewind spoke slowly.

"Bha-bring thy axe wha-with thec here, and-d also the magic band thou canst nha-not use but wha-which thou still retainest fha-from the evil sorcerer."

Kilian looked a bit sheepish, as if to say "do you think I'd try to steal it?" But of course he didn't dare glance at anyone else, because they would have told him that yes, that's exactly what they'd think he'd try. Still, he brought it out and held it up with his axe.

"Wha-wrap the band-d around-d the axe handle just below the head, and-d place it in mha-my mha-mouth."

This he did very carefully. Whitewind bit down on it and rolled it around in his mouth. When Kilian removed it, the band had become part of the handle.

"Wha-when thou holdest thy axe, thou wilst nha-now be able to speak wha-with animals one time each of thy days, and they wha-with thee," Whitewind declared. "Mha-makest certain that thou usest it wha-with care, or thou mayest hear what thou wouldst not."

Kilian's face brightened as he turned away and played with his axe. Alex limped forward more eagerly now.

"Ah, bha-brave bha-barbarian," Whitewind began, at which Alex beamed. "Take thy arrows and-d touch one of them to each of mha-my hooves." Lex carefully took his four best arrows out of his quiver and bent over Whitewind's legs. As each arrow touched a hoof, the materials sparked and exchanged. Magic-like bone replaced metal and stone. Whitewind looked at him carefully and cautioned:

"The others thou hast found mightest also repairable be. Usest them all wha-with great caution, fha-for they wilt hit — even shouldst they need to teleport thereto accomplish. Thou wilt know when they wilt needed be."

Alex wrapped these four special arrows carefully and separately, as well as the other broken ones from Whitewind and Mike, then put them back in his quiver and carried it away to compare them with Kilian.

Whitewind now looked at Mike – and his face showed confidence rather than the hope with which he had viewed Kilian and Alex.

"Come fha-forward, holy warrior" he called. "Touch thou the pommel of thy compa-a-anion Trail-healer to mha-my horn and-d receivest thou wha-what is left of its power."

Mike balked, for he knew the terrifying value of that gift: Whitewind could not live long after such a transfer. Yet his alignment could not let him refuse such an aid to the cause of righteousness. So he knelt in front of Whitewind and unsheathed Trail-healer, whose blue-steel blade and bronze pommel glistened in the late afternoon sun. He held it by the blade and lowered the pommel slowly onto the horn. As it touched, it seemed as if sparks flashed and lightning arced, engulfing both sword and horn. Yet the light didn't burn those who looked at it as it shimmered in iridescent swirls. These subsided into a steady glow, which faded slowly as if drawn inside itself. When Mike removed his sword, Whitewind's horn was now bronze and Trail-healer's pommel gleamed like pearl.

"Thy gift is lha-limited-d," he explained in barely a whisper. "Thy healing power ist now doubled whene'er thou holdest this sword of thine, but there be nha-no other extra benefits therefrom." He coughed twice and then panted out: "Thy sword wast well-named-d."

Mike rose, bowed deeply and honorably, sheathed Trail-healer and quickly motioned Heather up to Whitewind. She stumbled forward, crying softly, and knelt beside him and hugged his neck tightly. His eyes were glassy and blood drooled from his mouth and nose: He was obviously fading fast. Whitewind said nothing as Heather clung there, her face buried in his mane; but his skin began rippling up and down his body. Before anyone quite knew what was happening, Heather's brown leather armor became a snowy white, and Whitewind's skin turned to a worn brown. Kilian had to pull her away as Blue Cloud whispered to her "Thou canst teleport as wha-we do. Takest thy care when thou dost. Treasurest thou thy gift as he hath thee and thine."

Patrick now knelt in front of Whitewind and began the blessing again. Though it wasn't one of his seven sacraments, this blessing seemed to share their sacred character and was wonderfully appropriate for Whitewind. Echoes of the 23rd psalm came to him instinctively as he placed both hands on Whitewind's forehead and composed the death blessing: "May our Lord and God guide you through the pathway of the stars – out of time and matter into His eternity. May He welcome you there and give you rest in fresh green pasture near clear cool water." As Whitewind's breathing slowed and then finally stopped, he added:

"Be at peace, my friend," then under his breath, "as you wait for us and all creatures to one day join you."

Patrick stood up and backed away as Whitewind's body began to glow a bit, then faded. Something seemed to hover near them, then appeared to wander off as if it were looking for something, or someone. The other unicorns seemed very placid and unmoved as they ignited the holly branches some-how: either by horn or hoof rubbing or something. This time even Patrick didn't care how they did it. But as the fire reached higher, each of them – Alex, Kilian, Heather, Michael, and Patrick – felt their bodies become strengthened. Lex's leg showed no bite-mark and Kilian's shoulder was no longer bro-ken. Michael's side and Heather's hands looked as if they had never been cut, and Patrick's shoulder and arms no longer bled. Even their clothing, what little was left on each of them, looked both cleaned and mended. This was Whitewind's final gift; it seemed to flow into them from his other gift to each of them.

As the fire died down and the unicorns started drifting away, Alex and Mike brought the sorcerer's dagger over to Patrick and tried to get him to keep it.

54

"We each got somethin' and you got nothin'," Alex argued, "so you take it."

"After all, fair is fair," agreed Mike. "We would be unjust if you did not get something. You did kill him, you know. And you saved both my life and Kilian's."

"No, Mike, I didn't", Patrick replied somberly. "Lex chased the bounty hunter away, and it was the unicorn who told me about the antidote still in my blood. Besides, I got you all into this in the first place by not running away when we had the chance."

"That don't matter," interjected Kilian as he came over leading Heather who rested on his right arm. "You always get us into trouble, but Heather an' me want you to have the dagger anyway. Maybe you'll learn how to fight decently some day," he said mockingly as his left hand shot up quickly and messed up the half-elf's hair.

They smiled at each other for a moment, then Patrick shook his head slowly and opened his mouth to argue again, but Sunbridge stopped him politely with a soft nudge. He then explained to the others very gently: "Though thy dagger-gift to him be proper, be ye advised that he also wast healed, and thus also a gift hath received: his blood wilt always the antipoison containeth, but only whilst he be alive." Then he looked directly at Patrick and warned: "I am told that this gift wilt cost thee, for thy blood now only slowly itself replaceth wilt."

Sunbridge nuzzled his arm affectionately once then stepped back, looked at them all and said: "Be safe home, unicorn fha-friends, we need ye still" before he scampered away and disappeared into the foliage.

Chapter 7
THE JOURNEY ALL THE WAY HOME

When they looked around they noticed that all the other unicorns were gone and the fire was out. The three dead holly branches they had set out to get that morning were piled neatly for them near their packs and Patrick's shirt and armor. After cutting and bundling the branches onto the carrycart, Patrick once more tried to give away the dagger, but Mike and Lex and Kilian were adamant that he keep it – and learn to fight better. Seeing no other choice, Patrick then blessed the dagger. It seemed to feel OK in his hand after that.

As the day grew late they escorted Mike back to his burnt-out camp. Alex and Kilian helped him rebuild his shelter, Kilian's axe doing wonders on some nearby saplings, while Heather sewed together what she could of the bear fur and Patrick lit the fire and prepared their food as he brooded. He had never killed before, and the dagger reminded him of it. He had made a "friend" only to lose him. And he almost lost his other real friends through his own overconfidence. He had grown up a lot that day, and it had taken its toll on him. Half-elves don't really live much longer than humans, they just mature slower.

They left Mike in pretty good shape – with half a camp, and pieces of "bear rug" instead of a cloak to sleep under – as they took the new road northward. They quickly left the Markasandra and had just passed David's ford far up on Fogle Creek as dusk descended. By the time they reached the wood-lot it was getting dark, and Alex's boss, Tim, was angry – especially since Lex had rushed off without letting him know. But since Tim also attended St. Stephen's church, Patrick, as one of the clergy there, was able to calm him down with the offer of a gift. Tim had wanted the carrycart, but Patrick was able to mollify him with one of the toys plus a promise to share the carrycart's design with him before the next new moon. As part of the bargain, the whole episode was "forgotten" and Lex would get paid for all day. When Tim remembered how good Patrick had been to him and his kids at church, he even volunteered to explain to Alex's mother that his tunic and leather vest had gotten shredded as part of his work so Alex wouldn't get chewed out so badly at home either.

Even though Heather was supposed to have been back hours ago, Kilian's silver tongue explained her way back into her compound. Moreover, his own parents were always happy for him to be with Patrick any length of time. They seemed to feel Kilian needed all the cleric help he could get, and that the two of them would get into less trouble than he would alone. They were wrong on both counts.

When Patrick finally got back to St. Stephen's church he just had time to stash the wood and the bag of toys, remove his forest clothes, and throw on the proper robes to help with the evening shriving. Afterward Father Roger Crooner, the older cleric, noticing the difference in Patrick, inquired rather gently what had kept him out so long getting the holly branches.

"You wouldn't believe me," remarked Patrick.

"Try me," he replied in his usual grandfatherly way.

"Well, there was this unicorn being chased by shadow bears and a sorcerer and..."

"You're right," he interrupted, "I don't believe you. I'm just glad it wasn't anything dangerous."

....

Two days later the moon was full, the first one since the vernal equinox. Evening turned to night as Maundy Thursday, the first of the services for the three Christian high holy days, was letting out from St. Stephen's church. Patrick locked up the golden vessels and put the other things away quickly. He felt irresistibly drawn outside into the moonlight. He knew from experience it would be useless to ignore that urge, so he changed into his boots and sweat-stained buckskin leggings and green tunic-shirt. Picking up the belt with his water skin and medicine pouch, he noticed the dagger he had attached to it, and again felt uneasy. Yet the feeling wasn't because of the dagger but from something intangible connected to it. Patrick passed this feeling off as remorse over having killed someone. He told the other clerics he was going out for his usual walk and prayers and meditation, but he didn't tell them how long he'd be gone.

As soon as he emerged into the warm early spring evening and noticed the shimmering edge of the pale yellow moon poking over the eastern hilltops, he knew he had to go to the mountain. Something there was calling him, summoning him. Just after crossing the gray stone bridge over the gully on the east edge of town, he stashed his equipment belt in some bushes by the rail fence next to Alex's house. Then he went in to ask his parents if Lex could go running with him in preparation for some upcoming foot race or other. Lex was out feeding his calf; but his parents, even though they didn't like this "running business" especially after dark with all the wild creatures about any more than Patrick's parents did, were not about to stop their son from hanging around with one of their own clerics. When Alex came in a few minutes later, he caught the faraway look in Patrick's eyes, and pretended to have forgotten something in the barn. So while Patrick kept the family busy with a short religious story, Alex smuggled his sword to the barn. When he returned, his father made them both take off their tunics and leave them there.

"It's too warm for braves like you two to be wearing shirts while working or running," he claimed, building on their pride. Both Alex and Patrick knew he suspected something, however, and probably wanted to discourage them from getting into trouble in any of the inns in town by making them go out without any armor or even a shirt. Yet they were both able at least to recover their weapons, and the lack of armor didn't bother them since, as brand new braves, they were still in the show-off stage and neither of them really liked wearing a shirt anyway.

A quarter hour later, after a brisk two mile run, they found Heather and Kilian "well occupied" near the old quarry above the lake. For some reason they almost seemed to be expecting Lex and Patrick, though they themselves didn't even know why. Kilian, for example, had brought along his axe, which he almost never carried in town, as well as his dagger. When Patrick explained that he and Alex were headed for the holly grove, they jumped at the chance to come along. To go back for Jake, however, would have been too risky.

They traveled southward, silently and swiftly, as barbarians, rangers and half-elves can do when they need to. When they passed the now dark woodlot the vernal moon was still rising, and the trees were barren enough yet for its pale opalescent light to display clearly the path up the mountain. By the time they reached the top it had just passed its zenith and was headed toward the ancient temple. As they approached the holly grove they halted, for they saw a human-sized figure silhouetted there. Its armor and sword were dark against what appeared to be patches of fog rising behind it. They drew their weapons as the creature turned toward them. Then its sword caught the moon's reflection on its blue surface, and they all relaxed and ran eagerly over to Mike.

While they watched, the "fog" seemed to congeal into something like pearl, then roll out from the holly grove straight over the valley toward the Lord's ancient temple. Perhaps it was their imagination, but the star patterns seemed to continue that opalescent trail beyond the temple and up into the night sky.

As Heather and Kilian held each other tightly, Patrick almost automatically knelt in wonderment, and Alex and Mike instinctively held up their swords in salute when some tiny bright pinpoint of light appeared and then seemed to beckon from the far end of the trail of stars. In the distance behind them they could feel two "presences" gallop toward them and stop. Though they could see nothing even in the bright full moonlight, each of them felt the friendly touch of something brush down against their foreheads. They could feel a slight wind blow by them as these galloped onto the white trail and up through the field of stars into the night.

"Run well, my friends," Patrick whispered. "The trail is short, and your Lord and ours awaits you at its end. Rest in His peace."

As the shimmering moon trail seemed to unravel and dissolve behind them, each of those watching knew they would make it. And each, in his or her own way in the silent corners of their own hearts, rejoiced.

Chapter 8
ALONE AND EMPTY

Dwarven Proverb:
Beware the Invisible Parasite, the Guild of Terror

Not everyone rejoiced in the defeat of the assassin strike force: As the door shut behind her she could sense that something was out of place. Though everything in her petite and elegant salon was still exactly where she had put it, Nadine knew something was different than when she had left it this morning. As the court musician with access to the duke's household she had developed the artist's sixth sense, and she used it to her advantage – but oh so delicately.

Her slender, aristocratic figure was perfectly accented by her scarlet gown trimmed in black lace, and by her graceful demeanor. Her long, elegant hands and aquiline face, framed by strawberry-blond ringlets guarding a high nose and hazel eyes that had lost their twinkle, belied her age. Even the duke, who as a child had been taught by her to sing and dance, was reluctant to bring her age to mind. Perhaps he had never outgrown his juvenile fear of crossing her, but neither had anyone else.

Nadine's mother had died giving birth pre-maturely to her baby sister Annette. She lived for only three weeks, even though Nadine cared for her every minute of the day and night and prayed for her fervently. When she died, so also died Nadine's faith in God's mercy. Her father, William the Magician, who prided himself on having the most elegant home and best wine cellar in the city, was so distraught by his wife's sudden death that he stayed close to his cellar most of that year. Nadine and her little brother Kresov buried their sister and survived as best they could in a home cobwebbed with grief and poisoned with drink. Though inwardly she had buried her religion with her mother and sister, outwardly she still put up a good show of devotion. Neighbors even called her the "little nun."

Eventually, in between journeys to the wine cellar, William tried to put his family back together. He would let his children into his laboratory to help him, tried to be affectionate with them, and later that year even gave them resonant magic daggers. That was it!

Nadine drew back the purple and teal, salamander patterned tapestry concealing the niche next to the fire place and slowly slid open the door to her secret vault. The poison-needle trap was still set, so she knew no one had been in there, but she could sense a change in the magic "aura." All her potions on the top shelf seemed OK, as did the poisons – each in their own compartment down below. Her pearls and ruby were still there, as was her small gold locket with the image of her mother engraved in it (and the scratched-out place where her father's image used to be). It had to be the pedestal in front of it with the "fishbowl" and the dagger next to it.

Within the "fishbowl", a cubit in diameter but only a span high and enclosed completely in glass, was a model of the whole dukedom with desecrated dirt from each section of it therein. Glowing in the space under the glass dome could be seen the weather control spell, and any of the magical creatures holding it back. Already the spell had taken over the city; but that meant only a little "insurance money" for pageants and parades – no real power like they would have over food if they could extend it to the outlying areas. Flickering in the north and northeast were mere traces of pegasi and glow dog images. Their shattered communities could no longer hold back the spell. Unfortunately, the unicorn image was still there; and though yesterday it had seemed to be fading, today it seemed stronger than ever. Her cunning analytical mind could only conclude that their raid had failed. Soon, very soon, she'd have to explain this failure to the assassins' guild – and be prepared with another plan. She'd think about that later. Right now something else was still wrong here. Because of her identical dagger laying there touching the bowl, she could see just the pinpoint of an aura that would show her where her brother Kresov was. That's it! The aura! It had a different feel and a different hue. Someone other than her brother was holding his dagger – someone with a different moral alignment.

Denial raced through her mind: maybe a thief stole it and sold it; maybe he lost it or loaned it to someone in battle; maybe there was some good reason why the unicorn images seemed stronger and the quarterghost and shadow bears showed no traces at all. Maybe ..., maybe ..., maybe nothing. Little by little the clammy fingers of fear closed their grip around her and devolved into the cold dull realization that she was now the only one left from her family.

She just sat there, staring blankly at the dagger and the fish-bowl as the city's walls of shadow seeped in through her leaded glass windows. No music from her dulcimer; no fire in her blue-enameled fireplace; no tears slipped through her polished marble face. She had mastered her grief during her mother's funeral, and manipulated it to her advantage during her father's. All that the spectators saw was the outside of this orphaned twelve-year-old girl and her eight-year-old brother following his coffin and crying profusely. They couldn't read the satisfaction in her heart.

The old bishop alone suspected that she "mourned too strongly", and wondered about William's death. That he could have "accidentally" consumed the poisoned mushrooms he had been preparing for clairvoyance potions was attributable to his feebleminded condition. It, in turn, had come from the poisonous fumes from an alembic of quicksilver put in the al-chemical furnace. But how the alembic got there no one cared to ask – though only his immediate family had access to his precious metals. Finally, concern for the rest of his flock got the best of the old cleric. So he went alone to the churchyard at midnight with candle, incense, scroll and relic to summon William's ghost back from purgatory, if it was still there, to bring whatever healing he could to this distressing case. As the smoke from the incense reflected in the candle light took on William's features, the bishop put forth his one question: could Nadine or Kresov have had any motive to kill their own father? Reluctantly William's ghost whispered his confession that when trying to hold and comfort his children after his wife's death he had found Nadine very enjoyable to hold, much like her mother.

"Night after night I'd hold them both and tell them stories. Kresov grew tired of it, but Nadine still sat with me each evening after supper. Still I controlled myself – when I wasn't drinking. Nadine did have access to my laboratory and was skilled in poisons, but she could never have killed her own father…not my Nadine…no.…"

As William's shadowed form started to sink back into the soil of the churchyard, the bishop called to him: "William, my son, wait and live with reality." William stopped and rematerialized as the bishop continued to plead with him: "You are hiding something from yourself, and trying to hide it from God."

William looked ashamed as the bishop went on gently, in a truly fatherly way: "God can only forgive us if we allow his grace into us. You are holding some memory away from him – sadly, a memory so troubling that evil has been growing from it. Is there something that happened between you and your children that I can help heal, for both your sake and theirs?"

William felt so low his form seemed to lose its shape and flow over his grave and onto his wife's. He coalesced into a kneeling position and it seemed to the bishop that he appeared to be sobbing profusely. Slowly he started to admit his attempts to drown his anguish at losing his wife with his abuse of his wine cellar, and mistaking Nadine for her one evening –

kissing her in ways that only a husband should do to his wife, never a father to his daughter.

"She didn't know what I was doing until it was too late. When I came to my senses a few hours later, Nadine was huddled in the corner of the dark room, trembling. I tried to tell her how sorry I was, but she would never forgive me – never even speak to me," he related through sobs. "Nothing I tried seemed to get through to her; she would never forgive me. How could my wife forgive me? How could God ever forgive me?" he continued sobbing.

"Why did you not seek forgiveness through the church?" the bishop asked gently. "God has given us that power, out of love for you..."

"If my own family could not forgive me, I was afraid to mention it to anyone else... I just buried it deeper and deeper within my inner soul, hoping no one would find out..." He trailed off into tears so profuse it felt like dew was settling on the grave.

"Are you truly sorry for all your sins?"

"O, absolutely!" he pleaded, "more and more every day."

"Then God has given me the power to forgive you in his name," the bishop declared. "Whether or not any other human ever forgives you, by my words of absolution God will absolve you of this and all your sins."

William started crying so intensely that the bishop had trouble holding back his own tears at this point, but he bent low on his cane and whispered the absolution chant while making the sign of the cross with the relic: "Ego te absolvo ab omnis pecatis..." as William's form now dissolved back into his grave without the chains he had forged for himself.

....

During the next few years, as Nadine showed more grace and talent in the arts, all the socially eligible young men were attracted by her elusive beauty. Anyone who pursued her was rebuffed almost violently, even Simon Whitcomb, a son of one of the nobles. Because of this seeming penchant for chastity, the novice mistress of St. Genevieve's Abbey, during one of the Bishop's canonical visits, had suggested Nadine be invited to join the convent; but she noticed a passing, involuntary grimace on the old bishop's face. He simply indicated very vaguely that Nadine might not be quite ready, and that other candidates should be looked for instead. Nevertheless, the novice mistress visited Nadine on her own and even mentioned that she felt strongly that at 17 years of age Nadine belonged in the convent despite the bishop's misgivings.

"I am flattered and I thank you very much," Nadine replied sweetly over the edge of her tea cup; "but you know I still have to care for my little brother."

"Oh, I discussed that with the bishop," replied the nun. "I was hoping he would agree to take him into the boys' boarding school at the cathedral; but he hinted that I shouldn't even ask you. I wonder what his objections were."

"I wonder too," Nadine replied – more to herself than to the novice mistress there. After finishing the tea and a little small talk, the nun left. She was afraid to speak to the bishop about Nadine again, and didn't dare mention that she had visited with her once – contrary to his advice.

A month later the bishop was found dead in his cloister garden: a poisoned dagger wound in his side and his alms purse gone. His cane was broken, and a torn piece of black lace was still clutched in his left hand. Two leather-clad, green-cloaked visiting thieves from the Fox Clan who claimed they had found his alms purse outside the church were hanged for the crime soon thereafter.

....

The darkness deepened in her salon, but Nadine didn't mind; she was at home in the darkness. Stoically she changed into her working outfit of soft black leather and netting and gloves, all covered by a sleek black hooded cloak. She picked up the case of raven's feathers she would leave on windowsills this evening to call the assassins' guild together the following night, and replaced her dagger in its sheath on her belt. Quietly she slipped out the secret door behind her fireplace into the mechanisms of the clock in the city tower into which her second floor apartment had been built years ago. Catlike, she dodged the gears and pulleys which moved smoothly in a strict precision to which she had grown accustomed and climbed easily down the ornamental ironwork on the outside of the dark brown timbered and pale yellow stucco tower. The flickering light of the pans of oil suspended overhead from brackets on the buildings' walls, and reflected in the canals around the Duke's island, made it easy for her to hide in the shadows as the last of the evening's revelers made their way home for the night. As she disappeared into the narrow alleys of the city, only the flies nearby could hear the Nightshade resolve under her breath that whoever killed her brother would pay dearly – very dearly.

Though still long before dawn, the street cleaners and garbage collectors had begun pushing their handcarts to the garbage scows, the suspended oil lights had all gone out and the bakers were already on their way to work by the time Nadine returned home.

Chapter 9
THE GUILD MEETING

The guildhall walls dissolved in the black, feathery shadows cast by the three flickering candles on the oval table, around which sat and stood the assassin "family." The black leather wingback chairs seemed to envelope each "full" member in a sheath of darkness, so that no one was ever really sure he saw or could recognize any of the others. Because they were thoroughly integrated into this well ordered town populated for the most part by good, kind people, few of the assassin family feared arrest or even suspicion. All had "legitimate" cover jobs; most in the various levels of bureaucracy in the city or valley governments. Yet most as well had belonged to the family for so long, and had grown accustomed to wielding its power and enjoying its wealth, that they had a vested interest in preserving the "status quo." Almost since the time when the first duke had moved his palace from the knob top castle down to the "Duke's Island" the city had been big enough for someone to get lost in – especially if one wanted to. Neither their neighbors nor even their own families knew much about what kind of work cach of them did, and only the Nightshade knew what each of them really did. Usually their "jobs", either in the city or out in the broader Markasandra Valley, had no witnesses and left no evidence. Between protecting itself and its "turf" from free-lancers, and covering disquieting situations with a few bribes (or a "gift" contract) here and there, the family members took care of one another. And if things ever got too hot, a scapegoat could usually be found among the many visitors in this city of converging roads and waterways.

Like any parasite, the guild had a vital interest in keeping the city alive and functioning well. "Protection fees" became such an expected part of life, like taxes and tithes, that no one really noticed them much. When business was good, the "fees" were raised a bit. Never too much, or the populace might decide to "take their business to the competition:" raise taxes to increase the investigative police. When business was bad the guild backed off a bit – always with the threat that "you'll pay later."

But the guild had never quite been able to expand beyond the city. Members who were sent out to Lakewood or Dennistown couldn't compete with the local free-lancers; and those apprentices who tried to infiltrate the farmer clans either married into them and went straight – if they were young enough – or just disappeared. With the guild in control of the city bureaucracy it would seem possible to just slow river traffic down enough to "close" the city to products from Dennistown or Lakewood or the valley clans until they "came around" to making arrangements with the guild's legates. But attempts to close the city to outside products had backfired.

Though their wagon trains and barges were kept out for a week or so, whole clans came with the next shipment the following week and camped just outside the city walls in the floodplain. The merchants did a flourishing business for three days; but the raucousness in the camp all night and the groups of young bucks, half drunk, roaming the streets and insulting the townspeople – but never touching them – terrorized the city. Though no one ever saw them do anything wrong, boats were "found" up on the walkways, many a door would be opened only to find a wall of empty wine bottles leaning against it ready to fall into the house, and statues would be discovered wearing funny clothes. During the day some of the clansmen and their children would go swimming naked in the canals – disrupting river traffic and startling the ladies of the city, especially when they did the backstroke. The children got into everything: the drawbridges, the windmills, even the aqueducts and fountains. Most of the townspeople were afraid to leave their homes. Thieves who tried to infiltrate groups of clansmen were lucky to escape with their lives. And usually each time a group from Dennistown or Lakewood or the valley came, one more assassin would disappear – and another family ring would be lost forever.

The police, of course, saw nothing. They were kept busy picking up garbage and rehanging the oil lamps they found floating in the canals. Nor could the duke do anything with his clansmen vassals – especially since the leaders kept him and the entire Royal Council busy trying to explain why despite ancient treaties the city was closed to their goods. The discussions always ended with the duke finally agreeing to lift the ban. Through it all the city made money. And the young bucks of each clan, like Alex and his buddies Reuben Playbear and Eric Dancingbear, actually looked forward to finding new ways of causing as much trouble as possible without doing any damage. But the culture shock (never knowing who or what they would meet in the streets, in the canals or even in the fountains) was just too much for the city folk. The guild knew when it was beaten, and backed off – but they never forgot.

Only relatively recently had the family council decided to try another tactic and invest in some dark magic research. After several false leads and a few vanished magic users, they finally came up with the weather control device. Some guild members had expressed reservations about such strong collusion with diabolical powers, letting them infect the very fabric of their area. But Nadine reminded them that diabolical power was already at work in the valley where some magic user spells that controlled elements like storm or earthquake or fireball or lightning were all diabolically engendered. "Did the Assassins' Guild want to cede such power to the magic users?" she asked them all. "Are we not better than them?" Those who had asked the question about how dangerous and irreversible this device might be withdrew that question lest they be viewed as disruptive in the guild – and perhaps even be given a gift contract.

But implementing the device by insinuating it into the natural magic fabric of the Markasandra Valley brought them into direct conflict with the behind-the-scenes caretakers of the dukedom: the pegasi in the flat northern grasslands, the glow dogs in the glens and clearings among the Eastern woodlands and orchards, and the unicorns from the mountain "knobs" on the southern borderland. It was also possible for the Paladin community of the Holy Cross fortress, the protectors of the western backwater area, to halt the spell – but only if they found out about it. Fortunately that hadn't happened yet, so the unicorns remained the only obstacle.

Unlike the glow-dogs whose cavernous burrows were commonly known, the unicorns were much more elusive. And also unlike the pegasi who were big enough to be spotted from a distance both on the ground and in flight, Unicorns were smaller than elk and more reclusive. A direct attack first had to find the herd. Catching their scouts with the help of corrupted ex-rangers should have closed in on the herd's whereabouts. That process had started. Connections had been made; one unicorn had already been harvested and another was being pursued. Earlier in the day everything in the fishbowl had looked promising. What had happened?

The guild had again convinced their sorcerer into going with the strike force. Even though he was formidable enough by himself, he and the guild team had also taken along the unholy implements to summon the shadow-bears, the droghedae. They had already linked up with one of the free-lancers in Dennistown who had scouted the area. Together they should have been able to wipe out the unicorns rather easily: capture a few unicorn scouts, find the herd, throw a fireball or two, and let the shadow bears then hunt down singly what was left of the herd – child's play. But Nadine knew that for some reason it hadn't worked. So as "the Nightshade" she had no choice but to convene the guild family council before word of the debacle drifted back into the city.

From her hooded chair at the small end of the oval table she could see all the other guild-family members through her black mesh veil, but they could barely see each other and could not make out her features clearly. So had it always been with "the Nightshade", the guildmaster of assassins. In an affected voice, deeper than natural, and with the unseen aid of a crooner's mini-megaphone, she began dispassionately: "Evidence has reached us of a setback in our removal of the unicorn obstacle."

She had made an admission of weakness, a chance to be attacked.

No one said a word. Few would dare even consider it.

The older guild members probably knew the nightshade's identity; but they also had children and grandchildren, some of whom were being taught by Nadine this season. They knew she was ruthless enough to exact vengeance upon these little ones if an attack were made against her. And they knew that she knew that they knew this. The others may only have suspected her, but were afraid to act – each for their own reasons. Nadine knew this too, for she had been in that position, and consequently could out guess them and anticipate their moves. She looked around at their chairs and shadowed faces wondering who would try to attack her next – and who would fail.

"Though none of you chooses to ask," Nadine took a deep breath, gripped the armrest on her chair tightly and continued, "our strike force seems to have been …eliminated. Clansmen are suspected."

Shock gave way to outrage as each member of the guild family felt its pride insulted again. One after another the "sacred" family rings appeared on the table, pinned there by each member's dagger: the call for a vendetta. The family's honor must be preserved. The insult must be avenged.

Nadine looked over the table at the anger surfacing and applied her delicate manipulation. She had already managed to turn the anger over the failure of the strike force away from herself for underestimating the risk toward some unknown "clan" enemy. She watched that anger ripple through the room.

"Guildsmen," she began in a deep, almost sweet voice, "your wishes are noted; but we are professionals. We have established methods for dealing with those who dare interfere with us. This time we will attack them in their own heartland – but with the finesse for which only urbanites are known. Let the usual inquiries be made. We will convene the eve of one week hence and determine the most 'honorable' action. Let George be so notified."

Each refingered his ring of alignment reflection and rose slowly, one by one. Beginning with the newest of the guild members, they disappeared into the darkness behind their chairs. As the last two members rose together one asked Nadine: "Is there no trace of Kresov?"

No trace," she replied laconically; then with just a hint of a threat in her voice: "Why do you ask?"

Family ties were sacred even among assassins. But though they both knew Kresov was Nadine's only brother, they also knew better than to express any of the sympathy each of them instinctively felt for her. If even a trace showed in one's voice, it would be his death warrant. So the other elder replied obligingly as they disappeared: "We may again have need of a sorcerer."

As Nadine slipped home through the shadows of the waxing moon she remembered how she had used even the full moonlight to allow the former nightshade to be lured by her delicate beauty into trusting her. She had recognized him at the bank by his hands and voice, and to his surprise did not repulse his clandestine advances. One evening he had been "working late" at the bank, and never returned to his wife and family. He was never seen again, but his ring and dagger were now worn by the new occupant of the nightshade's chair. Any stalk of affection for Nadine grew bitter fruit.

As she continued her way home, almost invisibly darting from one shadow to another, she mused on how much like a unicorn's supposed teleportation that action was. Then the thought struck her: "If we can't eliminate the unicorns, we can open up and expose their habitat so thoroughly that they'll have nowhere to hide. Then they will either abandon the valley or become easy assassin's prey. But to clean out the woodlands the Duke will need a reason. I can make the area around the city so soggy that the city dwellers will be easily manipulated into clamoring for new wooden embankments and a series of valley dams. The need for wood pilings and branches for weaving into the mud embankments will quadruple. Even druidic sensitivities will play into our hands: To save enough trees to grow properly and make the druidic communities happy, we'll just naturally have to clear out all the underbrush to make up for the extra wood left standing. Soon, very soon, the unicorns will have no place to hide – and the druids will be responsible for it," she plotted. Now, however, she had her brother to avenge.

Chapter 10
THE MEDICINE COMPANY

Despite the sultry feel of the day before yesterday no storm had occurred during that night or yesterday either. This morning, though cool, was just pleasantly appropriate for a Thursday in early April. George Paddlefoot, the itinerant halfling trader, had just finished loading his locked boxes of jewelry and his papers and bottles into the double-keeled 2-man paddle boats for the backwater section of his territorial travels when the daily courier reached him. Among the rush orders of medicines in the pouch was the usual instruction scroll from his company with the totals-due for each of his next few established customers. But at the bottom, on the left wing of the company emblem, someone had blackened in one of the eagle feathers.

George ordered some more bread and soup, and some for the rider and oats for his horse as he secretly examined each envelope to see which contained the extra letter: the guild's instructions. Reading of the disappearance of the strike force puzzled him since he had seen them just a couple of days ago and reported the capture and "conversion" of parts of their first unicorn. He remembered watching how eagerly the droghedae had devoured what was left of the unicorn – even the dark hide with white flecks or stars in it. "There's just got to be evidence of them somewhere," he reasoned. "The clans can't hide everything, curse them. You can bet I'll find it! Kresov still has some of my medicine making equipment he was going to use on the unicorn's horn and blood. I had better get my stuff back – and maybe I'll even get his too."

By the time the rider courier had finished his soup George had his inventory list and itinerary ready for the "company." He sent back the original dispatch, replying that he would indeed take the rush order to Dennistown – and he had blackened in a feather in the other wing of the emblem to let the guild know that he understood the assignment and would report to them personally five nights from tonight as they insisted.

As the courier rode off northwest to the city George saddled his pony, gave his assistant charge of the cargo and the two guards, packed his saddle bags, and set off east toward Dennistown. All along the central low ridges of the Marksandra valley life was breaking out of its winter shell. A green tinge had already appeared in the tips of the willow strands and to the pasture-lands. The first traces of white were breaking through their coarse black coatings on the wild crabapples; and even on the knobs themselves, the barren stubble of wintry tree silhouettes softened into a pale gray-green lacey mantle of new shoots from each branch. The prairie land had been burnt and the fence rows cleared. Freshly plowed fields passed him one after another as the pony trotted along the dark blue dwarfstone road. On one rise he caught a glimpse of the Springfield windmills and soon thereafter came to the fork that led there. But he turned away from the route that led past these to the wharves and glass furnaces of Lakewood, and instead galloped south toward Dennistown. As he passed the still-barren orchards and rode through the split-rail fenced pastures, black and white faced dairy cattle watched him go by. Everywhere spring was finally taking hold. That was bad. Spring made people become more active and feel better with new life. They didn't need his "medicines." Business declined. That was bad.

He rode into the corral at Silverhorn Tavern just at dusk, and considered himself lucky to have made that good a ride on small hoofs. His dark blue waistcoat and white shirt were covered with dust and his collar chafed under his black neckerchief. His knees and thighs ached, and his dark gray leggings were soaked with equine sweat that gave him a displeasing aroma. He dismounted and gave the reigns to "Cutter," the ruggedly affable ex-cowboy, who had saved his money and was buying the tavern. While stretching a bit to put his little joints back into place, George asked politely how his wife and children were – and listened patiently to the usual children's anecdotes. As the children's stories went on and on, he glanced around, while still trying to smile, and noticed that Kresov's horse and buggy were missing. As he kept listening and smiling his face started to hurt. Sometimes, especially when he was tired or worried, it was difficult to keep up the pretense of a good alignment.

George was finally able to sneak in a word and ask if there was still a room open for the night. Cutter spit out his wad of Indian gum, wiped his mouth with the back of his hand and answered: "Oh sure, just head on in 'n' Sky'll take care of you. Tell her I said to treat you real nice – like she did the kids this morning when..." But by now George was halfway to the log and stone tavern, having taken all the "niceness" he could stand in one day.

Cutter's part-elf, part-halfling wife, Deborah Morning Sky, was cleaning up the common room and getting ready to stoke up the fire when she spotted him. "George, what a pleasant surprise to see you again!" she exclaimed as she bounced her way over to him and gave him a big hug. George smiled even though he felt like vomiting.

"What brings you back so soon? Your friends moved on to the "elegant" Golden Carriage House in the middle of town just after you left. Why don't you look there for them? Or did they go back to the city already. Wonder why they came..."

George knew better than to try to answer all of Sky's questions even when he wasn't feeling tired. Tonight he just held up the courier pouch while she continued "welcoming" him.

"Oh, of course," Sky replied more gently, her mothering instinct taking over, "you just rest. Which doctor did you give the medicine to? That's OK. The room on the left is open. I'll send up some hot water and towels right away. Do you want supper?"

"Just shut up and leave me alone" is what George really wanted to say, but he merely nodded and smiled politely as he dragged his body up the half-log stairs. "No wonder the city couldn't handle the clan invaders," he thought. "You'd chatter someone to death. Just wait till your crops fail and no one pays their bills and the guild buys this place out from under you. We'll just see how you smile and talk then." He nevertheless washed, ate, set out his clothes for Sky to clean, and was sound asleep when the full moon reached the ancient temple that night.

The next morning George was back in his fake character. He played with the kids in the yard a while and noticed with silent disgust that the purple crocuses were blooming in the new grass. Upon leaving he told Sky he'd stay there that night too. "As long as I'm here I may as well stay for the services."

He made the last of his legal deliveries in the morning and then strolled through town, across the square and over to St. Stephen's church. That high holyday, Good Friday, everyone who could get away from work was at church all afternoon. Usually the youngest (or healthiest) cleric in the parish would be the one to carry the large cross from place to place while the other clergy, in blood-red robes and black stoles, read the passion. The crowd followed and begged for mercy for their sins. At the eleventh station the blood of Christ, consecrated by the oldest cleric the evening before, was brought out of the tabernacle in the special glass chalice made last advent. The left hand of the cross carrier was tied to the cross and the palm sliced open with the point of a nail – letting the cleric's blood drip into the chalice and mix with Christ's. Helped by a "Cyreanean", the crossbearer would then struggle to carry the chalice and cross outside to the fire-site, the twelfth station. The faithful followed, crowding around to see the shattering of the chalice – and watch the price of their salvation seep into the barren ground.

George went there too – not really to watch this and see, but to be seen. His customers were always ready for him and more of his "magic powder" or "candy" as some of the younger customers called it. They always had the appetite, but couldn't always sneak money or small precious items out of their homes to pay for it. Sometimes he'd deny kids who couldn't pay. Other times he'd spread his poisons around rather freely – baiting his hook to trap them. Then, when he really wanted something any of their families had, he knew he could squeeze it out of them. Yet so far no one suspected the traveling dealer in "fine crafts and medicines" of carrying stolen goods and dangerous medicines.

One of his regular customers, William Wheatfield, Jr., or "Weed", the young delivery boy for the smaller of the general stores in town, worked his way over to him through the crowd. As neither of them had anything with them, George just whispered, "At ten tomorrow, usual place." Then they slowly drifted apart as the crowd moved to the next few stations where the cleric was cut from the cross, bandaged and absolved all there in the name of the Christ he had represented. The remainder of the afternoon was taken up with administering comfort to any of the faithful who wished to confess their sins individually and get spiritual advice as to how to overcome them.

Chapter 11
NEWS IN THE TAVERN

That evening the taverns were full. Silverhorn was no exception. The upper and lower rows of pegs all along the entry walls of well-trimmed yellow poplar held cloaks, hoods and hats from various sized customers. Not only was there the usual Friday night crowd – like "Rips" the barbarian fur-trapper from up in the knobs as well as several of the deer and horse and ox clan farmers including the Redox brothers: Charlie and Jack and Brad – but many other clansmen who had come into town for the "services at the cross" were there too. Alex had come from work with his Bear Clan buddies Reuben and Eric. Even Kevin Robinsong, the local bard who sang for his drinks, had brought a visiting fellow bard, William Coltan or "Colt" whose lute playing kept the halflings stomping on the dwarfstone floor surrounding the large central fireplace.

Everyone was hungry, for church law prohibited eating anything that day between sunrise and sundown or drinking anything besides plain water. The tavern crowd was rowdy, their empty stomachs having absorbed quickly the tavern's beer and wine and ale. The quote from Psalm 104 verse 11 engraved above the bar seemed as if it had been inspired specifically with them in mind: "They give drink to every beast from the field. Here the wild asses quench their thirst."

Minor scuffles broke out at human-sized tables in the smokier section further back from the dance floor. There tables of clansmen would taunt each other somewhat good-naturedly, then toast each other. At their own tables they would sing and sway together, but also smack one another for grabbing the wrong stein of beer or tiny "deer's horn point" cup of the tavern's questionably legal specialty: fiery "magic" water which shone as clear as moonlight. Indeed, the place was so busy that Sky had hired a couple of her relatives to help that evening in addition to her fellow druidess, Brook, who worked every Friday and Saturday night.

With all the well-lubricated jaws about George got an earful of everything that had happened recently in the town. With just a word or two he could steer the conversation into the direction he wanted it to go – and steer it back out before anyone realized that they were being pumped for information. He found out that Kresov and the three guildsmen had been seen for a few days around town, usually complaining about the rustic conditions. They would head out south of town each day, and were seen with Troy heading up Gunner mountain last Saturday. But George knew this, because he was there when they got back late Saturday; so he pumped for more information a little harder. At the bar near the tavern entrance he overheard Brad and Charlie telling Eric about how bad the crop forecasts were for all the clans. Over near the fieldstone fireplace he listened to Kevin commenting to Colt how lousy the music was during the Palm procession last Sunday but that it was better on Thursday. Near the large oak staircase going up to the sleeping loft he learned how on Sunday Kresov and the guildsmen had moved into town. He heard Rex the deacon tell Howard, the parish almoner, that the shriving had gone slowly on Monday but had gotten better on Tuesday because the front must have come through without the rain.

"Right now everyone needs rain, since the winter and spring have been real dry so far," chimed in Forest, a local druid school teacher. "Ground's too hard to plant the potatoes."

"Yeah," Rex replied, "that's what I was sayin'. The people thought gettin' rid o' their sins might bring the rain."

"Didn't work, did it?" remarked Forest.

"Wasn't s'posed to," retorted Rex. "Our prayers don't work that way."

"Ours do."

"Really? Then why aren't we plantin'?"

Forest swallowed hard on that one and murmured: "I'll talk to the Prince of the Air about that."

While the discussion/argument continued, George kept listening and kept asking about the "strangers." On Monday they had stuck pretty close to town, getting some unusual looking arrow heads put on four of their shafts. No one had seen them since Monday afternoon except Harry Crier, the town's roving watchman, who claimed early Tuesday morning to have seen a group of five people heading south of town before dawn. One of them looked like a woman – with a long dress or robe and a delicate walk. "She" seemed to be carrying an ominous-looking basket. Harry said that he thought it was their lunch, since the others carried swords and bows. But he hadn't been able to see them clearly 'cause it was still dark.

George now had a little more to go on as he moved from group to group. Was anyone else out south of town on Tuesday? Someone must have seen something! Forest, when George mingled into his group by the stairs again, replied that one of the little sisters in his druid "family" had been out south all day Tuesday – and had come in much later than expected.

"Come to think of it, she had on different color leather armor." George's ears perked up. Black perhaps? the assassins' armor? "White instead of her usual brown." George's ears "unperked." "Girls get away with everything," he claimed. "She comes in much later than she promised from getting the holly branches for some cleric, and her boyfriend still talks her way out of being grounded. They were out again late last night when she should have been at the full-moon service in our grove. That's why he's here without her tonight. She got into deep trouble for that one."

"Who's here alone?" George asked, not seeing anyone there by himself.

"I told you! her boyfriend yonder: the ranger talking to Alex."

"Who's Alex?"

"The barbarian in the gray leggings and sleeveless tunic. He does a lot of woodcutting in his Bear-clan lands just east of our sacred grove, so we keep an eye on him. Don't you know anyone around here?"

George let slip: "Only the important people" before he could stop himself, to which the druid replied, "Well, excuse me for livin'!"

George beat a hasty retreat and mingled his way over toward the bar where Sky had just refilled Rips' mug of ale. She was now arranging the second round of ale steins on her tray for the ranger and barbarian, and had grabbed a bowl of their special crisp-fried 'tater skins for them. He heard her call out, "Should I draw one for Patrick this time, too?"

"Naw," they shouted back, "he can't come – too weak."

"What about Heather?"

"Grounded, 'cause o' last night."

As Sky brought the drinks and chips over, George kind of ended up behind her, facing away, sipping his wine and leaning against one of the huge oak support beams holding up the loft.

"What did you do you scoundrel!" she asked Kilian half jokingly as she set down the ale steins.

"Oh it was great, almost like a vision of heaven..."

"Yeah, it was hard t' d'scribe just how good it was..." broke in Alex.

"Fiends! both of you!" exclaimed Sky as she tossed the 'tater bowl onto the table. "How can you brag about it on the same girl. And I thought you really loved her. And you," she turned angrily to Alex, "even wild as you are you should have had more decency than to ... than to ..." she dropped the tray and turned away toward the bar trying to hide her face. George ducked away from her and bumped into Rips – who let loose a cavernous belch and staggered away.

"No, wait, it's not what you think," Kilian shouted. "It was a religious experience ...."

"Call it what you want, you can't justify it," she replied indignantly; then with pain in her voice: "You knew better; you've been waiting to get married..."

"No, no," broke in Alex as he stood up, red-faced, "you got it all wrong! We watched two unicorns go up to heaven."

"Sure you did," she replied cynically, "and I'm a fairy godmother and my husband is an enchanted frog and the moon is made of green cheese and..."

Lex shrugged his shoulders and sighed: "Just ain't no reasonin' with the woman," as he sat down and buried his face in his second mug of ale. But Kilian was not so easily put off. For though his honor could be questioned he would not allow Heather's to be challenged so lightly – even by Sky.

"Look," he said firmly as he pushed away the heavy table and slowly rose to his feet, his dark eyes glistening with barely controlled rage: "I swear before all the saints that Heather's still a virgin. And I don't like people thinkin' and sayin' otherwise, even friends. If Lex says we said good-bye to two unicorns, believe him. Anyway, you can ask Patrick if you still don't believe us. But that's why he's not here."

"Huh?" replied Sky, now completely confused and becoming more and more embarrassed as the conversation continued.

"C'mon, Lex, let's blow out o' this place," grumbled Kilian as he started to step over the bench. Alex proceeded to down that mug of ale in one chug and get up, but stopped and rested one foot on the bench.

"No, wait," protested Sky as she held out her hands in front of her but not quite touching Kilian. "I'm sorry. Let's start over again. Where is Patrick?"

"He's recovering from the blood loss during the service this afternoon."

"But, he was OK last year. What happened this time? Was his hand cut too deeply?" she asked.

"No, woman!" Alex burst in loudly feeling the ale a bit, "we said blood loss. Part of his gift from Whitewind meant his blood ain't gonna' replace itself so easy no more. Shoot, it'll be three days 'fore he can do much o' anythin'. But we didn't know that, that's why we all gave him the sorcerer's dagger."

"Shut up," growled Kilian under his breath.

"There ain't no trouble," Alex replied, smiling broadly and swaying a little. "He tried to kill you and Mike with that fire-ball and those hu-u-uge shadow bears," he added accompanied by wild gestures that set him even more off balance. "Anyway, we ain't the ones who killed him, Patrick was."

"Yeah, but you chopped up the assassins in the web."

"That was the fun part!" bragged Alex smiling even wider, his face beaming. "Let's do it again!" He reached for his sword, which wasn't at his side as he had expected, due to the tavern rules, and finally lost his balance. He swayed back and forth twice, then ended up sitting down hard and letting loose one of his wild and deep barbarian laughs.

Sky sat down quietly and asked Kilian to please start from the beginning – which he did while Lex stared blankly at the bowl of 'tater skins and nursed Kilian's mug of ale. Sky grew more and more wide-eyed as the tale unraveled, but she listened patiently. A little further away, watching the fire and just barely within halfling earshot, George heard – not everything – but just what he needed.

....

As he wandered out to get his mules and supplies, Rips ran into Cutter just inside the stable door and asked: "You ain't gonna be closed tomorrow just 'cause a' church are you?"

"Yeah, we are," Cutter replied, grinning mischievously as he continued coiling up the rope. "I want the kids to see the bonfire. B'sides, Sky 'n' me d'serve a break once in a while too, and we're gonna' take it."

"Shucks! that means I don't get to celebrate Easter. At least you got a family. There ain't no fun up in the trapping camp.

An' it just don't seem right takin' a jug home and celebratin' all by my lonesome, do it?"

"Tell ya' what," Cutter suggested, "Come with us tomorra' night 'n' I'll buy ya' a drink free afterwards."

"Well, nah, it ain't that important that you all should go to the trouble..."

"Won't be no trouble," insisted Cutter, "so don't go givin' me no excuses. Sky 'n' me can use your help, big as ya' are, lettin' the kids see 'n' keepin' hold o' all three o' them. Then you can stay overnight 'n' have Easter dinner with us."

Rips paused a moment, then shook his head slowly and replied: "It ain't no good, Cutter. I just can't take advantage o' y'all like that. Y'all rent your rooms 'n' I can't pay for one. Iff'n y'all were an ordinary family it'd be diff'rent. I can't do it. I ain't good enough for insides – but I thank y'all anyway. I usually just crash down in the orphanage stables on the way back to the hills. I'll be OK," he replied as he turned away and led his mule across the stable yard toward the corral gate.

"Hold on, Rips," Cutter shouted after him, "I got a compromise. Come with us like usual, then bunk in the stables here 'stead a' at the orphanage. You can still head back t' camp after dinner 'n' make it there 'fore dark. What d' ya' say?"

Rips' face brightened and his brow twitched as the arguments Cutter gave battered the reluctance in his mind. "I thank ya' kindly, Cutter, but I still don't see how I can. I'd embarrass you all. I ain't even got no decent clothes – all wore out 'n' dirty."

"Shoot, Rips," Cutter replied as he hung up the coil of rope, "You know we ain't formal. Anything's good 'nuff here – y'already been inside in 'em tonight, ain't ya'?"

"Well, maybe, iff'n you're real sure y'all don't mind..."

"Rips! you know I don't say nothin' I don't mean. Now you be here tomorro' evenin' in time to help us get the kids to the bonfire. No more argument."

"OK, OK," he replied backing away and smiling wryly. "I'll, be here – 'n' I'll look forward to it all day," he shouted over his shoulder as he led his mule out the corral gate and up toward his camp..

....

The next morning at breakfast George pursued his questioning with the delicacy of an acrobat. He found out a little from Sky who the ranger was she seemed so enthralled with last night by teasingly threatening to tell Cutter about the two of them talking so quietly. She laughed it off, shaking her wooden spoon covered with oatmeal at him and threatening in turn to wallop him if he didn't behave himself better.

"All these creeps treat me like a child just because I'm small," he grumbled inside himself. "One day they'll learn to fear me. One day they'll regret their size and their attitude of superiority. Someday I'll get even with them all." But he just smiled at the baby girl and two small boys at his half-size table in the kitchen with him. When Sky went out to the chicken coop for another half-dozen eggs, he asked Ricky, their 7 year-old, if he knew Kilian; and Ricky, still at that trusting age, gave more information than George could possibly use – most of it correct.

After finishing off the other six eggs, two slices of ham, eight biscuits and a bowl of oatmeal, George paid his bill and went into town. As he was leaving, making sure Cutter noticed, he gave the kids one little toy ball to play with (and fight over). George thought how satisfying it was to be able to sow dissension even while appearing to be generous. Maybe even one of the younger two would swallow it and choke to death. Then the place would at least be a bit more somber. No one deserved to be as happy as they seemed to be.

Chapter 12
MASQUERADE IN TOWN

George walked his pony the mile and a quarter south into town, because he still hurt from the long ride the day before. He thought of his own children, and the meddlesome wench he had married a few years ago. She had finally given up on him and taken their three girls with her back to her family. They lived somewhere west of the city, across the barrens, in the farmlands of the Markasandra delta: on the edge of the duke's jurisdiction. Always griping, she was never satisfied no matter what he brought her. She was always claiming he never trusted her, wouldn't confide in her, stayed away too long, never loved her, only used her to move up in the world. "Damn right I did," he thought to himself, "and you bought my pitch lock, stock and barrel. So what, your uncle needed someone to handle his territory for him. So he retired early – with a little persuasion from the guild. Go, stay away, all you do is cost and never give. See if I care."

By now he had reached the Golden Carriage House and tied his pony in front of it. Across the courthouse square he could see the Monsignor puttering in the rose garden along side St. Stephen's and a plan took shape. He looked through his saddle bags a moment and found his dark gray travel hood, a faded red tunic and a hand-size leather ball. Ducking between buildings to change his white shirt and dark blue dress coat for these, he pulled the hood over his slightly graying hair so that only his child-like face showed. As he kind of wandered over to the monsignor while tossing the ball up in the air and catching it, he practiced raising the pitch of his voice.

"Good morning, Monsignor," he said eagerly with a little bow, the way the sisters had taught all the children to do. "Can Fr. Patrick come out and play?"

The old cleric looked up, and with his fading eyesight looked around to see who was talking to him. "Come here, young man, so I can see you when you talk to me. Now what was it you asked me?"

George tossed up the ball "obviously" as he came over so as not to have to get too close, and asked again with a touch of fake fear: "Please, Monsignor, can Fr. Patrick come out and play with us this morning?"

"No, young man, he cannot. He is not well today. You will have to do without him. He should not be spending his time playing with children anyway. You run along now."

"Please, Monsignor," replied George bowing again, "is he sick in his stomach, and does his mommy make him take that pink vomiting medicine like my mommy makes me?"

Monsignor Kieley straightened up slowly, letting the vertebrae in his back line themselves up at their own slow rate. He wiped his forehead with his episcopal purple handkerchief and looked intensely at George – but still couldn't see much of anything. "No, son, Fr. Patrick is a grown man, or elf, or whatever. But he is sick, or weak, or whatever. Anyway, he cannot play or do magic today, or was it tomorrow, perhaps next week; or was he going to sing and play? No, no, I will get it, just give me a minute."

Monsignor Kieley was starting to get confused. This is what George was waiting for. Whenever the Monsignor got confused during a sermon he would start to ramble. This time, with a word or hint now and then from "the little boy near him" he'd ramble through all of Patrick's history from even before he entered the seminary. He'd tell how Patrick's parents were lost in the last flood when they were passing through the area: How his father, who was a magic user or carpenter or mechanical builder of some kind, had tried to help some halflings with their belongings while the water was rising – when their own wagon broke loose and careened into the river. His mother was caught in the wagon and drowned in it though the basket Patrick was in floated clear. His father tried to swim to the wagon as it was sinking, but got his bootlaces caught in a submerged tree that was being swept along unseen and was pulled under as he struggled. The halfling couple never found a trace of either of his parents, so they adopted Patrick and raised him as their own with real deep love. On and on and on the monsignor went about how he had gone way far away to the seminary in the Duke's city and had learned some magic too, in the same new school that that nice young apprentice Lawrence Gmelin had attended, but he couldn't remember its name. Yet Patrick was always happier in the woods, even though Gmelin and most magic users, as well as Patrick's own halfling parents, were city people. Must be the elf part in him....

By now George was hoping he could get away before anyone with better eyesight came along. Luck was with him. The few people passing by the churchyard had business to attend to either in the church or the rectory, or someplace nearby in town, and so avoided at all costs getting into a conversation with the monsignor. They waved politely from a distance or tipped their hats and called to him, but never came close. Just as George had moved him from talking about the "rank indicated by the colors of clerics' robes" to colors of roses in the garden, a gang of boys came running down the street shouting after a runaway pig. George saw his chance, shouted "I gotta go", kissed the monsignor's hand and ran off with the "other" boys: leaving the monsignor talking about his roses – to his roses.

Around the corner, near the school outhouse, George had started to change back into his adult clothes when he heard the clock in the church tower chime for the hour, and then strike the bell ten times. He remembered that Weed was to meet him here – but he didn't have his "magic powder" with him. He put back on his disguise so no one would notice the "two boys" talking on the school playground.

Weed was late. But he came drifting in almost oblivious to everything around him. George had to repeat his questions a couple of times each to get an answer, but he expected this because he knew these effects in his "clients" and how such phases would come and go. Fortunately, he knew as well that Weed would not remember much of what he said or did during these spells.

Since Weed was really familiar with not only the townspeople but also the clans, due to his deliveries, George verified some of the information he had received about Kilian and Patrick, and obtained some about Heather's "family." It was the typical instruction and prayer commune of druids of various ages, which some clans call a school. Most of the "students" on their ranch just east of town had just reached puberty and were being prepared to go into farming or to carry on the "family." Every once in a while one might even find a bard in one of the families; but this family was too ordinary (and a touch too wild) for that. Other than the fact that Heather was just a quiet little druidess, fond of plants and gentle with animals and deeply in love with Kilian, there wasn't much to tell.

With questions about Michael, however, George struck pay dirt. Weed's family and Mike's lived behind each other in the hilly area on the southeast edge of town. Despite a difference of four years in age, the two boys had played together easily because each was the youngest in their families. Mike suddenly had a little brother and Weed acquired a big brother who didn't pick on him. They had had the usual children's "adventures" climbing trees and catching crayfish in streams, but little by little they grew up.

As Weed floated in and out of his mental fog, George trailed him through these stories. It wasn't easy to tell who did what or who all was ever with them, but Weed kept reminiscing: "Just before Mike entered the Paladins..., not too long ago

..., maybe ..., we took a whole week trip to the Rock Creek Gorge. It took us a whole three days to ride there on borrowed horses; I got real sore, but it was fun. I ain't never been so far away. We went right through Springfield and up into the head-waters of Blue Lake. I never thought my parents would let me go. They wonder why I get dizzy and forget things. They'd be real scared if they knew we killed a humongous snake there. They ain't even seen the skin I still have."

George mentally asked himself why he hadn't required it from him yet, and knew he would soon. Weed rambled on: "One time, however, when Mike was home on leave, we went back to Rock Creek again with Patrick for some reason. I just don't remember, probably to get some special components for a magic or clerical spell. My parents like Mike and Patrick a lot, so I get to go with them. Coming down from the sandstone double arch in the rainbow cliffs area we lost our trail and I was scared. So was Patrick, but he wouldn't admit it. Mike was great! When he was checking out one of the leads by hanging by his hands over the edge of the cliff his foot hit an old sword. It was a bit battered and rusty, but it still sparkled. Mike claimed that it must have pointed out the path we wanted to take to get off the cliffs, even though we hadn't come up that way. I tell you, we were all real glad to get down. It was so hot, and the climbing had scratched all of us so that we all just shed our clothes and jumped in one of the creek pools to cool off and sooth our wounds. Good thing nobody came by and saw us. When we got back home here, Mike cleaned the sword real good and Patrick verified that the sword was indeed magic. They then looked at each other and realized that they had the power to turn it into a holy sword. We gathered the materials, carved mike's holy symbol on the hilt, and waited for sunset. At the last moment of daylight, Patrick consecrated it with the ancient blessing spell and holy oil and cleric's blood. I ain't never gonna' forget watching its glow change from white to blue as he did this – all while Mike held it by its blade straight up out in front of him."

"So that's it," sighed George dejectedly. "Of all the dumb luck! Five 'kids' who happened to be in the wrong place and they mess up an elegant plan. A whole strike force wiped out just because they had a holy sword which interferes with dark magic. Cruel, miserable fate! and the guild'll blame me. Life leads you on then slaps you in the face. I curse all elves! I curse all humans! Curse them all!" He suddenly realized how loud he had gotten. So had Weed, but he didn't know what George was so upset about.

George turned on him: "So you want powder, huh? No way! You hear me? No way!"

"No, you can't cut me off. I need it!" he pleaded.

"Too bad, "you have the wrong kind of friends," George sneered as he stalked away.

"I'll tell on you," Weed whined.

"Go ahead," George threatened; "and see what happens to you – and your parents. How're you going to like being in jail? No powder, and knowing you marked your parents for death."

It took a moment for the words to sink in. Then Weed ran after him "No, please, not my parents. They ain't done nothin' wrong. Please!"

George just kept walking as he glanced disgustedly at Weed who clung to him, begging. "Even one word, and your family goes on the Guild's list. When you least expect it," he snapped his fingers, "they're gone. No prayers, no confession..."

"Please, Mr. Paddlefoot, I'll be quiet. Please don't hurt them," he sobbed.

"You'd better be quiet," George warned, and then stopped walking; for they were getting too close to the street. "And I might even give you some more powder – if you do something for me."

"Anything" Weed begged, "just don't hurt them. I gotta' have the powder. Anything you want, just tell me."

"I only said I 'might' give you some powder," George replied coldly as he pulled Weed off him. "We'll see next week."

"Yes, sir, anything you say. But please let me have more powder, and please don't hurt them. I'll do anything, anything!"

"You're damn right you will," George thought to himself as he crossed the street, leaving Weed standing there alone on the playground, trying to dry his face with his sleeve and already shaking a bit. The threats had made the fog wear off early. Soon, too soon, Weed's convulsions would start. George changed his clothes quickly and walked in the front door of the Golden Carriage where he was greeted by the desk clerk.

Chapter 13
CLUES INSIDE THE GOLDEN CARRIAGE

Matthew, the deskman, recognized George and greeted him politely. He had shown him into the restaurant many times when he had been entertaining customers: usually the local "healers" and the few jewelers in town. To George's surprise, he motioned him over to the desk almost surreptitiously. In a low, almost secretive voice Matthew explained:

"Mr. Paddlefoot, we have a rather embarrassing situation here. Some guests from Russelburg checked in last Sunday, but we haven't seen them since Tuesday. Early Tuesday morning the magic user had the night clerk put his spell book in our lock-box, and it's still there. The maid cleaned the room that day, and Wednesday as well – since the beds were used Tuesday night. In fact, the room was extremely unkempt Wednesday afternoon when she finally went in."

"How so?" George asked nonchalantly, trying to hide his interest.

"Good morning, Mrs. Ruhner," Matthew called politely to a rather ample but elegant, no-longer-young lady dressed in a beautiful gray gown and cloak trimmed in sable. As she slowly strutted by, her gold-capped cane placed delicately in front of each step, he inquired: "Is everything to your satisfaction?" But as it was beneath her station to reply, her serving maid just nodded curtly in his direction. When they were out of earshot, Matthew continued, still in hushed tones: "Where was I? Oh, yes. Well, some of the sheets and towels had blood on them, as did the rug by the window. There was only a little alchemy equipment around, even though there had been a whole table full of it the day before."

Matthew didn't see George's brow tighten as he went on: "But strange as it seems, their carriage was out front Wednesday morning. So we put it in the stable for them and waited till late Wednesday to clean their room – as I said earlier."

Matthew looked at him helplessly. "I don't know what to do. If I notify the town watch or the field sheriff, he'll ask why I didn't contact him sooner. And if there has been any trouble, there'll be investigations. That would mean closing the back rooms. You can just imagine how upset that would make the owners. What would you do?"

George, jolted out of his reverie of imagining the guild's delight at the local gambling competition having to close down, remembered quickly that above all they wanted no notoriety. If the Paladins ever got wind of the existence of the weather control spell . . ." Oh, oh, of course," he replied, "You've done the right thing, of course. There is no reason to cause commotion, and perhaps even worry your other guests." His eyes wandered in the direction Mrs. Ruhner had taken.

"But where do I go from here? I have their room rented for tonight."

"Don't worry, George replied with a wink while letting his lower lip protrude a bit and kind of "patting" the air in front of him with his left hand in a gesture of confidence; "I think I can help."

"Oh please do so," replied Matthew, his light blue eyes almost pleading with him. "I'd be very grateful."

George almost slipped out of his fake alignment by starting to ask coldly "How grateful?" but he caught it quickly enough to stutter: "How..gr-..a..m-many days do they owe for?"

"I have to bill them for Sunday through Wednesday," he replied. "I can't get around what people saw and what they gossip about. They were strangers here, you know."

"Yes, I know," George replied calmly. "And I think I know why they left so soon. Here's my suggestion: I'll pay their bill and take their baggage back to Russelburg. When I find them

I'll get them to pay me back before I give them their stuff. But for your sake, I suggest that we do this very discretely."

"Of course, of course," replied Matthew almost obsequiously, "I'll get everything ready at once. How can I ever thank you?"

George again suppressed the desire to let loose "I'm sure you will find a nice financial way year after year" only because blackmail would blow his "good" cover. But Matthew could sense some tension in him, and so looked at him surprised at some emotion he had seen flicker in George's eyes. So George quickly covered this with "as a little sign of gratitude . . ." Matthew's face paled. "How about having the kitchen fix me a bit of lunch for the road?"

George could see Matthew's whole body relax as the "cover" took effect. Instead of a fellow conspirator, George again became in Matthew's eyes just another typical halfling. Matthew smiled broadly and proclaimed "You'll have the best picnic lunch we've ever made! In fact, why don't you watch them prepare it while I get all the visitors' baggage together? I think I can even arrange for you to sample it as it's being prepared. No, better yet," Matthew announced gleefully, "go into the dining room for a special lunch here, complete with a bottle of sparkling wine; and take the basket as well!"

For once George almost enjoyed pretending to be good. He trotted joyfully into the dining room and was lost in halfling rapture for the next hour. The four druid matrons at the next table doing their monthly "recipe exchange" visit to the elegant local eating establishments marveled at his eating capacity. They requested and recorded his assessment of every course he ate. When he finally emerged, Matthew and the security guard handed him the huge, richly bound spell book, and had him sign for it – as was required for anything released from the strong-box. George hesitated for a second; but then, not wanting to attract attention, he went ahead and signed his own name.

"I'll make sure it gets delivered right away," he promised as he paged through it, looking at the pretty but indecipherable symbols. After checking the spell book to his satisfaction, and paying handsomely for the room, George stopped in the kitchen to give his compliments to the chef and pick up his food basket. As he was leaving he noticed the several large piles of firewood for the five ovens stacked next to the kitchen-house.

"Where did you get all your firewood?" he asked Mary Lou, one of the dishwashers, in a casual, friendly manner.

The auburn-haired, abundantly freckled eighteen-year-old looked up surprised at the question. "They deliver it from the woodlot just south o' town, sir, four times a week," she replied – stopping a moment, happy to have an excuse to dry her hands.

George, seizing the opportunity, rummaged through his side pouch for a little container of hand cream and handed it to her gallantly, while asking casually: "Who brings the wood?"

Mary Lou opened the little waxed paper envelope of cream as if it were a box of rare jewels. Though just an insignificant sample to George it was probably the most expensive gift she had ever received – and she was enthralled with it. Hoping not to arouse suspicion, George dared to ask the question again.

All apologetic, Mary Lou replied eagerly "Oh, sir, sometimes the boss-man, Big-Tim, he delivers it in his wagon and we all have t' help unload it. But most o' the time Lex brings it on in," she kind of drawled out as she rolled her eyes a bit; and George could almost feel her melt inside when she talked about Alex.

"He carries those big bundles all by hisself on his shoulders and I can watch his muscles tighten in his arms and back – especially in the summer when he's only wearin' the leather vest. Little bitty drops o' sweat kind a' glisten on him. I waits for him with a dipper o' cold water afterwards and he smiles at me. One time one of the other girls noticed a copper-head snake coiled in the wood bundle he was carryin' and screamed, spillin' milk all over him. He killed it easy and gave it to the cook, then started to wipe the milk off hisself. I grabbed a cloth and helped wipe it off. I actually got to touch his arm and chest."

Mary Lou suddenly realized she was talking to a man (or halfling) rather than another adolescent girl like herself, and started to blush and say, "Oh, thank you, sir, for the cream, thank you, thank you."

"Think nothing of it." George replied politely, then more friendly: "Do you know where Alex lives?"

Mary Lou blushed more and more, replying as she looked away, "Oh, I couldn't say, sir. I ain't s'posed t' gossip and I gotta get back t' work."

George very consciously and obviously looked up at the packet of cream in her hand, then directly at her face with a fake hurt expression. She felt ashamed for being ungrateful, and proceeded to describe his whole family: from the older brother who worked in the wood shop to his sisters whom she knew from Sunday school instructions, to his little brother who already showed barbarian tendencies and the three real little ones whom she didn't really know. When she mentioned his father's barbarian background from the outer reaches of the Bear Clan and his mother's relatives in the Ox Clan near the backwaters, George had what he needed. He picked up his heavy basket of "snacks" and said good-by politely, apologizing to her boss for keeping her away from her work so long, and leaving her in a dreamy "puppy love" mood all day.

George tethered his pony to the rear of Kresov's carriage or "buggy" and loaded his basket of food and the spell book in among the equipment they had salvaged for him. He eased his way through the unpaved back streets and set off northwest toward Russelburg, the duke's capital city. The bright yellow forsythia flanking the road and the new white and pink billowy blossoms in the orchards decked the whole valley out in Easter colors. The daily freight wagon came toward him and passed on by, as did two couriers and various holiday travelers. Some of the farmers returning home from their fields or from the trading posts George regularly visited waved and shouted "Happy Easter." George waved back only because he had to.

He made it to Hauber's landing by nightfall, and took notice of the fact that his assistant had not returned. That was OK, since two and a half days is rarely enough time to cover the whole backwater area, and it meant that he'd have a quiet evening. He checked into his regular room in the lodge and got ready for bed, only to remember as he was blowing out his candle that tonight was the paschal vigil – with its river baptisms and candles and bonfire. So he dragged himself out of bed, threw a little water on his face and got dressed again for the ceremony. Though the people of St. Brendan's parish saw him at the service all right, he was only really about 10% there. Fortunately, a little old lady halfling next to him kept nudging him whenever he started to nod. She also kept smiling at him affectionately, but he didn't notice.

....

The bonfire at St. Stephen's church also went well, with Lee riding on Rips' shoulders the whole time, holding onto his ears and bushy red hair. Afterward he fell asleep as Rips carried him home slung over his shoulder. Both Cutter and Rips enjoyed sharin' their drink while Sky put the little ones to bed. As Rips headed back to camp the next day after the noon meal he knew he'd never be just an ordinary customer at the tavern again. He'd always have to visit the kids before he got too rowdy; and no matter how drunk he got he'd never let Cutter defend the place alone.

....

The next morning, Easter Sunday, George slept late, had his usual huge breakfast, and drove the carriage along the river northwest into Russelburg. Even though they were covered with fresh daffodils this time of year, he was relieved to see the stone embankments, the old dikes transformed into causeways, come into view before him. He ignored the greetings from the folks on the string of small dilapidated houseboats tethered between the drawbridge and the southeast corner tower where gambling barges operate in the summer. He made it inside the city without attracting attention.

George went immediately to Kresov's rented stall in the municipal stables, but had difficulty finding a porter to carry the baggage to his boarding-house nearby because of the Easter Day festivities. He settled in and lit a fire, while he waited till the "nymph dances" and flag-studded, paladin-guarded regatta were over. As he tried to muster up the courage to face Nadine and tell her about her brother, he fortified himself by polishing off the remainder of the contents of the food basket which was ample even by halfling standards. The cozy feel of the fire and the effects of the food and wine, however, were just too much for him to handle in the tawny afternoon light.

Chapter 14
THE SPELL BOOK

George awoke with a start. The room was dark: the faint amber glow from the fire place only barely touching the pervading deep shadow. There was a figure in that shadow – dark robed, coming toward him, slowly. The figure stopped directly in front of him, towering over him as he sat there. In a deep, almost spectral voice it whispered: "Think carefully and speak quietly. What did you discover?"

"Who are you?" George responded.

Quicker than lightning the figure's right hand flashed downward, stinging the left side of his face as a ring inside the leather glove crushed his upper lip against his teeth in the blow.

"I ask the questions here!" the figure growled as George swallowed his blood and tried in vain to protect his face. "Who attacked our strike force" it asked as it grabbed George's arm and began twisting it.

The blood dripped from George's mouth as he tried to relate the story – from the tavern talk and the children and the hotel – while each detail he reported brought another twinge of pain to his contorted arm, which felt like it was ready to break at any moment.

"Why did you not question Troy?"

"Because I couldn't find him," George replied gruffly.

Pain shot through his arm as one of the tendons in his elbow snapped. "I want the real answer," the figure intoned.

"No, please!" begged George "my arm!"

"The truth!" demanded the figure.

"I was afraid . . ." gasped George as he stretched to relieve the tension on his tortured arm.

"You lazy, spineless coward! Had you no fear of the guild? We will teach you fear . . ."

George felt his shoulder blade begin to grate against his chair and crush the muscles between them. "No ...I was afraid the paladins would get wind of my mission ...No, please! ...the ...No, my shoulder! ...the weather-control...."

Suddenly his arm was free. He held it close to his body as the elbow and shoulder throbbed. He held back his tears.

"You will find and question Troy to verify your information before you present it to the guild."

"How?"

He felt again the sting of the ringed hand as the figure hissed: "Question not!" Then more softly it directed: "You will have him summoned here. There are other practitioners of magic – good ones, unfortunately; but certainly one can be persuaded to do this."

George again started to ask how, but covered his mouth with his right hand – both to stifle his own words and to protect his face. The ploy worked. The Nightshade almost seemed to chuckle: "So you protect your mouth so you can continue to eat. Good, you are still more halfling than you are assassin. Stay that way. It is a good front; and you would be no good to us if it was known that you associated with the guild." Then in a sterner tone she added: "Think, if you feel yourself capable. Are there not other ways of persuading than by force and threat? Is there not a magic item we – or you – can trade for such a service?" she alluded as she glanced around the room, noticing the spell book and the few items of Kresov's other magic equipment. "Besides, what need have we of alchemy equipment without our sorcerer?

"Troy must have it," George dared to reply. "The blood in the room indicates that he ransacked it the evening he escaped from the ranger."

"Then perhaps the spell book will suffice," she hissed as she started over toward it.

"No!" gasped George, suddenly seeing his only treasure, the recompense for both the hotel bill and his alchemy equipment, slip through his hands.

"What?" shouted the Nightshade as she wheeled around to face him. "You dare to contradict me?" she growled as she advanced on him.

He jumped out of the chair and tried to dodge her but she was too fast for him. She caught him by the throat and bent him back over the arm of the overstuffed brown leather chair, slowly squeezing the life-breath out of him. His hands were too weak to pry hers loose, and his arms were too short to reach her body. He could feel his lungs contracting: gasping, begging for air. Then suddenly it was over.

His body dropped to the ground. As he lay there curled in a heap, drinking in the air, he heard the Nightshade say with disgust: "You are of no use to us dead." When the figure turned to go and just before it disappeared George heard it command him: "Have Troy at the guild meeting Tuesday evening!"

Three short hours later morning arrived; but only the chiming of the city's clocks and the ringing of the angelus bells announced that fact. Heavy, slow-moving clouds released a steady rain over the city and probably over the whole valley as well. The good earth and its farmers were more grateful for the needed moisture than were the urbanites. George begrudgingly paid for a healing spell for his shoulder and the tendon in his elbow. The cleric's actions and words seemed so much like just a good massage and some self-hypnosis that George wondered why he couldn't heal himself. But it had never worked when he tried it. And it felt so good when he visited them.

After that, he tried in vain to see Master Edgar: the ranking magician in town. Unless one was part of the Duke's inner circle, requests to see the court magician rarely succeeded. Depending on the attitude of Jules Hoarfox, Master Edgar's steward, most other clients were either postponed or shuffled off to his assistant. Apparently George's "tip" to Jules had not been sufficient, so he got only as far as Lawrence Gmelin, Edgar's apprentice. Most people, especially those with any halfling or gnome ancestry, would have been very pleased with the short, dark-haired and bushy eyebrowed slightly chubby barbarian. Despite having been picked on as a "pup" by both his older and younger brothers because he didn't do as much hunting and crazy howling at the moon as they all did then, Gmelin remained delightfully affable. Though they still considered him the "lost sheep" of the family because he had moved to the city and submitted to the discipline of study, even they liked him too.

Gmelin really believed not just in magic, but in its inherent goodness and natural efficacy as part of God's creation. His enthusiasm gave confidence to all those he prepared for the spells Master Edgar would weave – thus augmenting their effects. He and Patrick had become friends in magic school; for both could see the fingerprints of the Creator in the world around them and could follow the movements of that Divine Hand in the tempo of life. When they graduated from magic school and were accepted as apprentices in different parts of the dukedom, their paths diverged but their friendship remained. Patrick had completed his apprenticeship in just one year, partially because his Master, James Meaderer, developed a terminal illness. They both worked extremely hard, and were aided by other Masters, so that Master James could bestow the journeyman bag before he died. Rather than striking out alone as a junior mage, Patrick had followed a calling to the altar. This meant that, after ordination, he could use sacred spells as well as natural ones. Gmelin continued natural research in ancient sources [medicines] under the most elegant of the local experts: Master Edgar "the cautious." Both these two youngsters looked forward to the ever less frequent occasions that they could get together – and play wizard ball and reminisce and wrestle with the kids and discuss magic research and share insights – and enjoy some of the expert cooking by Meaghan, Gmelin's charming halfdwarven wife.

As one who sought to serve the creator – by entering the auras, the broken traces of God's gentle magic that still permeated the world, and letting himself resonate with the natural harmony in creation – Gmelin was the antithesis of a sorcerer. George despised him. He hated his reverential curiosity and his awe-filled wonder at even the most insignificant and financially useless aspects of creation. George was positively sickened by Gmelin's genuine friendliness and altruistic service. Insults bounced off him, and he was so naive that deceiving him or stealing from him was such a non-accomplishment that it held no thrill. It bothered George to be in the same room with him.

This time George simply refused to talk to Gmelin. He rang again for Jules, and with a much larger bribe (that Gmelin neither noticed nor suspected) managed to get an appointment with Master Edgar for the next day. The remainder of the morning George spent in the archives of the diocese filling in the background notes on the five "culprits" from the centralized lists of the baptismal and registration certificates. He was glad to be out of the dreary rain.

All that afternoon and evening as he made his usual rounds of the taverns in his neighborhood, slyly renewing his "business" contacts, the thought kept haunting him that these culprits were insignificant, mediocre people. Worse than that, they were as naively good and trusting as Gmelin, yet they had wiped out a sorcerer's strike force. Was this just an unfortunate set of circumstances, or was there something or someone he was overlooking?. That thought bothered him.

....

Master Edgar was extremely pleased to get a look at Kresov's spell book. So when George explained that the person he was seeking might know Kresov's whereabouts, and whether or how he could be returned home, the good magician agreed to summon him merely for the privilege of copying what he chose from the spell book and holding it until Kresov's return.

"After all, little one," Edgar explained condescendingly as he accepted the book from George, "My esteemed colleague, Kresov, will need this book when he returns. I will simply borrow it a while," he continued as he began to peruse it while calling out to his apprentice: "Gmelin, prepare the magic inks and parchments for spell copying."

His powder blue eyes lit up as he stood there holding the book in his left hand, deftly paging through it with his right. Every once in a while he would grimace and rapidly flip by a spell; but curiosity kept him moving the pages. Suddenly his face went ashen and he slammed the book shut – letting it drop through his hands and crash onto the inlaid wood floor. Gmelin came rushing in crying "Master, Master, are you all right?" He almost knocked George over as he hurried over to steady Edgar who stood there shaking, hands covering his face. Slowly he forced his composure to return to him. Shocked and embarrassed, he looked down at George – who had just picked up the spell book and was hugging it tightly.

"I had no idea ..." Edgar stammered out. "I ... I ... am appalled! A sorcerer! We suspected at times, but this compels us ... A sorcerer, a contaminer of our delicate techniques and coaxing ... Yet he had always been so elegant ... How could he do this to us, betray us in this way? Do you know what that spell calls for?"

Suddenly Edgar realized who else was in the room. "Oh, of course you don't. You aren't of our kind: you can't read magic. But even your little mind would be offended by it. I can't believe it of him! To kidnap a three-week-old baby and cut open its body and crush its still-beating heart into the sacrificial mixture. May the Lord have mercy on us!" he gasped as he made the sign of the cross. "Truly I shall have to inform the Magician's guild immediately."

"Are you sure you want to do that?" asked George in a vaguely threatening manner.

Edgar, taken aback by the boldness of George's question, looked at him in dismay. "Why, whatever do you mean?" he asked as he rested his left hand gently against his pallid cheek.

"Only that you have no evidence that Kresov ever used the spell. He may instead have been working on an anti-dweomer to it. Does he not deserve the benefit of the doubt? Should he not be asked before he is accused?"

"George, little one," replied Edgar as he twirled several strands of his long golden hair with his delicate, well mani-cured hands, "you are naive like all your halfling kind. The price one pays even to copy such a spell usually includes blas-phemy and often involves ritual murder itself. A good-aligned magician could not even study such a spell without risk, let alone copy it or work on it. But go on thinking the way you do – perhaps you, like Gmelin here, are better off."

Being classed with Gmelin made George want to vomit, but he controlled himself. After a suitable pause He asked: "When will you begin the spell?"

"How could you even think that I would ... no . . . never would I give in to the temptation to sorcery!"

"I meant the summoning spell."

"Oh, yes. Well, 'dear' underling, I'm afraid I'm just not up to it after looking through his book. Run along."

"Is your word no good?"

"I do not have to answer to you about my word," Master Edgar replied indignantly as he turned and reached for the bell chord. "In fact, as a royal council member, I do not even have to speak to someone of your station."

"Then I will be forced to take the spell book to a cleric. Do you wish them to know what kind of spells some members of your guild deal in? You can imagine the reaction the 'under-lings', as you call us, would have to such a disclosure."

Edgar's hand released the cord. He dismissed Gmelin and told him to wait outside the chamber for further instructions, then he turned to George. "That book must not leave this room."

George held the spell book tightly as he replied: "You have already agreed to a most reasonable price for it. Just summon the person I wish and bind him to me – I even have the rag soaked in his blood that you need – then the book is yours."

Edgar sat down, defeated. He could never go back to being an outcast from polite society: thought of as dangerous, or at least abnormal. He had worked too long for acceptance to let someone else's cheating force him again to wander from town to town, hiding his profession. If word of any sorcery ever got out, petty clerics, always ready to pounce upon evidence of di-abolical collusion, would make sure that neither he nor any other magic user would ever be trusted again. It would then be just a matter of time before mobs of underlings, all too eager for any excuse to loot the wealthy, would ravage his laboratory and his home. Even if he would be lucky enough to escape with his life, he would see his books and notes burnt and his friends turn away. Driven from town to town, requests for shelter denied at any price, his health would soon give way. Within a few weeks he would be dead of starvation – and the bitter loneliness of a broken heart.

Edgar looked at the parquet floor and the inlaid oak fur-nishings around him. He fingered the brocade trim on his ex-pertly stitched sarum-blue linen robe. It was all too much to risk. Could he even trust the other members of the Mages' Guild with this revelation? Finally he said softly:

"You are right, little one. No one must know the contents of this book." Then in a resigned, almost distracted tone he continued: "I will need to mix his blood with some of yours to bind the spell to you. Come with me into the laboratory."

As Edgar trudged into the next room George followed a bit apprehensively – and shut the door. An hour later he was home having a large lunch to replenish his strength from the morning, and to prepare his report for the guild that night.

Chapter 15
THE GUILD AND THE HUNTSMAN

As scheduled, the guild members had come together just after the rainy darkness had swallowed up twilight. George began his report with a step by step account of the disaster, and continued by relating all there was to know about Heather and Mike and their families. As they had no real clan connections, and since they were members of groups potentially competitive to the guild, it was decided to "accidentally" eliminate them sometime during the next year.

Alex was another case, however. His death needed to be both a fitting insult and a warning to the clans that their turf could be invaded just as easily as they could invade the city. Kidnapping and dismemberment of the whole family seemed to be the method of choice among the guild members. Lining up the severed heads orderly – from the oldest to the youngest – in front of their farmhouse would provide an "elegant" example, fitting the guild's purposes well.

While George was describing Patrick's background a scuffle broke out at the door to the inner chamber. They all turned to see a lanky outdoorsman grappling with the two guards there. Conscious of most assassin-style tricks, he had turned them against them. Already one of the guards lay writhing on the floor, gasping in pain, both hands holding his groin. With the slightest gesture from the Nightshade the lower section of the table where there were no chairs – that is, the "stand up" men – closed in on the intruder. They had him disarmed and pinned to the wall before he realized it. George continued:

"Our noisy intruder is named Troy. He is the ex-ranger or huntsman who was our contact in the Dennistown deanery. He is also the only surviving member of our strike force. He was summoned here by magic to give his report, for he seemed reluctant to face us after his failure ..."

"My failure?!" roared Troy. "It was your lily-livered magician who waddled around playing fighter who ..."

He had been cut off in mid word by a backhand blow from one of the guards. "We do not abide the slander of a guild friend. Restrain your tongue if you don't want it cut out."

"You skunk turd!" Troy spat out. "You chicken brains think you never goof up. You ain't no better than any other possum-breath low life...."

The razor sharp dagger came up from cutting his chin and lower lip and was held in front of his eyes by one of the hitmen. Troy suddenly became silent as blood trickled down his beard. George sauntered over to touch him – releasing the summoning spell's compelling power on him.

"Perhaps our dirt-grubber will learn his place," he continued as he resumed his story. "Patrick may present a challenge. Oh, not in himself," he added quickly as strange looks surfaced on the faces of some of the older guild members. "He is a member of both the junior mage's guild and the diocesan clergy. An outright attack on him like we have planned against the clans could bring the ire of both those organizations upon us."

"Is it not in our interest," interjected one of the elders delicately, his right hand raised palm up and fingers uncurling in mock question, "to keep those two groups far from each other? Can we not devise a death for him such that the magicians can be led to believe that it was due to his contamination of their spells with his religion," he suggested; "and the clerics be 'persuaded' conversely that his death was caused by his magic that besmirched their order and angered their 'God'? Of course the 'accident' must leave evidence to that effect – but no witnesses. And a few other incidental casualties might even anger the underlings against both organizations."

"Excellent, colleague!" the Nightshade adjudged aloud. "Was it not reported to us that on the church door in Dennistown there is a notice," she continued subtlely, "that this insignificant cleric is to provide some entertainment at the orphanage next Sunday which did not take place during holy week? Could not a 'mistake' be arranged there? And while that event is distracting attention, our 'business' with the clan of this Alex can be taken care of." All nodded their approval.

"Let me have the pleasure," sneered Troy. "I know the layout of his farm well, and I owe that swamp rat one for this." He held up his scarred hand. "I'll finish the job this time, and throw in the flee-bitten ranger for free. What size pieces do you want him delivered in? and any of you want any particular slices or 'trophies'?"

"Not so fast," cautioned the other elder as he took a deep drag on his curved pipe. "We cannot afford any more of your mistakes. We will judge who is to do what. Just report what you know of him and his family – and I hope for your sake that your information is better than your fighting."

"Why you stinkin'…uh…'stingray'!" replied Troy in a tone that began with disgust and ended sycophantly as the hit man let his dagger-point rest on Troy's nose. And much to the guild council's pleasure, Troy continued by describing Alex, Heather and then Kilian thoroughly if not calmly. As the report went on about Kilian's father's family of half-dwarf wood-cutters and stone masons, and his mother's family of half-elf ranchers and foresters, with a thief or gambler thrown in here or there on either side, George corroborated the description.

"Where did he receive his ranger training," inquired one of the 'juniors', a not-quite-elder council member; "and does the thieving you attribute to him link him to the thieves' guild? After all, we would not wish to upset our 'little brothers'." Everyone chuckled condescendingly.

"That information was not in our documentation," replied George furtively; "but I'm sure our ex-ranger here can inform us."

Troy shot George an ugly glance and tried to avoid the question with more town gossip about how Heather and Kilian had met at a dance at church. As the dagger point bit into the surface of his nose and bits of blood mingled with the grime there, Troy came more to the point: "OK, he ain't no guild member."

"How do you know this?" asked the original questioner.

"Well...uh... (the dagger point slit a little farther) I paid to have him black-balled."

"Clever! What about the ranger part?"

"Shoot! he can't be no ranger. There ain't no cat-scratchin' rat-raunchy rangers left in the whole stinkin' valley! Ain't no rewards, and they're all too dog dung lazy to go across the mountains to train for it."

"Enough!" commanded the Nightshade. "Take our 'guest' out and gag him, then wash out his wounds. Moonshine and salt should suffice."

"You low-down slimy dog slobber..."

The door closed behind Troy and his four captors as the conference continued – interrupted only slightly by muffled screams from the hallway.

"Have you anything more to add to your report?" the Nightshade asked George.

"No," he replied, after just the slightest pause, having decided to keep his suspicions to himself.

"Out with it!" demanded the Nightshade as she pounded the table. "What are you trying to conceal from us so unsuccessfully?"

George, terrified now, blurted: "Only that these characters are too weak to have wiped out our strike force. I don't like it. There has to be some other force at work. There must be something we are overlooking."

"You worry too much, merchant," replied the Nightshade with disgust – trying to hide the implication that perhaps she might have miscalculated the strength of their foes. "They are no threat, just a nuisance. Do you think we are too out of practice to handle a few underlings?"

This comment drew smiles and nods from the others around the table. The Nightshade continued: "Let us prepare our attack, gentlemen. While George arranges for a fireball potion to explode during the magic show, another force can be eliminating this Alex's family."

"Simple, but will that not alert the others?" inquired one of the other juniors.

"May I finish!" roared the Nightshade, as the junior cowered in his chair. Then, regaining her composure, she continued "Can we not arrange for the others to 'happen' to be at the orphanage just at that time? Perhaps the ranger can be hired by the medicine company to help with something outdoors, such as ...yes, ...perhaps pony rides – in conjunction with the magic show. And do not the druidesses visit there each Sunday morning also? So if our company provides "iced cream" by hiring the druidesses to stay and help the cleric make ice there, the ensuing chaos among the urchins will cover any potion release. And even if any little ones do survive, who would believe any tale from the 'children of lust' living in the orphanage?"

All pounded the table in agreement with this plan. Its insidious delicacy demonstrated to them why the Nightshade maintained her dominance. To cover his embarrassment, the junior member asked: "Will not the paladin become suspicious when this happens to his friends? Might that not hinder his elimination, or at least start him talking?"

"He has a point," spoke up a third elder. "Paladins generally are dumb, like most righteous types, but they aren't all completely stupid. Once in a while they just might notice the obvious. The less evidence we leave, the better. And if we leave no paladin to talk ..."

"At least someone here is thinking as one would expect of a guildsman," replied the Nightshade. "A little royal influence could arrange for a particular honor guard for the orphanage from the paladins' fortress that Sunday. And with the slightest royal suggestion through their liaison here in town for specific duty assignments ... all could work to our advantage." Then softer and more vehemently she proclaimed through her gritted teeth as she leaned forward and held her clenched left fist in front of them, "and those who do piece together the anatomy of this operation will begin to sense our power and fear us all the more."

"But how are we sure all will be inside when the blast occurs?" asked another of the "juniors." Nadine was beginning to notice how boldly even the younger council members were becoming in questioning her. It had always been traditionally allowed and supposedly encouraged; but no one had dared exercise that privilege until recently. She realized that it was a sign that things were slipping a bit; so she resolved on a purge or two after this job was completed. But to restore order right now she rose to her feet and tore into him.

"You call yourself an assassin, yet you cannot predict human behavior? Have we not just now described the making of iced cream? Are you so dense as to fail to realize that wild horses could not drag any of them away from it? Could you not see the plot as it unraveled here before you?" she gestured. Then with venomed eloquence she shot the words at him: "Now shut up, and show us that we haven't wasted our time in training you!" all the while thinking to herself: "for you, there won't be any next time."

"I still don't like it," remarked George.

"You don't have to like it, merchant!" she screamed, leaning across the edge of the table toward him. "All you have to do is carry it out!"

As the details and assignments were worked out, the meeting broke down into small group planning conferences. Nadine sat back down and allowed the guild to make its own arrangements to carry out her plan all while "avenging its honor." George moved from group to group, coordinating details and updating notes. As each group concluded, it dissolved quietly into the darkness at the edges of the chamber. After extinguishing the three candles, Nadine wended her way home through the valley fog – all the while preparing her diplomatic charms for the duke and his courtiers.

Chapter 16
PREPARATIONS FOR DISASTER

Dwarven Proverb:
Be Patient with Those Who Hear the Angels Cry

The next morning the low-lying traces of red in the eastern sky were quickly swallowed up by the heavy gray folds of clouds rolling in from the southwest, and the rains started again. By mid-morning the rain had already filled the fountains to overflowing and had raised the level of the lagoons a full two fingers; and it showed every intention of continuing to drench the entire valley all day. The duke's subjects were very prophetically reminded that spring had always been the season not just of tornadoes but of floods.

George "arranged" for and picked up his cyanide salt crystals, having forged a Springfield prescription for them; and he retrieved the emerging-fireball potion materials from the secret drop point that the guild always used behind the fancy entrance sign to "Madam Jane's" exclusive ladies' goods shop. Today he made sure that both these items were in waterproof oilskins as he packed them in his saddle bags and headed off to Hauber's Landing.

He actually preferred riding in the rain: There were few passersby and none of them shouted friendly greetings; and he could almost watch the blossoms and delicate spring flowers being beaten to death by the cold, driving rain. At Hauber's Landing he found his assistant and the two guards warming themselves around the hearth in the boarding house they often used. He took malicious delight in sending them out in the late afternoon rain to the orphanage to make arrangements for the company-sponsored "iced cream" to be part of the magic show on Sunday. He found Billy Carter, a Fox-clan delivery boy, huddling in the stables near his soaking wet pony cart and hired him for almost nothing to help his assistant find Kilian and arrange for other ponies for rides next Sunday. As he listened to the drumming of the evening rain on the wooden roof, and the howling of the wind outside the shuttered boarding-house windows, George wondered whether this was just a normal spring storm, or something more. It seemed as if the clouds weren't just dropping their rain but that it was being squeezed out of them. He thought of his assistant wandering through that bone-chilling rain, trying to track down Kilian and contract with him for pony rides that same Sunday. George leaned back, puffed slowly on his pipe, and reflected how being the boss had its advantages.

The next morning, after a huge breakfast, George set off in the rain himself for D-town to make the final arrangements for the materials for the iced cream to be delivered in certain very specific ways. He explained to Stan, the middle-aged red bearded general store manager, that he wanted Weed to do the deliveries because he "saw how hard that boy worked, and wanted to give him a chance," but he wanted to do it anonymously – to see if he might be cut out for bigger jobs. Stan thought the idea of giving local boys a break was great, so he eagerly agreed with all the unusual and strict timetable requirements George proposed. George really liked dealing with gullible people.

Knowing he could trust Stan to make Weed follow these arrangements precisely, George headed north to spend that night in Springfield and Friday in Lakewood before returning Saturday to Hauber's Landing. A chilling wind followed the rain on Friday, causing whitecaps on Blue Lake and tearing off the last of the crabapple blossoms. And though the sun eventually shone on his travels, George watched with glee as each little stream he passed or crossed eroded more and more of the nearby fields. He knew how it hurt the clansmen, and he liked that fact.

....

That Sunday Weed wasn't too sure that he liked his delivery job at all. He could understand making medicine and food deliveries yesterday even in the drenching rain, but why he had to personally carry the heavy, wax sealed and water-tight pottery crock filled with rock salt through the soppy ground out to the orphanage escaped him. The bag of dried peaches in his backpack wasn't so bad, but why he wasn't allowed to pull the crock in a dog wagon or a pony cart like he would with other groceries just didn't register with him. Maybe the ground was too soft after all the rain for the dog to pull the cart safely; but at least "Boss Stan" could have had Billy, the other delivery boy, help him carry the basketed crock. Weed just couldn't grasp that even on good ground the twenty pound crock he carried in its wicker basket could crack open in a wagon; nor had he remembered that Billy was bringing the cream from several farms. He had no idea just how much the rock salt he carried was worth. "It's all so gritty. What would anyone want all this much for anyway?" he thought.

After thinking about it for a couple of miles, he decided that he really hated this job – especially the odd hours. He had planned to go fishing Sunday afternoon, but had been told he had to deliver the bag of rock salt then and only then. That made no sense to him at all. He had argued with "tall Paul" the head clerk about why couldn't he deliver it on Saturday – so he could be free Sunday afternoon to go fishing at his friend Kenny's farm pond and so follow the third commandment to "avoid unnecessary work" on a Sunday. But he was told by Paul that the Boss insisted that though the beet sugar could be delivered to the orphanage on Friday despite the damp conditions, the rock salt had to be delivered at high noon on Sunday:

no earlier, no later, so that it could be mixed with the ice right when it was being made.

Though he hated it, he needed the money, so he trudged along his "short-cut" path, diagonal to the wagon trail to the orphanage. At one point he sank up to his knees in the mud and had all he could do to keep the basket upright as he pulled himself out of the mud. He almost wished he had taken the trail, even though the rocks there hurt his bare feet. While wiping some of the mud off his legs on the early grass and some of the violets' leaves he dreamt of the magic powder. It made no sense to him why Mr. Paddlefoot was mad at him; but then it made no sense why the rock salt, the sturdiest of the iced cream materials, had to be delivered only at the very last minute.

"Sometimes adults don't make no sense at all," he grumbled to himself as he pulled his brown leather belt a bit tighter around his gray tunic and adjusted his worn canvas backpack and hood against the chilling wind. "But they're the ones with the jobs and money," he sighed as he picked up the basket of rock salt again and continued up the hill toward the orphanage – and consoled himself with the thought that "fishin' wouldn't be no good on Sunday after this much rain anyways."

....

When Kilian told his parents about being hired to organize the pony rides they weren't too thrilled. It was hard for them to admit he could earn his own way in the world without their help. They recognized his hunting skill and ate the meat he caught and brought home, but still considered him their little boy, youngest of the brood. But since they couldn't come up with any excuse why he shouldn't be involved in a task this little – and also for a cause they, unlike most of the townspeople who disdained the orphanage because of the questionable legitimacy of most of the orphans, considered charitable and wholesome – they gave only minimal objections.

So Kilian contacted several nearby stables, slogging glee-fully through the rain and mud, eventually rounding up six ponies. He stabled them all at Silverhorn tavern Saturday night, and arranged for Cutter to help him take them the rest of the way to the orphanage Sunday after mass. The few guests that the tavern took in on Sundays, Sky, with Ricky's help, could handle for the couple of hours he'd be gone; and the little bit of extra money would be real welcome right now. But more than all that, any little joy they could help bring these outcast children was well worth whatever inconvenience might be involved.

None of the tavern's Saturday guests commented on the extra ponies in the stable that evening. Even Rips headed back to the orphanage late as usual without saying anything. Perhaps he thought there really weren't six ponies there – for he had been known in the past to see 'more than one' of what was really there; and he was in no condition to testify about how 'alert' he felt that night. He just headed back to the or-phanage stables, holding on to Molly, his mule, who knew the way better than he did most nights. Molly found him a nice empty stall, where he crashed as usual – and he slept clean through the mass the next morning. He was awakened by the commotion of the pony rides in the courtyard, but dozed off again lightly when the children went inside for the magic show.

....

After a week of rainy days and waterlogged fields, Mike was happy to be out in the sunshine. He whistled gleefully as he and "little" Ray Hillman, his tall, broad-shouldered com-panion paladin with dark thinning hair and full-trimmed beard, strode along the road toward D-town. It was Thomasday, the Sunday after Easter. All the paladins had renewed their faith oath while touching the hands and side of the giant crucifix, and now he was heading to an ice cream party and then to an overnight visit home. Mike couldn't imagine how he had lucked into such a blessing. Perhaps he was the only one handy last night whose family lived near the orphanage. He still couldn't believe this much good luck was happening to him; but he was sure that the Vincentian had indeed approached him and Ray yesterday evening and had given them the "task" of being the honor guard for the celebration at the orphanage today. Pony rides and the magic show were good enough, but this was to be followed by iced cream. Though it was really only for the orphans, there was always a little left over for the "workers" and guards. But more than all this was the furlough afterwards: they had permission to stay at Mike's parents' for the night (and for a festive post-Easter dinner) and return the next day.

Ray, whose parents lived south of the Markasandra in the Kumbarland mining regions deep in the knobs, just happened to be paired with him in the wrestling practice last night. And since paladins were always sent out in pairs (except when doing the isolation retreats), the two of them got the detail. This was especially nice, since neither of them had seen any family since the usual furlough just after Christmastime.

They wore their summer ceremonial uniforms of black tunic and denim leggings and well-shined boots surmounted only by the royal blue full-length scapular (with each one's individual coat of arms emblazoned in gold thread on the front of it) held in place by the sword belt. This time of year they rarely needed the black (winter) hooded cloak; and they sure didn't need chain mail to protect themselves against the orphans. After their roll call and faith proclamation at dawn, followed by mass and breakfast, the two of them had set off. As soon as they had gotten out of sight of Holy Cross fortress they carefully removed their scapulars and tunics, rolled their holy swords up in them and strapped them to their backs – so as not to get them dirty – and, since no one was watching, they ran and played their way to the orphanage. After washing up at the fountain outside the gate and getting back into uniform, they reported to Br. Ansgar, the chief monk.

Their services were soon needed in more than a ceremonial way, for the young-uns started to go wild when Kilian and Cutter came into the courtyard leading the six ponies. While each child (in groups of six) had a turn around the inner courtyard, Mike and Ray helped keep order as the others tried to wait in line. After a while when each child had had two turns and all the little races were done, they all started to lose interest and began to gather inside for the magic show – the final act of which was to be the making of ice for the iced cream.

....

As Weed rounded a bend in the wooded area between the orphanage and the last of the fields between it and Dennistown, he set down the bag of rock salt and took a short rest. A few minutes later as he got up to continue on the last bit of trail he saw someone small walking toward him, probably one of the children. As he drew closer, however, he recognized George, and felt both eagerness and apprehension rise inside himself. He knew George and he craved his magic powder; but though he didn't remember much of their last meeting, he knew he hadn't liked it.

George greeted him with a sly smile and said: "I've got a little bag of something for you."

Weed's whole face lit up as he began to imagine the bright colors and exciting feeling of the magic powder. "Great! I knew you'd come through. I just got to have the powder. I'll get you the money right away."

George's smile became a bit more sinister as he replied, "Oh, I have some powder, all right, but that's not what's in the bag. If you do a little job or two with this for me you'll see all kinds of bright colors again and feel more sensations than ever before." Under his breath he added "or ever again."

"Sure," Weed replied. "What job?" and "What's in the bag?"

"It's very special, a magic type of sweet-salt. Here, look at it." George replied as he opened the little leather bag and let the sunlight fall intermittently on some small white crystals.

"You want me to add these to the bag of beet sugar?" inquired Weed. "Will it make the iced cream better?"

"Yes," George replied smoothly, "and it will taste almost magical if you also sprinkle the dust from these crystals into the mixture of cream and sugar and fruit you give to the paladins."

"But won't that make the iced cream gritty and salty?"

"Not this special sweet-salt. That's why I keep it separate. In fact, it all really belongs in the iced cream. Smell how special it is," George invited as he held it out for Weed to smell. Weed hesitated, so George put the pouch up to his own nose and took a deep breath. (But Weed couldn't see that George inhaled through his mouth outside the bag rather than through his nose.) He handed it to Weed who took a big whiff of it and liked the burnt-almond scent.

"Does it taste as good as it smells?" he asked as he licked his finger and started to put it into the pouch to sample just a tiny grain of the special white stuff.

George grabbed the pouch out of his hand and examined Weed's fingers carefully. "This is for the orphanage, not you!" he shouted. "You are to put it in the iced cream only. I'll put a curse on it so that you won't taste anything if you try to sneak some again; but if you eat any of it, the curse will kill you."

Weed's eyes went wide with fear. He put his hands behind his back and declared "No sir, Mr. Paddlefoot, I won't take any. I promise, cross my heart. And I won't let anyone else taste, only smell it."

"No! No! you idiot!" George screamed at him as he jumped up and down agitatedly. "No one is to even know of the pois ... er...p... powder. No one! It is to be a surprise magic secret. Do you think you can get it into the iced cream stirring machine, when you help the druidesses add the rock salt to the ice, without anyone seeing you? I can trust you to do properly just a little job like that, can't I? Or are you totally worthless?"

"I can do it, Mr. Paddlefoot, honest I can," Weed promised. "Do I get some magic powder after it?"

"Sure," George drolled out slowly and sweetly, "on the way back from the orphanage."

Weed took the leather bag and carefully hid it in the burlap sack surrounding the crock of rock salt. They both started up the road again toward the orphanage. As they passed the washing-up fountain just outside the black wrought iron gate George stopped. Weed halted and looked at him questioningly.

"One more thing to get the powder," he instructed. "Make sure you save a little extra dose of the powder for the iced cream you give to the Paladins. After all, they deserve something special. And they ought to get some first. But don't tell anyone you even saw me. I want to bring in an extra surprise a little later."

"Anything you say," he replied eagerly. "Where do you want me to look for you later to get the magic powder?"

"Oh you won't have to worry about that at all," George answered evasively, "not at all…You go on in now, and I'll be in a little later."

Watching Weed go in the orphanage gate George hoped he'd remember to give the Paladins the double dose of cyanide crystals – for Paladins were usually strong enough that one or both of them just might survive the fireball blast even if no others did. That was one thing he could not afford. He decided he'd have to watch Weed to make sure he carried it out.

Chapter 17
TAVERN VISITORS

Sunday morning had been fairly quiet at Silverhorn tavern after Kilian and Cutter had left with the ponies. With no guests this week-end, the whole family had been able to go to early mass together. Afterward, Ricky and Lee had traded their church clothes for just short leggings or "shorts", and Anna crawled around in just a diaper. The two boys raced their pet turtles most of the morning after Ricky's chores were done, while Sky let Jake keep an eye on her baby daughter and she herself got a few moments of precious time to just be quiet and let the outside natural world restore her inner nature this radiant spring morning.

A little before noon five somber looking strangers rode into the tavern yard and tied up at the hitching post under the huge old sycamore tree. By the looks of them and their horses Ricky guessed that they had ridden all morning, and that four of them weren't too accustomed to it. Jake didn't like the smell of them at all – a sweet, city smell; but Sky finally quieted him down. She sliced some cheese and fresh-baked dark bread, drew some brew and ladled out the simmering tomato soup for them all.

Jake just wouldn't stay still: he kept pacing back and forth in the kitchen with Sky and kept whining. Finally, when Ricky came in from having watered the horses and brushed them – at least as high as he could reach, Sky picked up Kilian's magic axe to talk to Jake.

"Just what is wrong with you?" she asked impatiently.

"K-aa-eep ker-rwyat" Jake was finally able to reply – in growl-like words that only sky's ears could distinguish from low barking and whining. Standing directly in front of her and looking at her and Ricky he rumbled. "Ther-r-they her-r-ave 'sass'n s-smell, her-r-unikorn 'unters; en-n-n h-run h-is-s Tr-r-r-oy."

Sky went pale with fear, clasping her hands across her mouth. She knelt down directly in front of Jake and whispered, "Then Kilian and Heather and Patrick are in danger at the orphanage." Her eyes widened as she suddenly realized and said: "Oh no, maybe they've already been there!"

"H-n-no blu-uh-d s-smell, h-n-not h-yet."

"You've got to warn them!"

"H-n-no kan-n-n h-tal-l-lk ha-a-gin-n."

"I'll put a note for Cutter to read to Kilian on the axe. Give the axe to Cutter so they'll find the note. We'll delay them here as long as we can and try to find out where they're headed if it's not after them." She didn't realize how loud she had been speaking as she wrote and then tied the note to the axe. As she held out the axe for Jake to take the handle and note in his mouth, she stroked his head once and prayed: "May the angel Raphael protect you as he did Tobias and his dog." Then she opened the door for Jake and watched him bound northwest through the fields. Then, turning to Ricky, she whispered, "Go take off their horse saddles."

"Mom, I can't; they're too heavy for me."

"Didn't you do it before, to Kilian's horse – and Alex's?"

"They helped me so we could fool you," he confessed as he shuffled his bare feet on the floor. "I wish now we hadn't."

But Sky was lost in wishes of her own. She wished Cutter were home to protect them rather than with the orphans … and Kilian … and Heather and Patrick and … what about Mike and Alex?" she thought.

Just then she heard a crash from the dining room, followed by curses. As Sky ran in to see what was going on, Ricky went out and tried to do what he was told. What Sky saw when she entered the common room made her cringe. For, without Jake to watch them, Anna and Lee had wandered into the common room – with their turtles. Apparently one of the turtles had "found its way" into the lap of Grek, a balding dark-bearded assassin, while they were eating. When that city hit-man first felt it there he had thought it was a dried out piece of bread. But when it started to crawl up his arm as he picked it up to dunk in his soup he jumped up from the table screaming, knocking his chair completely over and spilling the pitcher of beer on the table.

Sky ran back into the kitchen to get some towels and hollered for Ricky – who was out trying to remove the saddles but was only able to undo the cinctures. She ran back into the common room to clean the mess up off the customers and off the furniture – apologizing profusely all the while. She had just gotten them calmed down (by promising them two free bottles of wine) and had gone to the cellar to get them. On the way back up it occurred to her that if those at the orphanage by chance were not their target, then Alex was their only other choice here. She was arrested from these thoughts by another low-pitched scream. Anna had crawled under the table and was pulling the leg hair off Alvin, another one of the crew.

Coming up through the cellar door Sky heard that assassin plead with the leader: "Come on, let me kill her. One more dead little vermin won't make any difference."

"Later, later," came the reply, "after we get the others."

Sky made lots of noise as she came through the kitchen. Her heart was beating so fast that she could barely stop herself from rushing in to try to snatch away her baby daughter. Still, when she nonchalantly sauntered in and saw another assassin holding Anna away from himself by the back of the neck she became fawningly apologetic.

"Oh, I'm terribly sorry. My children should know better than this. I'll take them in and spank them so hard they won't sit down for a week. Your whole meal is free. I'm so sorry," she said as she put the two dark green wine bottles on the table and reached for her daughter. "Here, let me take her before she tries to spit up on you."

As Alvin disdainfully let go of this "contaminating urchin", Sky snatched her up and carried her and Lee into the kitchen – very obviously scolding them both the whole time.

Ricky was waiting there for her and asked: "What did you call me for? I almost had one of the saddles off."

"Quiet!" she whispered bruskly; "go find your cousin Kristopher's house in the bear clan territory and tell his older brother Alex that these men are going to attack him and probably his whole family."

"Right now? But mom ..."

"Yes! Move! Now! Get there the quickest way you can!"

From behind her a deep voice stated ominously, "I don't think that would be too wise."

"Run, Ricky!" Sky screamed as she turned to face the intruder in the doorway and clutched her two youngest ones to herself.

Ricky slipped through the back doorway as Grek, followed by Marty and Troy advanced toward Sky with their daggers drawn. Alvin and Kruk were waiting for Ricky out front by the horses, where they had gone to retrieve their bows; but Ricky didn't run that way. Around and behind the barn he ran and clambered over the split-rail fence into the cattle pasture.

Troy tore Anna from Sky's arms at dagger point and tossed her to Marty who held her by the ankles and traced little designs on her back with his stiletto-like dagger point. Droplets of blood oozed from several of the cuts to fill in the traced outlines. Her crying had no effect on the stubby, ox-like assassin whose heart was deaf even though his ears weren't.

Lee was harder to pull away, but a dagger to Sky's throat helped her let him go. To stop his kicking and squirming, Grek just held him by the neck with the long fingers of his claw-like left hand and battered his face with front and back-hand slaps until Lee's jaw broke and he went unconscious. Each time Sky

140

tried to reach for him the edge of Troy's dagger sliced a little deeper into her throat – but just short of the jugular vein – for now.

Troy dragged her outside through the kitchen door and shouted to Alvin and Kruk: "Back here, you fools, he went behind the barn. Circle 'round the stable and shoot him as he comes out toward the road."

Kruk nocked an iron-barbed arrow and brushed on a slimy blue-gray oil, while Alvin ignored Troy and headed between the stable and the inn – toward them at the kitchen door – with sword and dagger ready.

Alvin spotted Ricky heading away from the road, northeast toward the pond, and called for Kruk, his fellow half elf, to come toward him instead of toward the road. But by the time Kruk reached them, Ricky was circling the upstream edge of the pond, trying to get to the fieldstone dam so he could climb down the embankment.

As Kruk came around the other side of the stable, he caught sight of him and took aim at the center of Ricky's back – knowing that the arrow would pierce the rib cage and plunge through the heart. Sky saw him aim and screamed "No!" Ricky, distracted by the cry, turned to glance back and didn't see the wet cow dung in the mud in front of him. When his foot hit it with his body twisted, he slipped and started to fall sideways just as Kruk released the venomed arrow. It struck him in the right shoulder rather than the center of the back; and the force of the blow catapulted him into a side channel of the pond. When the ripples stopped, neither Kruk nor Sky could see any movement among the low-growing rushes.

Despite Troy's insult-filled urgings, none of the assassins would venture after Ricky into the pasture among the herd of long-horned red and white mottled cattle moving toward them menacingly. None of them would order another guildsman in that pasture either – more because of the "droppings" than the beasts themselves. After shouting and hurling curses at one another for quite a while, they dragged their hostages with them to complete their original mission – with three other severed heads to be thrown in for good measure.

Chapter 18
TROUBLE INSIDE THE ORPHANAGE

As Weed worked his way through the gleeful uproar in the courtyard, he noticed Cutter and Kilian and Ansgar, the chief cleric or "monk" with his familiar: a small black fox with white snout, paws and stomach. He glanced at Little Ray and some other paladin, both covered with about three children each – and then he glanced again.

"Mike, is that you?" he cried as he set down the rock salt and ran over to him.

"Weed?" Mike replied, as he gently extracted himself from the clinging little ones and bounded over toward him. "Boy have you grown in the last few months!"

"You too," Weed asserted as they locked arms and wrestled a bit in typical boyhood playfulness, and then in the traditional Markasandra valley greeting they each tried to mess up each other's hair. This wasn't easy for Weed to do because of Mike's height and royal blue paladin headband.

After a few minutes of catching up on family news, Weed remarked "Hey, what happened to Trail Healer?"

"I'll tell you all about it later," Mike replied. "It was the dying gift of a 'friend'. It doubles my healing power. Look, after we're done here today, Little Ray and I get to spend the night at my parents'. Walk home with us and I'll fill you in about it all."

"Yeah, great, I'll meet you at... Oh wait a minute. I have to do another errand and ... uh ... report back to the store, sorry." Weed's voice trailed lower and lower. "I could catch up with you all ..."

"Weed!" Mike jumped in, "you've known me ever since we were old enough to remember. I'm your best friend. What are you trying to hide from me?"

Weed's ear tips started to turn red. He looked at the ground and shuffled his left foot in the dust of the courtyard – trying to think of a way to tell Mike the truth, but not the real truth. Finally he looked up a bit and stammered out: "I've got to meet someone for a few minutes."

"That's OK, Weed; Ray and I can handle a little detour with you on the way. It's just so good to see you again," Mike said encouragingly as he put his hand on Weed's shoulder.

By now Weed's cheeks and forehead had started to blush as well as his ears. He shuffled his foot even more and felt uneasy under Mike's friendly gaze. Mike's hand seemed to grow heavier and heavier on his shoulder. Slowly he almost whispered: "I have to see him by myself."

"Would he think paladins are the wrong kind of friends? But if you don't want me just say so straight out. You know I'd never do anything to interfere with your life."

Weed looked kind of glassy-eyed. He had heard someone say "wrong kind of friends" somewhere before, and it seemed to be connected with Mike somehow, but he just couldn't remember. So he just stood there, gazing nowhere, doing nothing. Mike just let him be, for there was no "healing" for what Weed was going through right then. All this time the little ones had become more and more demanding of attention. Two of them were already pulling on Mike's leggings wanting to be picked up and held. Ray in the mean time had sat down on one of the stone benches near the horse trough, and was covered with half a dozen friendly urchins. Meanwhile three others had discovered the sack of sweet-salt and had started trying to open it. When they knocked it over Weed snapped out of his trance and shoed them all away from it. Picking it up he went into the monastery-orphanage kitchen without looking back at Mike. The monk and his fox came out and started herding the little ones into the dining room.

At one end of the large, oak-timbered greystone room a stage had been set up; and while Patrick performed his songs

144

and dance and magic on it, helped by some little volunteers and some big ones, in the kitchen Weed was mixing the rock salt into the ice that Heather and her friend Violet had been making all afternoon in the outer ring of the iced cream mixer. While the two druidesses were chatting with each other and glancing at the magic show as they gathered the children's regular bowls and spoons, Weed managed to mix the pouch crystals into the iced cream mixture while working with the rock salt. He smeared some on the top edge of the iced cream maker outer bucket, so that he could "dust" some into the bowls as he helped serve them. George had managed to sneak in and had watched all this approvingly. No one noticed him then or when he pulled his own "bowl" out from beneath his child's clothing disguise.

The show ended with the making of the last little bit of ice in the inner ring of the iced cream machine, and that inner ring was ceremoniously carried into the kitchen while the monks led the children in some easy songs for the few minutes it took to churn the milky mixture into iced cream. When Heather and Violet brought the finished product out of the kitchen and started to dish it out the kids mobbed the table. Even the paladins and Monk together couldn't keep order. Kilian was right there in the midst of them all trying to get some, but Heather kept him waiting – handing bowls of iced cream each time to smaller hands than his. And Kilian didn't really know whether he liked better getting the iced cream or standing there watching her bending down to each child, leaning out of her white leather armor – more delectable than any frozen concoction. But Weed, true to his promise, snuck away two bowls of the iced cream for the paladins and liberally sprinkled them with the "magic flavoring powder."

Once George saw Weed accomplish this he put the rest of the plan into action. Into his "bowl", made out of some dull metallic material which had been dipped in dust and sand on the outside to look like the other children's pottery bowls, he emptied a glass tube of milky-white liquid that smelled faintly like old caves. Into this he set the wooden spoon the assassin's guild had given him – soaked in the igniting ingredient. As it all would soon start to bubble, he knew he had only a few minutes to place it with the other used bowls on the stage and get out of there before the whole place burst into a pit of infernal fire.

Unfortunately for him, some of the first children to get the iced cream started to react to the poison just as Weed was giving the dishes to the two paladins. Mike and Ray immediately set the iced cream down and rushed over to see what the matter was. It finally broke through inside Weed just what was going on and why George didn't want to add the special flavoring agent himself. He remembered the almond smell and should have known the danger even before the children started reacting to it; and he had finally realized who had told him he had the "wrong kind of friends." He ran over to Mike and grabbed him by both arms and shouted into his face: "Mike, they're poisoned. Do something!"

"Sure, Weed, it's OK, don't worry. I'm sure it won't be that bad; just too much sweets on top of too much excitement," he reassured him.

"No, you don't understand," he shouted at him, almost crying. "I put the poison in the iced cream. It was white crystals that smelled like almonds. Mr. Paddlefoot had me do it. He said it would make the flavor better. I didn't realize what I was doing. Save them, please, so many have started to eat it. Please!"

Mike grabbed him with both hands, looked deeply into his coppery-colored eyes and asked, "Are you sure?"

"Yes – as I stand before God!"

Mike ordered calmly, "Go tell the druidesses to take away the iced cream crock and prepare some raw egg, and you grab the iced cream away from those who haven't tasted it yet. I'll take it from here." Mike then shouted in a booming commanding voice that few had ever heard from him: "The iced cream is poisoned! Spit it out! Now!"

As the startled children reacted to his order almost unconsciously and instinctively, he turned his attention to the adults: "Monk, get your two helpers to separate those who have had no iced cream and keep them away from it. Ray, guard these while the monks then make the others vomit. Kilian and Cutter, get some buckets of water from the trough outside and wash this stuff off them lest they even lick their fingers by mistake; and then flush the stuff from the dishes. Hurry! All of you!"

As each sprang into action, Mike drew his holy sword and turned toward Patrick. More gently but just as firmly he said, "Cleric, you know what we need from you."

As Mike came over toward him, Patrick rolled up his left sleeve and tied one of the colored scarves he used for the magic show around his arm just above the elbow. Just as Mike got there, Patrick pulled out his magic dagger and truly made it his own by handing it to Mike with the request: "Don't let your holy sword draw a cleric's blood. The dagger has been used to kill; let's use it to heal."

Mike acquiesced. He slit Patrick's arm on the prominent vein inside the elbow and started leading him from child to child, letting Patrick drip blood in their mouths, and then massaging their throats himself to get them to swallow. Ray came over and started to help the children get their breathing back by holding them upside down by their heels and spanking them – much as the midwives did to start their breathing as infants. Heather and Violet and the monks had already started the others vomiting. The pet fox kept watch very carefully on the ones who had not yet even tasted the iced cream, and who were edging toward the stage where the bowls had been collected. As it yapped and growled at them to herd his "sheep" together, one of the slightly older ones, who was a year behind Ricky in Sunday bible and catechism school, noticed George's "bowl" starting to spark and bubble and cried: "Look, look, pretty fire magic, look," at which the fox, whose sense of smell (and natural sense of danger) were greater than humans began barking wildly.

Br. Ansgar, the chief monk, knew instinctively from his familiar what was wrong, as did Patrick as soon as he saw the traces of sparks and smoke. Just as Kilian and Cutter came in with the water Patrick shouted, "Everyone, down on the floor. Take shelter immediately."

But the chief monk didn't. He ran over to the stage table and picked up the bowl, burning his hands as its heat grew volcanic and larger and larger sparks shot higher and higher. He was intending to fall on it to shield his little ones from the blast at the cost of his own life, but Heather had run there too. She gave him a brisk and unexpected slap on the face, which so startled him that he dropped the bowl – just as she wanted. She caught it as it fell and disappeared. Almost immediately the entire orphanage was jolted by a tremendous blast centered just above the inner courtyard. Kilian and Cutter were knocked forward to the ground and their backs were singed by the inrush of the blast from the doorway. The six gentle little ponies tethered in the courtyard couldn't move as easily – and didn't escape the released infernal fire.

Chapter 19
LITTLE ONES IN DANGER

The rushes Ricky fell among were thick – just enough so that the arrow feathers got caught between the long sharp leaves and stalk of those plants as he tumbled through them. The arrow shaft and fletching were deflected there, so the arrowhead only grazed his shoulder while he fell. The cuts from the razor-like leaf edges caused such profuse bleeding that the pond water and blood washed away the bits of poison that had touched him. Still Ricky lay motionless in that deeper than usual part of the pond by the inlet channel, his head just barely above the surface of the water and mud, but hidden by the rushes.

As time passed, second by terrifying second, Ricky kept expecting the riders to come out and run their swords through him. When no one came and he thought they might have gone from the pasture side of the tavern back to its front, Ricky slowly stood up and peered over the edge of the dry, pointed rushes and cat tails. Mud and duckweed scum covered his shoulders and slimed down his back – and kept the blood in. He moved slower now, down the ravine below the dam and east around the druids' pastures, following the contour of the creek bed. He felt tired and his shoulder started to throb. Some of the rocks in the creek bed were moss-covered and slippery; others were sharp when he stepped on them or fell against them. To his right he could see the stone embankments supporting the wall around the druids' grove tower above him. He was tempted to try to climb it and ask for help, but he had been caught crossing their gully before and had been scolded so thoroughly by one of the guards that ever after he hid under the culvert bridge whenever he cut across their property to visit with Kris and his clan friends.

"Kris's parents are just a little farther," he thought as he picked his way over the rocks much more slowly now. "Just sneak under the bridge and up the branch on the other side ... Real close ... I'll just sit and rest a minute ... Just one minute . . . that's all ..."

He heard some horses coming down the road from the east. Afraid that it might be some of the druids returning from the headwaters of Blue Lake or the Kumbar-land mining region south of there he dashed for the culvert and hid there crouching in the darkness. A few moments later, once they had passed, he slipped out the other side and dragged himself along. Each step made his shoulder ache more – and drip more. He saw the tree line that marked the beginning of the Bear-clan lands and somehow he made it up the slope to the greenbrier hedge. The hidden tunnel through it there that the kids had made was still easy to crawl into. It was shaded and cool inside like the culvert under the viaduct had been. If only he could rest just a minute ... it would be so nice ... so quiet ... so nice....

....

As the unconsciousness wore off, Heather slowly became aware of the pain. First her hands started to itch, then burn. Then her face and chest began the tingling, stinging ache. She tried to move her arms to touch the areas and stop the pain; but each move hurt worse. As nerves transmitted, one after another, their hideous messages from her tender, burnt flesh she wailed – it hurt so bad. Her movements became wild thrashing, which only tore shreds of seared flesh off her arms and side. She wished she could cut off her hands and even her face – anything to stop the pain.

She looked down at her charred hands – forcing her eyes to open, trying to make the damaged muscles work. All was still darkness, for her eyes had melted and now only oozed out of their sockets. At that moment, guardian of life though she was, she wished for death. She could take no more.

The unicorns watched her helplessly. They had been frightened when what was left of her burn-ravaged body had first appeared in their clearing. Finally one of the scouts ventured toward this smoldering clump of rubble, then called to the others when it recognized Heather. Apparently, when the fireball blast knocked her unconscious the unicorn-skin armor continued teleporting on its own to the only place it knew as home.

By the time they had located and summoned Blue Cloud, Heather had slumped back into merciful unconsciousness. Blue Cloud's first thought was for the severely injured creature in front of her, and so she had several of the herd teleport her as gently as possible into a nearby shallow cave-creek pool, to let its icy spring-fed water cool the fire in her body. Sunbridge with his limited cleric ability made sure she could breathe. Even though her flame-ravaged face was submerged, a short piece of reed was all he needed. But soon a worrisome reality insinuated itself into Blue Cloud's thoughts: not only may they not be able to keep her alive, but their other guardians might be in as bad or worse shape. For the sake of the herd she would have to leave Heather in others' care and investigate this threat.

With the prospect of such a danger menacing the whole herd, Blue Cloud left instructions not to use the herd's one and only "return the dead" spell on anyone until she herself called for it. She had to investigate this threat: but where could she start? Heather could tell her.

Crowded with pain as Heather's thoughts were, glimpses of a group of children screaming and fleeing, some of them sick, intermingled with the all-engulfing flames and the shock of a blast came to Blue Cloud as she gently touched her horn through the water to the side of Heather's skull. There was only one place with that many children on a Sunday at this hour: the orphanage in the ruins of the ancient Knob Rabbits' monastery.

From the scenes she had seen in Heather's memory Blue Cloud knew that even if she left immediately she probably wouldn't get there in time, but she had to try.

....

"Let's kill these three now!" Marty insisted as he wiped the blood off his dagger point and tossed the baby girl back to her mother. "Nobody'll find them."

"Real smart, you city idiot!" Troy scoffed ironically. "We have to pass by here to get back to Russelburg. There ain't twenty ways out o' town like you pansies are used to – just one – unless you care to head southwest through paladin territory, or leave the roads to cross fields and cattle pastures. And since none of you got guts enough for that we don't need the field sheriff here as we try to ride by here later. Any more dumb suggestions?"

"Yeah, take your dagger and sit on it!" Marty replied.

"Go jump a sheep; it's the only female you could entice," Troy spat back at him.

"Break it up!" Alvin interjected, stepping between them. "We've got 'business' to do before word of the orphanage blast starts stirring things up. Let's take our mutual vengeance on the clan first; then you can settle things between you any way you choose."

"And I'll be happy to provide all the daggers and sheep either of you can handle," Kruk added with half-elf sarcasm.

Grek started to laugh – the deep, dark growl kind of laugh that puts fear in little children. But here it was infectious: first Alvin and Kruk, then even Marty and Troy joined in it in spite of themselves as they dragged their three prisoners through the tavern, out the front door and over to their horses. But as Grek tried to mount his, the saddle very slowly started sliding sideways. He got up on it, but the imbalance continued shifting the saddle to the left. Squirm and struggle as he might, Grek couldn't stop it from slowly tilting, and then sinking down the left side of the horse. As he sat there upside-down – head and shoulders in the dirt, feet still in the stirrups and rump in the saddle – looking up at the horse's belly surrounded by the whole assassin crew laughing at him riotously, he decided he didn't like it.

"Get me out of this, you bastards," he shouted. No one helped. Then he began to curse and kick wildly as they just continued laughing at him. When he finally got up, he walked over to Sky and knocked her to the ground with one backhand blow to the face. "This is your doing, wench!" he bellowed. "Now get up and fix them all right, or you'll watch me slice the faces off your babies."

Terrified, Sky did as he ordered. Twenty minutes later they were entering town: Sky riding double in front of Troy, barely able to stand the stench; and the two little ones, just barely alive, "cradled" by Alvin and Kruk. As they passed slowly through town, Troy made her wave to different people and return their "Happy Easter" wishes on this last day of its octave. But this Easter time was far from happy for her whose heart ached for her two littlest ones who were near death – and her husband and other child who were probably both dead already.

Chapter 20
MORE THAN FIRE IN THE STABLES

"What in tarnation is going on here?" Rips shouted as he awoke in the aftermath of the fireball blast. As adrenaline pumped through his system his eyes focused on the little secondary fires burning sporadically around him and his nose caught the scent of the burning thatched roof above him. Knowing how dangerous a fire is in a stable, he immediately stomped out what he could; but the heat from the roof told him to get out of there quickly. He went from stall to stall trying to lead out the two monastery plow horses and three donkeys. He noticed two-legged movement in one of the far stalls; but he could see nothing over the sideboard. As an old but sturdy-looking mottled gray pony whinnied and raised her head, he shouted: "Get that animal out of here now!" and then made two trips to get the other animals tethered outside. He tore up his shirt to cover their eyes, and even used some of the strips to bind them to the hitching post as far from the blazing barn roof as he could.

When Rips trotted on down to that end stall after his first trip outside, he saw what he thought was one of the orphan children trying to saddle that pony. "Hey, boy, lead that pony outside now. Carry that little saddle if you have to, then come and help me," he ordered as he went over to lead out the other horse. When Rips ran back in to try to lead out the three donkeys, he noticed the roof starting to fall in. He called again to the "boy" in the last stall to help, then with difficulty led the three donkeys outside by himself as pieces of smoldering wood and the burning straw stubble landed on and around him, singing his bushy red beard and leaving burn marks and soot streaks on his face and down his chest and back. Leaning up against one of the courtyard walls to try to catch his breath, he heard the old pony whiney again from inside the barn. He ran back in and saw George just finishing saddling his pony and trying to mount it as pieces of the roof dropped around them, making the pony jump away in fear. Rips grabbed George in one arm and yanked the pony out with the other just as that portion of the roof fell in too.

As Rips set George down and blindfolded and tethered his pony with the others he turned toward George and, with anger tempered only by fatigue, demanded: "Why ain't you helped? Boy, you better learn to move when you're called, or you won't get no other chance."

"Buzz off, creep, I'm not your boy" came the reply as George tried to untie the pony and ride off – knowing that he had to get out of there before anyone came to investigate the blast.

Rips lunged at him and caught him by the scruff of the neck, held him high with one hand and then tossed him into the dirt and singed herb garden between the wall and the hitching post. "Now get up and don't give me no more of your lip. You help put out this fire, or I'll break every bone in your body!"

George got up and tried to move closer to his pony but Rips stood in his way, eyeing him suspiciously. From his boot George pulled out a dagger and menaced Rips with it as he ordered: "Out of my way, you filthy ape, or you'll eat this steel."

By now Rips could see that this was no child, and he started to lose control. He ran at George, only to feel the sting of the dagger on his leg as he tried to kick it out of George's hand. George, more confident now, lunged at him; but Rips, who was used to being attacked by small varmints, easily dodged it and sent George reeling with a blow to the side of his head. This time Rips was able to disarm George by stepping on his hand and kicking the dagger away from it with his other foot. George had just reared up to bite Rips in the calf as Kilian came outside.

"Where is she?" he demanded.

"What!" Rips hollered, surprised as he turned to face Kilian. "Where is who?"

"Heather, she teleported with the potion."

"What in the world are you talking about?" wiggled out of Rips' mouth, followed by a "Yeaow!" as George bit.

Kilian spotted him there and ordered: "Stop him, he poisoned the orphans' iced cream."

Despite his leg wound, Rips spun around immediately and dove to grab George's left leg. Straightening up, he lifted him high and dangled him upside down. "There ain't nobody that low!" he said. George clawed at Rips' arm and tried to grab the red hair on Rips' chest as he held him there at arm's length, then tossed him back disgustedly into the trash at the edge of the courtyard.

Cutter and Ansgar had just come down into the courtyard from putting out the fire on the sod roof of the orphanage common room. They had sent the few older un-poisoned children to continue drawing water from both the inside well and the outside "washing" well so they could douse the little fires around the courtyard and barn. The monks gave up both their barn and the two nearby haystacks as hopeless, for they did not have the water or manpower to put them out. However, the heat from them as well as the blowing sparks kept igniting other smaller fires, which they could control. Fortunately, the stone walls and sod roofs of the orphanage itself were not very combustible from the outside, though they would have become "oven walls" had the blast gone off inside them.

Having been caught in the doorway when the blast went off, both Kilian and Cutter had been knocked to the ground and had bruises on their faces. Their hoods and leather vests had caught fire, so they had had to tear them off their backs immediately. They had rolled over in the spilled water to douse their tunics and leggings, but even these had large burn holes in them. However, Kilian's mind and thoughts were somewhere else: Having seen the traces of leather from the ponies' saddles among their melted and smoking hooves and teeth, and thinking the leather was from Heather's armor, he was starting to get hysterical.

"Where is she? Where is she?" he kept demanding of George whom he had picked up and was holding by the throat up off the ground.

"Calm! ... my friend," the monk said to him in a commanding tone of voice as he laid his hand firmly on Kilian's shoulder. Kilian immediately relaxed and let George drop.

This cleric, who had seen more than just the forests of this dukedom, had risked using a remove fear spell on Kilian to bring him back to rationality as Cutter and Rips saw to George. Cutter still couldn't believe what he was hearing about George, but trusted Rips and Kilian enough to know it was true. George began to sense this confusion, and waited till the other two were preoccupied with calming Kilian.

"You know they're going to kill me," George began as he brushed what grime he could off his clothes. "They think I'm somehow to blame for this. I just got here. I don't know what this is all about."

"Where were you when the fireball blast went off?"

"In the barn," he replied quickly, "just like I said." Then in a pleading tone George went on, "I just got here."

Cutter seemed to be weakening.

"Look, the saddle's still on my pony." George then showed Cutter the scuff marks on his neck: "See? ... Get me out of here before it's too late."

Turning his singed back on George, Cutter moved right up to George's pony and noticed that it hadn't been ridden for over an hour. As he was turning back toward George to ask him about that, he saw George try to hide the dagger which he had picked up from across the courtyard.

"I think maybe we'd better talk about this with the paladins. They won't let anyone harm you improperly."

"Fine, sure, I'll head there right now. My pony's already … er … still saddled. I'll meet you there," he replied as he tried to mount the pony and get out of the courtyard.

"Now wait just a minute here," objected Cutter as he reached out with his right arm to block George, the same way he would try to stop a two year old. "I meant the two paladins here. Be a good boy and come along."

"I'm not a boy!" George shouted at him as he jumped back and tried to get free of his arm. Unable to do so, he pulled out the dagger with his left hand to reach behind him and stab Cutter in the groin or the leg; but having seen the dagger a few moments earlier, Cutter was expecting it. He grabbed George's wrist as he jabbed upward with the knife, and his rough hand tightened around that wrist as the blade kept drawing closer and closer to his own abdomen. With a surge of strength Cutter nearly crushed one of the muscles in George's wrist, making him drop the dagger. Kicking and screaming, George was ferried into the orphanage commons under Cutter's arm. Just then Reuben Playbear, who always looked for excitement – and always offered help – and Eric Dancingbear and some of the other neighboring farmhands, who had seen the fireball flash and heard the blast in the distance, started arriving. Even Billy Carter who had been returning the empty cream jugs to the dairy farms came racing back. When he saw the remains of the six ponies he was glad his had been carrying the cream jugs with him instead.

With the assistance of these neighbors, the monks were able to keep the barn and haystack fires from spreading to any of the other buildings. It was fortunate that the orphanage was built in the ruins of an old monastery – itself built in the never completed old Knob Rabbits' church. Since the masonry stones were already there, they had used them rather than the typical waddle and daub – which would have been much more flammable. Even the little orphanage chapel had a low sodded roof rather than the wooden vaulting so typical of the area.

They were very lucky Heather had taken the blast outside. Yet it seemed she was not so lucky, for despite all their subsequent searching, none of them there ever found any pieces or even any trace of Heather. Kilian just sat there on the low stone wall near the well, his head down in his hands, not willing to face the fact that she was gone.

When Cutter carried George into the dining commons, most of the children turned their attention to the screaming "child" whom they expected to see spanked any minute. Raymond and Violet had gotten all of the infected ones to vomit by now, so only a few drops of Patrick's blood were needed per child. Weed stood there zombie-like, worried sick about his parents, while Violet and the black and white fox herded the children to and from the anti-poison and kept them away from any traces of the tainted iced cream. Even though some of the young ones were still sick and barely breathing, all eventually were antidoted. Mike helped Patrick lay down on the stone floor near the wooden stage area and held his arm up and applied pressure and a bandage to it to stop the blood flow. Mike took off his scapular, rolled it up, and used it to prop Patrick's arm higher than the rest of his body. Patrick knew he'd be sick for weeks, but it was a price worth paying for even one little one's life.

Restless as they were, the children kept asking about George and the racket he was making as he struggled against Cutter. Mike ignored them all and went over to Weed and put both of his big hands on his shoulders. "Are you OK?" he asked strongly. When just a blank stare was all that returned to him, Mike shook Weed and called to him deeply and loudly: "Weed! Weed! listen to me. You are here. You are with friends ... Weed!"

Mike shook him again and called his name louder. This time Weed's eyes started to focus on Mike's face and a weak groan escaped from his throat. Mike shook him again and again. Patrick couldn't stand it anymore. He rolled over on his stomach and struggled to get up. Little Ray came over and helped him stand. Then, understanding from gestures what he wanted to do, led him over to Mike and Weed.

"Hold on, Mike," Ray cautioned, laying one hand on Mike's right arm while steadying Patrick with the other. Mike looked at him, then at Patrick who was barely able to squeak out: "Maybe he's been given some other kind of poison. Let's try a little more of my blood. He's worth the risk."

Ray caught Patrick as his knees started to collapse. "Better give it a try, Michael, or this cleric won't give either of us any peace," Ray cautioned. So Mike and Ray forced a bit more blood out of Patrick; and Mike coaxed Weed to swallow it while Ray tried to get Patrick to go back over to the stage area to lie down again. But Patrick wouldn't go until he had given Weed his strongest cure spell. He tried to give himself one, but couldn't make it through the little ceremony. Ray carried him over to a big oak-plank table and gently laid his limp body on it while holding the cut on his arm closed and elevated. Ray stayed there, compassionately resolute, like a large dog guarding a wounded puppy.

Cutter was getting tired of George's squirming and kicks, so he smacked him twice and started dragging him over to Mike to ask what to do with him. The children saw this and started chanting: "Spank him. Spank him."

The fox looked at them broodingly and growled. They got quiet immediately.

George tried to hide from Weed, who was starting to become a bit more lucid: losing the glassiness in his stare and moving his head more. Mike shook him once more, gently this time. Weed recognized Mike and started to smile. Then he noticed George as he struggled under Cutter's iron grip, and started trying to get to George while crying, "No, no, not my parents ... Please don't let the guild kill them, please ... I won't talk ... I promise, no ... no ... it's poison ... you tricked me, I didn't want to do it ... I'm sorry." As Mike's strong arm held him away from Cutter and George, Weed finally collapsed on it in tears and deep sobs. Mike held him there while Weed's tears ran down his arm and dripped off his elbow and the words rearranged themselves in his mind. Mike could no longer escape the realization that his best friend had been poisoned by long use of the magic powder – and it tore at his heart.

Chapter 21
THE RACE AGAINST DEATH

Kilian was disturbed in his brooding by a strong tickle on his right cheek. Then he felt it again and smelled something kind of musty. Finally he heard Jake barking at him and opened his eyes to see him jumping around in front of him and the double-headed axe lying at his feet.

"What are you doing here, boy?" he asked, almost expecting Jake to answer.

Jake pawed at the note tied to the axe and kept bouncing around, obviously trying to get Kilian to go somewhere with him.

Kilian picked up the axe and tore off the note. He started to read it, then noticed that it was addressed to Cutter. He kept reading anyway. But when he read that Troy and the four assassins were at Silverhorn, he realized that they were after Alex. He jumped to his feet and started to follow Jake out, then remembered that the message really was for Cutter. Whistling Jake back to himself he raced back into the dining commons to find Cutter and give him the note.

Cutter handed George to Kilian while he read the note from Sky. Jake, next to Kilian, started sniffing George and then started barking wildly and growling at him. Kilian tried to ask him what was wrong, but the axe wouldn't work since Sky had already used it today. To calm Jake down, Mike asked Violet to come out of the kitchen and cast her speak with animals spell. When the others heard her explain Jake's account from Silverhorn, and his claim that he smelt Troy's blood on (or it seemed like "in") George, the pieces started falling into place.

Kilian picked George up by his shirt and shouted at him: "You! You planted the bomb that killed Heather!"

George answered with a gloating, almost diabolical laugh, then spit in Kilian's face. Kilian went wild – which was exactly what George wanted. At worst, Kilian in a violent rage would kill him, and then would be executed for murder; at best, the others would be so busy restraining Kilian that George would have another chance to escape by grabbing one of the children as a hostage. His plan worked. While it took both Mike and Cutter to restrain Kilian, George bounded for the door. As he tried to grab the tiniest and most frightened little girl nearby, however, the fox interposed itself. Growling and barking wildly and nipping at George, it halted him for half a moment while also alerting Jake. With one leap Jake was on him and knocked him sideways to the ground as he reached for the child. His head hit a leg of one of the heavy wooden benches at just the wrong angle but with enough force to snap the neck. As Jake dragged him over the flagstone floor away from the terrified children, George's head rolled back and forth on his neck, the bones grinding through the spinal cord. By the time Jake had delivered him to Kilian, blood was dripping from his ears and mouth. He was dead.

After a few minutes of stunned silence followed by confusion, Cutter picked up George's body and laid it on another of the long heavy oak tables. Kilian was stroking Jake and saying "Good goin', boy!" He wandered over to the body, looked down at it in disgust and said: "That was for Heather." Then he said "This is from me," as he spit on him – hitting him right between the eyes.

As Cutter finally got a chance to read the note his hands started to tremble with rage. "My family! They're trying to stall those guild cutthroats right now. I've got to get there."

"I'm coming too," Kilian added as he surreptitiously slipped George's ring off his finger and into his own pocket, then hurried out after Cutter.

Ray shouted across the room: "Mike, you go too. They may need a paladin to keep some order. Besides, it's your friend the assassins are after. Take the monk with you. I'll hold down the fort here."

"Somebody here needs me," Mike replied, as he glanced down at Weed who was crouched on the monastery floor, head against his knees and clinging with his left arm to a table leg to slow down the intensity of the convulsions.

"Somebody may need you more somewhere else," continued Raymond. Then glancing rather wistfully at Violet: "Besides, this charming and beautiful halfling damsel here and I can certainly handle anything that comes along. I believe the attack's over here, so with the farmhands' help we can watch over the little ones, as well as Patrick and Weed."

"Are you sure you don't need the head monk?" Mike argued.

Ray had had enough discussion by this point, but he couldn't simply order Mike to go since they were both the same rank. So he laid Mike's rolled-up scapular on Patrick's chest and gently draped Patrick's bandaged left arm over it. He turned to face Mike squarely and came to attention: feet together, body straight and tall, right hand holding his sword straight up along the left side of his head with the hilt touching his chest directly over his scar. Mike immediately snapped to attention too.

"Corporal," Ray began, "remember your oath. The faithful are in a clear and present danger. These little ones here are no longer threatened. What is your duty?"

"To protect the faithful of our church from manual or magical attack by evil people or evil creatures, and aid them on their life's journey, even at the cost of my life, sir!" Mike recited squarely.

"Then do it!"

Mike saluted by extending his sword in the most official manner, straight-faced and serious. He walked over to Ansgar the monk who was gathering up a few clerical items. As Mike approached but before he could ask him to accompany them, the monk looked up and said, "Yes, I'm coming too." And before anyone could blink they had disappeared through the large wood-framed doorway.

They caught up with Kilian and Jake and Cutter just as they had entered the front gate of Silverhorn tavern. The place was deathly silent. Even though Cutter had rushed through the entry-yard and raced in and out of the common rooms and the kitchen, Kilian was able to determine from the tracks Cutter hadn't obliterated that five horses had come and gone. At least one of them was heavier when it left than when it had arrived. The blood in the front yard sent Jake into a panic when he smelled it: and by naming first Sky, then Ricky, Lee and Anna, Kilian found out that it belonged to Anna and Lee. Cutter was frantic. He went racing down the road after them. Mike sent the monk after him, for the road at least was smooth and the path obvious, and Cutter himself might need a cleric if he found pieces of his family along the way. Mike also asked Kilian to send Jake along to make sure Cutter and the monk didn't lose the trail.

Kilian and Mike took the short-cut to Alex's clan's "roost." Kilian couldn't help but notice the "Ricky-size" footprints near the pond. The crushed reeds and the arrow were glaringly obvious, as was the blood on the stone dam embankment. Any minute now they expected to find his body. Instead they kept finding footprints, dribbles of blood here and there, and a large bloody smudge against the side of the culvert under the eastern highway.

Emerging from the culvert Kilian heard a group of horses coming east out of Dennistown crossing the road ten cubits above them. He thought he heard Troy's voice calling the mob to hurry, but Kilian couldn't get their attention from down in the gorge. As Mike emerged, he and Kilian climbed the sloping eastern side of the ravine quickly, but couldn't get over the thorn-bush hedge lining the road edge. Mike had started chopping through the hedge when Kilian, who had been searching the greenbrier-encumbered tree line, found more blood and

Ricky-size tracks. Calling Mike over, they started to squeeze their way, one at a time, into the greenbrier tunnel. As they crawled through the winding five-cubit-long, one-cubit high tunnel Mike was glad he had removed his scapular so it wouldn't be getting caught on the briars, but he almost wished he had on his armor. Then as screams from the farm on the other side of the hedge caught their ears, all pain was forgotten as they squirmed the rest of the way through the hedge tunnel.

....

Interspersing traces of her teleportation ability with each of her prances, Blue Cloud galloped north over the eastern fringes of Gunner Mountain. Her combined movements yielded an elusive, out of focus strobe-like effect that even if it were noticed would not be believed by passersby. Around the northern edge of the mountain, and then west between the new quarry and the eerily silent haunted lake she raced. Now, far enough to the west of Dennistown to avoid detection, she streaked north on her magic hooves, crossing the backwater road and several fields before coming to the Monastery Woods.

The haystacks and the barn roof were gone; in fact, that whole section of the monastery-orphanage complex was a mass of smoldering ruins. All that was left were some charred stone pillars (some of them fallen and crumbled) and smoking fragments of what had been huge cross-pieces. One big red-bearded human was directing a couple of the neighboring farmers in salvaging what they could of the orphanage's farm stock and equipment. One other neighbor was laying tracks southwest in the direction of the backwater and the Holy Cross fortress, while a delivery boy with his pony cart was making his way hurriedly toward Dennistown. Blue Cloud suspected they were letting the authorities know about the disaster.

She snuck in closer to survey the damage done to her littlest ones. She saw the burnt remains of the six little ponies, and cried. Yet miraculously she saw no children's bones or bodies. In the main hall there was one older youth crouched on the floor, huddled now up against one of the fieldstone support columns, and one small body nearby. The evil it radiated indicated that it couldn't be a child. Through the nursery window she could see that a halfling maiden and the guardian fox had already quieted down the infants and toddlers, and had gotten them ready for a late afternoon nap. The other neighboring farmhand was working with various groups of different sized children to repair what they could on the outside of the building, and for some reason they were scrubbing down the whole inside area of the dining commons thoroughly. Concentrating, she could sense the traces of poison being removed. Over by the stage, watched over by a tall, dark-bearded paladin, one other person lay resting – alive but very, very weak. She felt very close to that human, but could not quite tell why. All seemed OK here, or at least repairable. Yet she had this strange sense that her people were still in danger: that some evil was still afoot. The battle wasn't quite over yet. She wondered how her husband would have reacted to this situation.

The memory of her husband triggered her senses. She recognized the scent of his blood and remembered his "friends." Heather was burned, perhaps fatally. She now realized that it was Patrick who lay there weakened beyond belief. Signs of a strange, magic-like battle were evident, yet no other wounded or dead were in sight. Since the only living creatures around were "safe" humans: the tall paladin and the short female druid, she decided to risk putting her head through the open window and speaking to these two. Within a few minutes she knew the story and was on her way in a wide circle far to the north around Dennistown toward Alex's parents' home on Runningbear farm.

Only after Blue Cloud departed the scene and all was quiet, did Ray finally remember that as a paladin he too could heal; and he realized that there was one in front of him who needed that healing very badly. He reached down and laid his huge hands on Patrick's head and chest, and prayed. He felt the healing move through him into that half-elf. Little did Ray know that he had given Patrick the very gift of life that he needed.

....

Ricky woke to the dull thud of wood being split. First a block of twisted, left-over wood from work was slapped down on the stump, then came the sharp clopping chop of iron slicing wood. He hadn't remembered crawling out of the hedge tunnel and over to the orchard, but there he lay up against a tree, less than twenty paces away from where Alex was chopping firewood. He dragged himself over to him, shouting for him, but his small child's exhaustion-weakened voice couldn't be heard over the chopping – intense as Lex was on the work at hand. Finally as Lex reached down to pick up another of the logs, he felt the branch writhe in his hand. He instinctively let it loose, jumped back and raised his axe to slice up the snake he must have grabbed – when he noticed it was no snake, but his cousin Ricky's arm. He saw the wound on his shoulder, picked him up, and ran toward the house. Ricky just couldn't get him to listen that attackers were coming. Finally he pulled hard on Lex's ear to get his attention, but could barely blurt out: "Assassins coming here to kill..." and he went limp. Alex reached the front porch of the large cabin just as some horses were coming up the side lane. He yelled for his mother to come, left Ricky on the kitchen table, and grabbed his bow and arrows as he raced outside.

....

From one end of town to the other Cutter frantically sought evidence of where his family might be, but he was wearing out. Jake kept picking up the scent of the trail; the perfumy smell was easy to follow. The monk caught up with them both and eventually had to pace Cutter to get him to slow down to catch his wind. Out the east road they marched, past the druid groves, across the old stone bridge and into the Bear clan's farmlands. Jake raced on ahead through Alex's parents' gate, but Cutter and the monk couldn't keep up. Ahead they heard Jake spook some horses, followed by a loud wail. Cutter recognized his wife's cry, but just couldn't get there any faster.

Chapter 22
ANGELS CRY AT RUNNINGBEAR FARM

Kristofer was coming out of the barn with his father Rupert to see who the visitors were when Lex ran by them and cautioned through clenched teeth: "Grab your weapons 'n' gather the younguns inside. Danger!"

Lex moseyed down the front lane to "welcome" the visitors, but kept his magic arrow nocked. By the time he got there they had dismounted. He could tell from the perfumy smell that the three fighters he saw come toward him, shielded by Sky and the two little ones, were from the city.

Sky tried to do what they told her and greeted Alex pleasantly, "Hello, Lex, Happy Easter!" She felt the dagger in her ribs and continued, "Is this any way to greet your relatives?"

Lex just stood there. He could see the knife at the throat of the baby girl and under the chin of Lee, and knew that there must be one on Sky. Yet he thought he had heard more horses. He didn't like it.

"Lower your bow or she dies!" Marty ordered.

Lex panned his aim to cover all of them. Marty advanced, pushing Sky ahead of him.

"Stop where you are!" Lex ordered; "What do you want?"

"You," replied Marty with a sneer as he still kept coming closer. "Come with us quietly and we'll leave these three alone here."

"You skunk-tailed liar! I said stop. T'aint no way you're gonna let 'em go."

Lex heard some slight movement near the barn and glanced there. Grek started to rush him, dangling Lee. Alex panned back and Grek halted. Marty ducked behind Sky and started pushing her forward again. When she resisted his forward push, he cut into her. She tried to hold it in, but couldn't stop a tiny cry. Alex aimed at him and ordered him to stop. Marty kept coming – hiding behind and torturing Sky, as Grek and Kruk both rushed him. As Sky flinched in pain, Lex caught sight of Marty's left eye and let go the arrow. Marty ducked and pushed Sky in front of the arrow, roaring in laughter – then in pain.

As the arrow teleported away around her and into Marty's eye, Sky finally pulled away. The blood spurted out of the eye cavity, followed by a globby gray material as the arrowhead continued out the back of Marty' skull. He grabbed for his face but fell to the ground, dead.

Kruk avenged Marty by slitting Anna's throat and tossing her behind him as he rushed forward. Sky couldn't get there in time. Grek felt the next arrow, though he tried to block it using Lee as a shield. Around Lee and through Grek's throat it sped, and dropped him in his tracks.

Kruk hit Lex before he could nock another arrow. His broadsword shattered Lex's bow and cut into his elbow. But Lex grabbed Kruk's sword arm and wrestled him to the ground as he had many a steer. Kruk, however, was craftier than a steer and knew a few tricks of his own. Poison was his trademark, and it wasn't limited to his weapons. The studs on his leather wrist band included one that was hollow. All he needed to do was touch it to Alex's bare arm as they wrestled; but it had somehow rotated to the wrong position on his wrist. Squirm as he might, he could not turn himself to make that part of his arm touch Alex. The design on his belt buckle contained a poisoned needle as well. With a quick torso twist he let the spring mechanism release the needle from its sheath and stick out just enough. Lex saw it and tried to keep Kruk from rolling over onto him with a body slam and the added lethal scratch. Then there was the sword itself and its razor-sharp blade. Lex just couldn't watch all three spots and still use all his energy to wrestle Kruk into immobility. When he thought he had Kruk pinned, the assassin somehow slithered around and had the needle poised just a finger tip away from Lex's exposed left side. Lex saw the needle and arched his back to avoid it – allowing Kruk to flip over onto him as they both grappled – hand on hand – rolling back and forth on the ground. Jab after jab with Kruk's belt needle barely missing Lex's exposed sides and stomach; but soon one little scratch would end all this struggle. Sky watched helplessly, holding Lee and Anna's dead body, as a dark, hairy shape rushed past her; but she couldn't see it in her delirium.

Lex's mother screamed as the shadow passed her cabin window and then screamed louder as her son Kris staggered through the kitchen doorway – his right arm severed, dangling from above the elbow by just a few strands of sinew and skin. She watched helplessly as he collapsed on the floor in the expanding pool of his own blood. Outside she could hear her husband furiously battling the two intruders seeking to murder the rest of the family. For a few moments all she could see were strokes swung as more and more wounds appeared on her husband. Suddenly she heard: "In the name of God, desist!"

The battle changed as Alvin swung around to meet the tall blond paladin. A quick dart toss as he turned should have caught some part of that character's exposed upper body skin and let the poison-contaminated spike do its work. It should have been an easy target with no scapular to catch and wipe off some of the poison coating, but Alvin's aim seemed off. The dart veered ever so slightly to the side as it came toward the aura-shrouded paladin and ended up striking the log house walls instead.

"Damn your filthy god!" Alvin spewed out as he tried to raise his sword to intercept Mike's return blow. Having already had Trail Healer raised in attack stance in front of him as he called for the surrender, Mike instinctively responded to the blasphemy and dart attack with an incredibly strong counter strike fueled by righteous anger. Letting loose a heaven-piercing yell, Mike sliced down through the leather armor on Alvin's right shoulder and kept going. The lightning-sharp edge of the holy sword seared through the shoulder skin, shattered the shoulder blade and continued slicing diagonally right through the ribs. It cut the right lung in half, continued on through the heart and clipped off the bottom of the left lung before emerging on the left side with its trail of blood, bone fragments and pieces of intestine. As Mike's follow-through spun him away, Alvin wobbled, then fell forward into the huge puddle of his own blood and viscera.

Troy reared up to take one more swing at Rupert, trying to finish off what he and Alvin had begun before they could both descend upon this intruding paladin, when he saw Rupert looking not at but behind him. Troy veered to catch sight of Kilian coming upon him just as they were all halted by Mike's holy battle cry. Troy parried Kilian's axe swing and maneuvered Rupert between them. With a quick push, Troy flung Rupert into Kilian and high-tailed it around the edge of the cabin. By the time Kilian had steadied Rupert and followed Troy around the log house, he was through the small orchard and running toward the heavy greenbrier hedge.

Troy tried to climb over it and couldn't. Then he tried to cut and push his way through it, but kept getting armor and clothing caught in the curved thorns. By the time Kilian got there, most of Troy's right leg as well as his left arm and hand were in shreds: skin only adhering to the flesh in pieces here and there. His beard and the tatters of his clothing were hopelessly caught by the greenbriers that seemed to wrap tighter around him the more he struggled to escape Kilian. The fear from Kilian's shout of "Come out of there, you snake scum!" made him stop and turn around. He knew he could battle his way through this ranger, possibly even close enough to take another hostage. But as he turned to swing at Kilian, the hedge caught part of his sleeve, holding his arm tight. As Troy glanced down to look at where his arm was caught and started to try to unhook it, Kilian threw his dagger at Troy's exposed neck. It hit just below the jawbone, and drove up through the throat and back of the mouth, finally wedging its point in the neck vertebrae. With hands and arms caught, Troy couldn't even reach his own neck. He choked and gagged as the blood spurted first from his neck, and then from his mouth. He slumped forward, still held tight by the thorn bushes. The forest itself had now claimed the final price from one who once had known better, but had chosen to butcher it for profit.

On the other side of the log house just as Kruk was hoping to land upon Lex with the poisoned needle, the dark, furry creature that had raced past Sky took a huge leap onto Kruk's back – snapping at his head and ears. Thus distracted by Jake, Kruk was no match for Alex who pushed him over and off himself as Jake attacked Kruk's face and throat. Lex, who had been unable to stop Kruk from slitting the throat of the defenseless baby girl, jumped up and over him, grabbed Kruk's own sword, and drove it through his chest and into his unfeeling heart.

Jake had received only a slight scratch from the poisoned needle on one leg, so Lex immediately cut the spot out completely: hair, flesh and all. Somehow, Jake seemed to understand. He even stood still as the monk who arrived a few minutes later washed and bandaged the whole area.

Cutter came staggering in dripping with sweat and panting: the energy he had used on the frantic run through town having finally taken its toll on him. He hurried over to Sky and held her tightly as she continued clutching Anna's body as well as Lee, sobbing and screaming hysterically. As the monk came over, Cutter was finally able to pry Lee away from her and hand the barely breathing little boy to him. Ansgar said a quick prayer over Anna from that distance and went to work on Lee. With God's special help and hours of his own healing skill Lee just might make it alive.

Mike had stepped over Alvin's body and steadied Rupert as Kilian chased after Troy. Mike had started to look after Rupert's wounds, but Rupert instead dragged him into the kitchen of the log house where Kris lay dying. His mother had tried to bandage the arm back together, but couldn't stop the bleeding. Mike, however, knew some battle-wound skills – and he had Trail healer. He undid the wrappings, realigned the severed bone pieces, and laid his sword lengthwise along the arm: hilt on the shoulder, point extending beyond the fingers. Then he laid hands – and the tide of life turned again in Kris's favor.

Chapter 23
A Struggle to Recover

Blue Cloud arrived at the northern edge of the Bear-clan lands and cautiously crossed a couple of fields in the shadow of the edging woodlands. She carefully surveyed both directions along the road before attempting to cross into the entry lane to Runningbear farm. But as she came up that path she knew that secrecy was no longer needed. She saw her husband's three special fighters standing before her: Alex comforting his family and patching up Rupert his father, Mike bandaging their cousin Ricky, and Kilian and the orphanage monk trying to get the young couple there to be concerned about their hurt little boy.

Blue Cloud suddenly noticed their real heartbreak: the murdered baby girl. She heard the hysterical sobs and ranting of Morning Sky about how they had wanted a daughter so badly and why God had taken her away. Cutter was trying to comfort his wife with words like "It's OK, she's with God . . . She was baptized . . . God understands," but Sky couldn't understand – or control herself.

"That's easy for you to say!" she spat out. "You were raised Christian. Baptism means something to you. I don't care about life later, I want her life now! What kind of God would give her only to take her away? Why didn't He do something if He loves us as you all claim? Where is He when we need Him most? Where . . ." Cutter actually had to hold her tightly not just for comfort but for restraint. She thrashed about in his arms, then finally collapsed in sobs on his shoulder.

Blue Cloud couldn't stand it any longer. The herd had the ability to re-enliven dead which they could use only about once a year; for it would drain or cross-level so much of their own life power. She had intended to save it for Heather, for it appeared it would be needed there; but the sight of these innocent victims who had no part in her husband's charge or responsibilities almost broke her heart. She slowly stepped around these people and up to the baby girl's body. Saying her silent but powerful prayer to the One Lord of all the living, she gently touched the tip of her horn to the baby's neck to seal the wound, then touched her forehead – and felt their life-energy flow into her and let the spark of life return. As the Monk picked up the baby girl and gave her back to her incredulous parents, Blue Cloud, weakened by the gift of life energy from every member of the herd, disappeared silently and slowly into the forest.

Kilian realized that he suddenly felt weaker. Perhaps it was the post-battle letdown, or the run exertion finally catching up with him. Nevertheless, he sat down on the edge of the log porch. Jake came over and nuzzled him, but Kilian didn't even have the strength to pet him.

Lex stopped bandaging his father and sat down on the bench in the late afternoon sunlight suddenly feeling very weak too. Mike staggered over to the porch roof-post and held onto it as he slowly eased his way down to a sitting position on the edge of the porch, his feet dangling over the collection of wild flowers beginning to grow there again. For some strange reason it seemed his energy was all but gone.

The other members (original or gifted) of the unicorn herd fared similarly: Sunbridge and the whole crew near Heather could barely stand for a few hours. Patrick had been sitting up for a little while now back at the orphanage and was getting ready to gather his equipment to return to St. Stephen's church for solemn vespers. Instead, he slowly sank back down on the wooden table, barely breathing and unable to move or speak. Raymond called for Violet and the two of them tried to revive or strengthen him. They didn't know what had happened or why, but it would be days before he would be strong enough to return to the parish.

Heather did not fare as well. The traces of life energy in her were minimal as it was, and the tenuous hold she had on bodily life was still excruciatingly painful. Perhaps it was for the best that the channeling of the "herd's life force" into Anna took all that Heather had to give. It shows great love to give up one's life for another – even when there is little life left to give. Perhaps Anna would one day become a druidess herself and carry on where Heather left off. The herd would save Heather's Whitewind armor for her – though no one else would know about it until God's good time. For now, they let Heather rest in God's peace. In some suitably anonymous way, probably through a series of animal messengers, the herd would let the druid community – and Kilian – know what had happened. They would all have to do the best they could with him for quite a while; he had already heard the angels cry.

Ruth, Heather's mother, took it really hard. If it weren't for her younger daughter Rosemary needing her, she might have just drifted away herself. But their community claimed that such deaths were part of the ebb and flow of life in nature. She and her family would survive. Every now and then some of the druidic community, particularly the mothers, wondered if there was something more to life than just survival. They had no good answer.

By evening a patrol from the Fortress of the Holy Cross had arrived at the orphanage. After Raymond's report, a few of the paladins were immediately dispatched by the Vincentian to the Bear Clan farms to look for Mike and the rest of the crew. Retrieving them was easy – and the subsequent investigation by Field Sheriff Don Ironfist went very smoothly during the next few days. The "Fine Goods and Medicine" company was investigated and disbanded, and patrols of both paladins and ordinary troopers were doubled throughout the dukedom to protect Weed and his family.

The paladins were particularly troubled at their lack of ability to detect evil in the assassins. Even when they really concentrated, their sense of good and evil seemed to be disrupted. They suspected some kind of magical device, or perhaps a potion or spell. That very evening they were able to "recruit" a couple of the valley mages to examine the bodies at the bear clan farm, but these two refused to examine anything until a cleric had entered the area and blessed the bodies and equipment first. Fr. Gregory Oxentrail, the paladin's priest-chaplain, went into the spot with holy water-infused-blessings and a two-man paladin escort. Systematic removal of all the armor and equipment revealed that the rings had a disruptive effect on detection of evil.

By the next day those rings were carted off to the duke's city, where both the bishop's synod and the Magic Users' guild were most intrigued by this kind of property. The Royal Council decided on a combined team to analyze what was causing this – for neither the clergy nor the magic users guild felt comfortable trying to analyze this kind of device by themselves. In the course of the formal investigation, a good feeling developed between the clerics' organization and the Magic Users' guild. Working together on a tough problem generally engenders a mutual respect – and reduces prejudices. Moreover, they were each disgusted by what they discovered, and were pleased that they shared that revulsion. Apparently both saint's blood and daemon ichor had been somehow infused into the original formula of the amalgam for the stock ring metal. In the analytical process, however, the four guild rings were decomposed and destroyed. No one but Kilian knew of the one he had retrieved from George; but now he knew what it was.

Chapter 24
INSIDE THE MASTER MAGE'S QUARTERS

The Royal Council representative of the magic users guild did not take part in this analytic work, and seemed to distance himself from its results. This wasn't like him. Indeed, for more than a fortnight since Easter Gmellin had been worried about his boss, "Edgar the Cautious." Having been apprenticed to Master Edgar for over five years now, Gmellin could begin to sense when Edgar was just not himself.

Although users of magic never behaved normally by any standards, Edgar's behavior had not been quite the same since his session with George Paddlefoot right around the time Master Kresov had disappeared. Not only had Edgar dropped the large spell book that day and been visibly shaken, he progressively became more and more withdrawn. He had refused to see anyone all that afternoon after George had left – canceling abruptly two standing appointments with very wealthy clients. Jules his steward had dumped the problem of trying to satisfy these customers on Gmellin, telling him simply that "Master Edgar had acquired a new document and did not wish to be disturbed." So Gmellin had had to make excuses and try to enchant whatever he could for those special clients. Each of the spells they requested was way beyond his ability. It seemed almost as if those aristocrats knew it and wanted to watch him fail. When he admitted humbly that he couldn't do the spells, they left in a huff.

That evening, while listening to the rain on the roof, Gmellin began to connect the document Jules had mentioned with the spell book that he had seen George offer to Edgar. From the little he remembered hearing of the conversation between them that day, Gmellin began to suspect that it was connected with

Kresov as well. Unfortunately, due to the mystery involving Kresov's disappearance and the scandal the next week involving George's business, Gmellin didn't dare bring up the subject to Master Edgar or even to Jules – but he worried about Edgar anyway.

Things got worse. During the next few days, as the new moon approached, Edgar began to forget or ignore other appointments, and eventually cancelled all his appointments with all his clients. Emmaus Sunday came and Edgar didn't show up at church. "His" kneeling spot was noticeably empty. There was talk. Fortunately, everything that had happened at the orphanage and at Alex's parent's farm the previous Sunday gave folks much more to talk about. However, despite the "excuse" that Edgar might be investigating those assassins' rings, the clerics would not be convinced – since they were working hand in hand with the magic user's guild on that very project for the Duke. There would be more talk if Edgar didn't show up the next Sunday.

Gmellin not only sensed a difference, but knew instinctively that this was not his same master. The real Edgar had painstakingly crafted a personality that would be acceptable to the inner circle of the Duke's court. He had courted each of the wealthy and established families, and was loathe to have them consider taking their business elsewhere. Something suspicious was beginning to preoccupy more and more of Edgar's attention, and was possibly even eating into his consciousness.

For someone who makes his living using magic, this could be devastating. It is difficult enough to connect with or "hook" the subtle influences around us, the living and non-living auras or "fields", and delicately coax them into an intricate pattern. It is as intense a process as pulling celestial music out of a home-made fiddle. Concentration was everything. Finding the aura, enhancing it, weaving it into a particular pattern – focused by the spell components' images in the magician's mind – all this was a very delicate process. Being either distracted or preoccupied would automatically interfere with the very process of weaving such magic spells. It would be like trying to dance with one heavy boot on: it could be done, but would be very difficult to do correctly. Due to his reputation, any spell failure would lead to disaster for Master Edgar – and everyone associated with him.

When Gmellin very discretely brought up the matter to Jules, he was told to mind his own business. When he pointed out that business was in fact part of his concern about Edgar, Jules took notice. As Gmellin explained, "if Edgar doesn't snap out of his distractions soon, business is gonna' disappear." Jules eventually agreed that the two of them would have to get Edgar to start seeing clients again – real soon.

They decided upon a first step to try to revive Edgar's interest in things around him: wizard ball. Though Edgar probably couldn't be enticed into playing this weird game that had no magic about it but looked like it did, if they arranged a game that he couldn't avoid watching, his excitement would be aroused. So while Jules worked on convincing Master Edgar that he just had to go to church that Sunday to prevent his friendly rival, Msgr. James Beaumont, the rector of the cathedral, from having an excuse to check in on him, Gmellin and his wife contacted two other apprentices with kids, Jeff Bricker & Carl Hammermann, to bring their families over to Edgar's compound for a picnic & game after Sunday mass.

It worked. Though Edgar didn't remember anything about mass on that "Good Shepherd" Sunday, nor even notice the picnic going on in his own courtyard, he couldn't escape the children. He had always been very kind to everyone's children not just because it was the proper or philanthropic thing to do; he remembered being hungry (and lonely) as a child and was not going to let that happen to others around him. So the kids really loved him. They always piled on him, hugged and tugged on him, shared their food and toys with him, and made him play with them.

Indeed, Edgar's fondness for children, and his willingness to pay his apprentices a stipend that was large enough for them to support a young family, was the main reason that Gmellin had chosen to study under him. Other Master Mages were much less family friendly. Edgar could afford such largess – and he had gotten some very good apprentices in the process. Though they took longer to complete their apprenticeship due to family distractions, Edgar got great service from them and now had foster grandchildren throughout the dukedom and beyond. Having already achieved all the status he would ever reach by being chosen for the duke's inner circle, he now lived for and sincerely loved all the kids.

When the three apprentices started the wizard ball game, which was hardly more than attempting to kick a lopsided, oval-shaped ball around a triangular grassy court, the kids went wild – and drew Edgar into their enthusiasm. The ball didn't really bounce but seemed to have a mind of its own – just due to its shape. Edgar found himself cheering on Gmellin as he battled against Jeff & Carl (but more often against the ball) trying to get it into either of the others' home court – their apex of the triangular field. Before he knew it, Edgar was betting with the other two masters who had come to cheer on their own apprentices. After the game, they lingered over branded-wine or Brandywine and Jasmine tea and Meaghan's famous pastries; and they discussed spells and politics and the usual business of the magic guild just as if there had never been anything wrong with Edgar. That night, after they had cleaned everything up, Jules and Gmellin each went to their quarters relieved.

In the valley, it had taken several days for the clan members to come to grips with what had happened. They began to appreciate more and more the protection that the paladin fortress had been giving them all along, and at least for a few weeks many of them came back to church regularly. Their new-found appreciation of the members of this holy order of fighters blossomed into heart-felt cooperation like the blueberry blossoms coming into bloom on the roadsides, or the buds on the overarching trees maturing into full leaf. A couple of weeks later, when the paladins asked for help restoring the damaged orphanage compound, whole groups of clansmen overcame their loathing of orphans and competed with one another as they all helped rebuild the courtyard walls and raise the barn.

The only time that things got a little uneasy was in the removal of the debris from the inner courtyard. When hauling off some of the burnt timbers that had fallen into that inner part of the group of monastery buildings, some of the deer clan pulled up a few of the pavement stones that had cracked under the intense heat of the blast. Some of the other stones then crumbled into a pit beneath them with several soft thuds, and one metallic "clink." They had unwittingly uncovered the Knob Rabbits' burial chamber under the high altar of their original church. The clansmen scattered to the outer walls and started blaming each other.

Fortunately, Little Ray was again on duty that day and at that point checked for evil; then he marched right up to the pit and very reverently removed the rest of the covering stones. The clansmen watched with a mixture of admiration and horror as Ray examined the remains and then called for Br. Ansgar.

No one moved.

Ray called again, and again. Finally one of the older orphans ran and got Br. Ansgar to come out. Together they said a few of the prayers for the dead, then the two of them reverently scooped up the ashes and bone fragments into a blessed wooden box – like the caskets used for any children who died – and carried them away to the chapel for a reinternment blessing. Br. Ansgar ordered them all to come into the chapel with him for the prayers, to guard against any curse for disturbing the dead. They all came immediately. He then blessed them with holy water by dunking them in a trough of it. No one objected. In fact, the rougher he was with any of them the more protected they felt – almost like a re-baptism. Ray and Br. Ansgar then blessed the former grave site with the whole trough of water, and Ray leaned in and removed the metallic object: an old dilapidated sword with a black hilt embedded with one very tiny blue-white gemstone. What was left of its leather scabbard fell away as he picked it up and sliced the air with it for the first time in perhaps a century or two. As fascinated as the clansmen are with weapons of any kind, no one would come near that sword. They all claimed that it had an "itchy" feel about it. Neither Ray nor Br. Ansgar could feel anything about the sword, other than that it was well-balanced and had a bright blade and that the gemstone seemed to fit in the pommel of the sword without hurting the wielder's hand. The only inscription on the sword might be its name, or its heritage: Wanderstar.

Only after Br. Ansgar had taken the ancient sword into the chapel and Ray personally had filled in the gravesite could he get the clansmen back to work. At that point he was losing patience. He threatened them all with calling back the knob rabbits' spirits if they didn't help him repair the damage. Eric Dancingbear and Robby Deerhorn then double-dared each other to pitch in, which meant that if one did the other had to as well. That broke the "spell" of inhibiting fear, and they all redoubled their efforts to prove how brave they each were. Over the next few weeks they all helped as a matter of clan pride and hoped to be done for the duke's and the bishop's visit to rededicate it on Pentecost.

....

In the city healing was not going quite as well as in rebuilding the orphanage. Despite the wizard-ball game, it was clear that there was still work to be done on Edgar. Though he was able to begin to focus on his practice again, Edgar still seemed to be burdened by a secret worry – or a decision he was having to make – that was so heavy it appeared to hold his fate in the balance. Whatever it was had a strange grip on him and would not let go.

"Balance! Yes," thought Gmellin, "that would be a good next step." So he sort of reminded Master Edgar that it was time to recalibrate the mechanisms on their clock collection (which Edgar always insisted on doing himself but needed an assistant with the tools and timing device nearby). Next they moved to the gyroscopes and they both had fun playing with them – walking the 'scopes on strings and on fingers and even tossing them to each other – all while checking the mechanisms. It was the special 'scopes that both interested and terrified Gmellin, the ones Master Edgar had shown him how to build with magnets attached to the rotating wheel. Gmellin kept trying to understand elemental magnetism but just couldn't do it. He couldn't feel the magnetic force, but iron granules nearby would form patterns when the magnet came near. The magnets on the gyroscope would make the iron granules dance, but wouldn't affect silver or gold. What intrigued him the most was what it did to any copper piece or wire he would bring near the magnet-scope: it would bite him!

Edgar would always laugh at this, and remind Gmellin of the taboo against standing in water   or even on wet grass – when working with magnets and gyroscopes. Time after time Edgar would try to instruct Gmellin about elemental magnetism and the lines of force (or did he call them lines of energy?) and that the whole earth was one big magnet. That was why the little iron fish that the mariners dangled from a thread, once the fish had been "kissed" by the big magnetic fish in his laboratory, always swam north in any kind of weather – even the dreary rain they'd been having lately. That was also why the divining rods (or "witching wands" as the valley mages called them) would dip down whenever one came to water no matter how hard one tried to hold them back. Did not Edgar say that such lines of magnetic force ran even through our bodies? Then why couldn't we feel them even when these forces were using something we held? That kind of magic Gmellin just had trouble understanding.

Edgar explained again and again that "magnetism isn't something that humans can weave into a lasting pattern, like we weave designs into cloth on the loom or weave interlocking strips of cane together to make a basket or even a chair." Putting two magnets together only lets them interfere with each other; and moving a magnet in a pattern just didn't last. The pattern or design fades almost instantly. And just like when a part of a knot or a woven pattern or even a spider web is broken or missing, the whole structure starts to unravel; so also an incomplete magnetic pattern just would not hold. "But," Edgar pointed out, "if we use a machine, powered by our windmill on the roof or the water wheel in the aqueduct by our outside wall or even animal power in a treadmill to keep the magnet moving again and again in the same pattern, then we can get them to set up a field or weave a magnetic spell over a whole doorway or even a corridor. It is like an unseen dog that doesn't bark but bites with a thousand little teeth – especially if one is holding a metal sword."

What did Master Edgar call it, a charge spell or a "luck-trick" spell? Gmellin couldn't remember, but he could feel that same luck-trick force in the air just before each springtime thunderstorm. He could feel it and he could use it. Even long ago Gmellin had been able to master how to make the luck-trick spell "charge forth" from a glass wand if he rubbed it with a wool cloth. Miniature lightening would arc from the end of the glass wand to his target. More experienced mages could make longer arcs or even patterns in the luck-trick discharge. There were legends that long ago great magic users could call down the lightening from the clouds by weaving a luck-trick pattern for the lightening to follow. Some folk even claimed that druids had developed the same luck-trick skills and could call down lightning from storms too. Gmellin could believe it. He had been "bitten" by the luck-trick charge of the magnetic gyroscope enough times to know an invisible dog bite when he felt one.

"Druids were good with animals," he reasoned. "Maybe they had learned how to tame the luck-trick dog & make it bite where they wanted it. Strange, though," he thought, "my tools and my dagger can feel the elemental magnetism, and I can feel the luck-trick charge in the atmosphere. Yet, the animal magnetism in me can disturb how the magnetic fish swims, and my tools can hold on to or 'carry' the luck-trick charge. I wonder if some day it will all come together?"

Chapter 25
SIR WOLF

The next morning Gmellin moved Master Edgar from elemental magnetism to animal magnetism. Both Master Edgar and Gmellin had a certain knack with animals, almost a natural understanding. Extending that skill into a magical spell came reasonably easy to both of them, so this day's activity was more like colleagues sharing useful techniques than it was a master instructing an apprentice. First they would approach an animal, even a little animal, with a respect bordering on reverence. Next they would "call" to it, either verbally or mentally – or both. Each bit of response from the animal would be gathered, almost like the threads on a loom, and woven together to make a bond with the animal. Eventually the animal would trust and come close enough to allow them to touch it. Here the different special spots of trust and comfort – such as just below and behind the ears on a dog – would be the tool they would use to strengthen that bond. By the end of the process the animal would become almost a friend. Farm hands called it taming an animal; magic users called it animal charm or animal magnetism.

There was a two-fold difficulty to this type of magic: the diversity of the animals involved – and each animal's past history. An animal that had been harmed would take much more effort to charm. The harm had to be overcome or healed somehow. There had to be at least a trace of willingness to trust before an animal would begin to listen to any kind of a charm, even a healing charm, calling to its inner self.

The difference in species of animals also gave certain parameters, both physical and mental. Depending on the size of the animal's brain, there was a varying degree of mental energy emanating from it with which to connect. Other limitations were that some species had no ears, and so might need movements to connect with – much like the movements of the Arab pipers which are what really charm the snakes they use. Some practitioners consider that action a type of hypnosis.

Magicians would weave all these elements together: animal curiosity or hunger, desire to be accepted and loved (or at least petted), and certain movements or sounds – or even smells. All of this might be important in making that "trusting" connection. Once the connection was made, however, the real work started: the mage had to communicate with the animal. This was done by picking up signals that the animal was trying to send – but so faintly, almost in a whispering mode. A squirrel might move its head or its tail in just a certain way if danger was near, for example; and the magic user had to be able to pick up on that. Only after a message was picked up could the charmer relate what he wanted the animal to do – all in terms of the needs that the animal had already just communicated.

An easy example of this animal body language is the way a cat will rub against one's legs. This means territory or safe area. If the mage reinforces this request by gently enveloping the cat, all the while communicating mentally in a very respectful tone, the charm can begin to work. Unfortunately, there is always a chance that a charm will fail – particularly with dangerous animals because of the trace of fear in the magic user. A distraction of the animal during the charm attempt could also disrupt the spell, leaving the magic user particularly vulnerable because of his own trustingness while in the presence of the dangerous animal or reptile. Just as many a member of a hunting party failed to return from mountain lion or buffalo hunts, so also some legendary mages attempting to charm large and dangerous animals or reptiles had "bitten off more than they could chew" and had had parts of themselves bitten off in return.

The most difficult and dangerous animals to try to charm, however, were those who used tools: humans – and others like them. The more complex the individual, the more difficult to really know him. Though some humans can immediately take to each other or fit, many have a wariness that the merchants call sales resistance. It takes more than just words or motions or smells to charm humans. It takes a good first impression as the original strand of trust. Then the mage uses that starter to connect with the aura glimmering around the person and weave a bond with himself. It is complete when the will of the charmed one, though essentially still free, is so wrapped up in the desire to serve or please the charmer that he can't even tell he has been charmed. Some claim that romantic love or infatuation is much like this.

After Gmellin and Edgar had practiced a bit on some small animals, they both worked together on a special request that day. Sir Robert Fielder, the Count of the City and captain of the Duke's knights and royal guard, wanted to have a large wolf that he had captured charmed and attached to himself, so he could show off at the next hunt. Here Gmellin's natural affability set the stage in the knight and helped relax him and lessen his fear while Edgar worked separately with the captive wolf.

Edgar started slowly, working on Prisoner Wolf, picking up some signals of anger at being caged and fear about what these humans were going to do with him. Slowly Edgar began to communicate a sense of what chivalry required of a captured noble: great respect and proper treatment even while in captivity – almost like being made part of the tribe. With considerable mental effort, while feeding and stroking the wolf in ways that no other wolf could do, Edgar was able to relate that idea of chivalrous station to how one wolf could be accepted and treated well in another pack. Was such pack acceptance unlikely? Yes, but if one proved oneself in a crisis, the other wolves would give welcome and perhaps even a special status.

Slowly Mr. Wolf began to like that idea, and even started to imagine the status that the knight and his human pack might be willing to bestow.

Then came the switch: Gmellin was brought into the room with Citizen Wolf and Edgar, and together they began to build up the self-esteem of the wolf to the point that captivity could be a badge of honor. While the wolf got used to the traces of the smell of the knight on Gmellin, Edgar went back to the knight to speak to him as a fellow member of the Duke's Royal Council about how valuable that wolf would now be. The level of care and companionship – though not like a dog, for he would not want to break the wolf's independent spirit – would need to be truly as noble as he would want if he were in the wolf's place.

Eventually, by going back and forth, Gmellin and Edgar were able to heighten the respect and even desire of the knight and Sir Wolf for each other, to the point where a formal introduction could be successful. Gone would be the wolf's memories of capture and confinement – replaced by the thrill of a human touch that healed. Gone also would be the knight's fear of reprisals and attack; modified instead by a fear of offending an equal. A distant sense of respect began to emerge, from which Edgar and Gmellin wove a bond of trust – much like how a matchmaker would set two lovers together, and let them build on the best in each other. Finally, the wolf and the knight revealed their names to each other through the magic users.

The spell worked. Sir Robert was delighted with this new addition to his household and treated him chivalrously. The rest of the family, and the servants, kept a respectful distance. Sir Wolf never lost his cunning in the hunt – or in sniffing out an enemy of the knight, or his children. And the Duke and the rest of his courtiers were very impressed.

Edgar and Gmellin were both weary by the time the spell had been completed. Once the two-week guarantee trial period had passed, worthy payment would be forthcoming. After a relaxed (and late) lunch, Edgar saw other clients (whom Gmellin had prepared) and seemed to be his cheerful self.

The next few days went by almost normal – as long as Gmellin kept Edgar busy. But neither Gmellin nor Edgar could keep up that intense a pace. Gmellin tried going back to his studies, what he still needed to learn for his transition from apprentice to junior magician or journeyman. This meant leaving Edgar alone to work on his own projects for a few hours; but things just didn't "feel" right in the house when Gmellin did that. He was apprehensive about leaving Edgar alone over the weekend.

Slowly Gmellin closed in on what that uneasy feeling was: he could sense that Master Edgar was still deeply worried about something. Unfortunately Jules was no further help. He took care of Master Edgar after hours, but kept a professional distance. Having gotten Edgar back in the magic business again, Jules was reluctant to risk crossing that professional boundary: not wanting to delve any further than necessary into Edgar's personal issues. As long as the spells were still functioning – and the money was coming in – Jules was happy. Gmellin was left to worry alone. He didn't know what to do or who to turn to. If Edgar were to get so distracted in the middle of a spell that the spell was ruined, his reputation (and Gmellin's) would plummet. Edgar could retire and live off his savings. Gmellin and his family would starve.

Worse still, if some concern was gnawing at Edgar's consciousness this seriously, it had to be a really big problem. It might be a problem big enough to harm the whole dukedom. Could it be connected with the battle a week after Easter at the orphanage? Could it have something to do with Kresov's sudden disappearance? If there were something "out there" that was attacking mages, Edgar would certainly have put his innumerable defenses in place. No, the problem was inside, much like an important decision weighing on him that wasn't yet resolved to anyone's satisfaction.

Gmellin needed to talk this out with someone, but no one was available. Jules was unwilling to broach the subject. Meaghan, his wife, was not a magic user and would have trouble really listening to him anyway with all the noise the kids usually make. He didn't dare discuss it with any of the other apprentice mages. If any one of them were to gossip about it, he'd be dismissed from Edgar's service and blacklisted among Mages everywhere. Besides, most of the other apprentices in the city didn't know any more about this kind of a distraction than he himself did. Few if any of them would have any good advice about how to heal it in one's boss.

Since this trouble might need healing, Gmellin would have liked to have taken the matter to a cleric, but didn't know any of them in the city who were sympathetic to magic. Moreover, if he went to them in an ordinary advice conference, they would be free to blab Edgar's problem all over the city – and would be more than eager to do so. But he couldn't really talk about it "under the seal" of confession because there had been no sin committed – or had there? And even if there was, it was not his own sin, so he could not bring it up without being guilty of calumny or false accusations. Still, he just had to talk to someone. Finally, as he was walking home with groceries Friday evening in the spotty spring rain showers, he remembered his classmate Patrick.

Jules took care of Edgar that Saturday while Gmellin made preparations with his family for the next week's ordeal. With Jules' help, Edgar made it to mass that Sunday and seemed reasonably well-composed. Only Gmellin, and now also Jules, could tell the difference. Jules, however, looked more haggard than usual. Watching Edgar carefully, keeping him from sinking into a dangerous distractedness from reality, had taken its toll on Jules. It gave a new meaning to the term "rough weekend."

In a few moments' conversation after mass, Jules and Gmellin agreed that they had to resolve this soon. Jules reported that when he had reminded Master Edgar about the monthly Mage Guild meeting Monday evening, he had seemed agitated and distressed rather than displaying his usual delight at the chance to be lionized by the younger magic users. Since the first post-Easter meeting was the only meeting each year when apprentices, particularly those getting ready for their journeyman exams, were allowed to attend, Gmellin would shepherd Master Edgar that afternoon and evening. Jules was grateful for the respite. Gmellin could rather easily keep an eye on Master Edgar all while he himself, as expected, would be meeting all the Master Mages who might be on his exam board a few days later.

Jules was apprehensive about Gmellin's need to be gone for a couple of days after the annual soirée to gather the components he would need for whatever spells might be on those exams. But Jules was even more upset at the realization that after those exams Gmellin might be gone for much longer periods – leaving Jules alone with a no longer completely functional Edgar. Gmelin promised to visit with "a trustworthy cleric, one sympathetic to magic illnesses" while on his spell-component hunt; so he might have an answer to Edgar's illness when he returned. Jules seemed relieved, and even offered to pray for the success of that endeavor. This was a significant concession, for Jules' normally cynical attitude did not take easily to prayer.

Monday's activities went as well as anyone could ask. Because the Mage-guild annual meeting was a major social event, few clients expected to get to see Master Edgar that day. The few that did manage to prevail on Jules to let them have an audience with Master Edgar were easily satisfied – and were very apologetic for disturbing a Master Mage on so important a day. Edgar ate it up – and it was also just enough exertion to keep him from drifting back into despondency.

That evening Edgar looked truly regal in his black robes trimmed in red velvet: three crimson bands on each sleeve and similar panels down the front of the robe. Only a few other mages were permitted the crimson trim, which signified admission to the Duke's inner circle. Other masters had to settle for a yellow or goldenrod colored trim: the color of one of the gifts of the Magi to the Infant Christ. Lesser mages, those not quite of Master status, wore only two stripes of velvet trim and no front panels. Junior mages or journeymen got just one band of velvet – but they were very proud of it. Apprentices wore a plain black robe, much like a monk's habit but without the scapular. Yet they, like all magic users, were permitted to wear hoods.

These black hoods, for magic users, were much more than simply a device to keep one's head and shoulders warm and dry. Just as each knight had his coat of arms emblazoned on his shield, so the insides of the magic users' hoods were striped and patterned with distinctive bright silk colors. Each mage had his (or in a few cases, her) family colors, or silks as they called them, lining his hood. Everyone in the family, everyone who co-lodged together and formed a miniscule co-lodge or college, even apprentices, were permitted to wear those colors until they attained journeyman status. At that point they could retain those silks, those college colors, and be forever a part of that particular family or school of magic; or they could devise their own colors. Any special exploit could be incorporated into or allow a modification of the design of the silks – but only with the Duke's permission and the guild's concurrence. Often, after a special heroic task, some symbol of that task became part of the magician's colors or a knight's (or even a cleric's) coat of arms.

In addition to the robes and hoods, any devices of special honor or medallions or trophies from battles with magical creatures might be worn for these ceremonial functions. For more ordinary occasions, mages wore a simple plain white or gray robe in which to work – or just a tunic & leggings, or even less than that – depending on the temperature, circumstances and type of spell work being done. In some smelting or device construction, or even more often in potion making, even these utility robes got in the way; so a leather apron over their boots and leggings was often all that protected both the masters and apprentices from sparks or any other ill effect. Spellcraft could be as dangerous as blacksmithing or any other craft – and often just as strenuous. Some of the younger apprentices didn't mind the hard labor, though, for it gave them muscles that helped them compete with the farmhands or the other smithy workers for the young ladies' attentions. The difference was that they had brains to go with the brawn.

Chapter 26
THE SOCIAL

That Monday evening was pleasantly cool after the damaging Saturday thunderstorms. The formality of the robes with the colorful hoods draped down their backs did not add any stifling to the party atmosphere – and they really looked sharp. Crowds of townsfolk would line the streets around the guildhall entrance to see the arrival of each master with his retinue of students, apprentices and journeymen. The storm debris had been swept away and the pink and white dogwoods and azaleas were in full bloom both in the courtyard of the guildhall and along the street in front of it. Music played from the open balcony over the Guildhall door, street vendors sold refreshments, and banners featuring all the silks in the guild lined the nearby streets. Even for those not permitted inside, it was the only place to be and be seen that evening.

Inside the guildhall, there was a truly magical feel. This was the one night a year when only practitioners of magic were allowed into the courtyard. Indeed, rather than hire more accomplished musicians, only bards who had studied a tiny bit of magic made up the quintet on the balcony. Because of that exclusiveness, a communality or family atmosphere reigned. Even those working as servants in black denim leggings and white tunics bringing drinks or passing around tidbits of food were first or second year students in the Guild's portion of the Cathedral School. There was a spirit of fraternity that evening that was more than just the bond of a common profession. It was more than their common reverence for true knowledge and understanding. Though there might be a few magic users among them who had multiple professions or responsibilities, that night they were all simply drawn together by a love for magic – and a delight-filled awe for the God who shared such power with His creatures.

Gmellin loved it. He enjoyed meeting everyone: the big guys as well as the middle management in the guild from the city and the surrounding countryside, and even the students. But he couldn't just party. This was an ice-breaker to allow the examiners and the examinees to get to know each other just enough so as to reduce any apprehensiveness on either side that might affect concentration – and thus also affect the efficacy of the spells on the test. Master Edgar had coached Gmellin to pick up on any reaction just slightly beyond ordinary affability in the other mages to whom he would introduce him. That might indicate who would be sitting on his board of examiners later that week. And once one knew the questioners, guessing the likely spell questions would be easy. That was essential, and was understood to be an aspect of the test (the one aspect with which the apprentice's master could legitimately help) so that each examinee could intuit what spell components he would need to gather in the few intervening days before the journeyman test.

One of the first guildmasters Gmellin met that evening was a favorite professor of his that he hadn't seen recently: Master Leo Ridgewalker. Gmellin remembered his class five years ago on True Essences and how it had set the tone so well for all the following courses on medicines, herbs, metallurgy and alchemy. The laboratory work among the alembics and retorts and crucibles of purifying materials added a graphic touch to the rather dry philosophical and mathematical classroom studies. It was in this class that he had been lab-partnered with Patrick. They found that they both really liked the awe-filled approach Master Leo had exuded whenever he spoke of seeing the hand of the Creator in all the elements of this world. That kind of appreciation had drawn these two students together and had left them both with very fond memories of Master Leo.

Tonight Gmellin thought he detected in him that sparkle of which Master Edgar had spoken. Yet he wasn't sure whether it was anything more than simply the delight at seeing an old friend again – coupled with Master Leo's almost leprechaun-like affability. Gmellin could have spent all evening just visiting with him alone, and had trouble pulling himself away from him. If only he could remember what kinds of spells Master Leo might ask. Perhaps Patrick, who was still too weak to have made a trip to the city even for this gathering, could help him remember.

Moving through the room Gmellin met several of the professors whose eyes betrayed no special twinkle, whose attitudes ranged from a genuine welcome to a newcomer, the future generation, to annoyance at having to put up with such juveniles. Paul the Master Juggler was friendly enough, but was more interested in a couple of other apprentices. Gmellin felt very relieved. Dexterity and balance were not his strong points, and everyone knew it. Fortunately, the whole appearance or illusion school of professors were the least likely to be on his journeyman board. After all, the guild really wanted their students to succeed, so they played to their strengths even while assuring a certain amount of breadth of magical discipline.

Master Roderick Hayfield gave him a polite nod, but nothing more. It was the least someone from the charm or influence school could do. And Master Edmund Paramenter of the Craft or design school just never made eye contact as he hurriedly brushed by both Gmellin and Edgar.

Close on Master Paramenter's heels was his co-worker, Master Roy Oysterman. He deliberately stopped to say hello to Edgar, yet seemed a bit more interested in visiting with Gmellin. Master Oysterman's construction techniques in both wood and stone bordered on sculpture: crafting an edifice or structure so that it seemed to have grown directly out of the landscape. His apprentices learned how to almost speak to the materials (and to Mother Nature) to weld them to the earth and seemingly pull the bridge or fortress or home directly out of the terrain. Though Master Paramenter could make an overall design for a city that would enable it to flow and live and function, Master Oysterman could use his brand of magical craftsmanship to bring each structure of that city to life. Gmellin had always been fascinated by his skills and appreciated that same reverential approach in his classes that he had seen in Master Leo – though those two masters seldom traveled in the same circles. Gmellin now suspected that they would both be on his board of examiners, and he was ready for them. Prayer would certainly help with these two, but he would still need to go over with Master Edgar the next morning what spells – and hence what components and what tools – he would need for each of them.

Since there would be four professors on his board, two from his school of Making Good Medicines or Magical Essence and one each from two of the other three schools, Gmellin still needed to determine who else from his school (since Edgar could not be part of his test panel) and who else from either the Influence school or the Illusion school might be chosen. Unfortunately, it was beginning to get late.

Master Phillip Treebark wandered into the periphery of their group, but couldn't seem to get through Edgar's admirers. He got pulled away before Gmellin could make eye contact. Master Joseph Warden, whose family had been city defenders for generations and whose older brothers still filled several of those posts, struck up a delightful conversation with Edgar about magical enhancement to natural defenses. Their lively discussion about the crafting of various magical weapons beyond the oft-requested magical swords kept Gmellin fascinated for a drink and a half – but betrayed no sparkle.

Master Peter Dubious from Dennistown, who had known Patrick's halfling adoptive parents and who had taught their class how to see through illusions, came by arguing most politely with Master Henry Ralston, who advocated that all physical reality was mere illusion to the mind of God. Even Edgar got drawn into the conversation, leaving all the students, apprentices and journeymen to attack the food table unrestrained by their masters. Again, Gmellin detected no sparkle from either of them, and time was running out. But at least his stomach had stopped growling.

The guild's Master Advocate, Nicholas Earthenglow, wandered by for no particular reason. As head of the charm or influence school, with red velvet stripes similar to Edgar's, he mentioned to both Gmellin and Edgar how pleased Sir Robert had been with the charm spell on his wolf. He teased rather playfully that Edgar might want to switch schools and join his. When Edgar rather humorously declined, he proposed the same thing to Gmellin – but with a decidedly different tone. Though there was no sparkle in his offer, there was a probing intensity that had the feel of a mind touch – something the valley mages called ESP. When Gmellin politely declined, blushing and stammering a bit as he bowed in deference to a master's offer, Master Nick departed with a half-smile on his lips. As soon as he was out of hearing range, Master Edgar confided to Gmellin that that half-smile was as close to a sparkle one would find in a lawyer. Gmellin now knew three of his examiners.

Subtle hints showed that the evening was winding down: the band's music became more and more restful; the food trays were not replenished and empty ones were removed; and no clean tankards were left near the keg. As the magicians took the hint to begin to depart, Master Phillip finally got to talk to Edgar. He seemed, however, slightly more interested in Gmellin. Phillip was a potion-maker with aboriginal ancestry. He could trace a portion of his family to the inhabitants of the region before the Celtic and Norse had crossed the ocean and mountains and settled in the Bluegrass and Knobs that the duke ruled. Edgar was polite to him, but felt his materials and methods were inelegant, too druid-like. Edgar didn't really want Gmellin's approach to magic contaminated by Phillip's rather grubby techniques and work-methods. He was one of those masters who thought nothing of doing hard labor along with his apprentices.

He seemed to relish the adventure of finding new medicine materials – often in the worst of places. His normal work clothing was indistinguishable from a common laborer or a servant and was often an embarrassment to those of the guild in the Duke's inner circle. The hard work at cauldron and forge, field and wilderness, had kept him thin and had given him a rugged complexion that was the antithesis of Edgar's. Still, Master Phillip had "cleaned up well" as the valley mages say and looked strikingly handsome in the black robe with golden stripes and his pine green and lake blue color-coded hood. As Phillip kept trying to engage Gmellin in conversation and Edgar kept trying to keep them apart, Gmellin was sure that a sparkle would have betrayed itself had Edgar permitted it. Now there were four.

As the first and second year students of the Guild's Magic Academy cleaned up the guild hall that night, Edgar and Gmellin almost floated home. Spells and potions can be bought and sold, but true camaraderie is priceless. Edgar slept soundly that night, allowing both Jules and Gmellin that same kind of relief.

Chapter 27
CLASSMATES SEARCH AND RESCUE

The next morning Edgar helped Gmellin sort out what he knew and what he needed to refresh from his studies. They also strategized about what spells might be encountered. Master Phillip would be sure to ask druid-like spells or potions, so some basic materials needed to be hunted down in the wilder portions of the valley. The construction techniques of Master Roy required tools readily available in the city, so Jules could arrange to have them delivered. Master Nick's test would most likely be resistance to charm – all interwoven into a legal argument or discussion. Gmellin's natural naiveté, combined with having been fore-warned and hence fore-armed, should see him through that ordeal. But Master Leo's classes were so long ago that he couldn't recall the things he had been tested on then. Gmellin explained to Edgar that he would just have to stop and visit with Patrick while he was in the valley gathering rustic components. Perhaps Patrick could help him recall the thrust of Master Leo's style of questioning. What Gmellin did not tell Edgar was the other reason for visiting with Patrick – the search for what was ailing Edgar and hence how to cure it.

Early that Tuesday afternoon, after assuring his wife that all would be well and that he would be home by nightfall the day after tomorrow, Gmellin rode northeast out of the duke's town. The white dogwoods formed a lacey under canopy all over the knobs, and marked the fullness of springtime in this "west of the mountains, west of the ocean" territory. As the pale green of the weeping willows and the carpet of Bluegrass on the Knoblands and Kumbarland plateau combined with the last of the yellow or purple or white crocuses, he thanked God for the sprouting of new life all around him. He enjoyed this first part of the trip in the pristine afternoon, and noticed a few groups of young druid matrons who had taken their school classes outside to enjoy their studies in this delightfully refreshing springtime environment. These groups reminded him of Meaghan and his kids, so he refocused his efforts, but only collected a few fresh components along the way. He arrived in Bloomfield by nightfall, just in time to send a note with the overnight courier to Dennistown. He needed to let Patrick know he'd be visiting with him the next day, after an evening of tracking glow dogs and a morning of gathering spell components from the meadow-lands.

Gmellin knew where the glow dogs' burrows were, but wanted to see them in action to verify the location for the next morning's search. Much like fireflies or glow worms, these miniature dogs had glands with the same material that would blink on and off as soon as darkness fell. They were fun to watch playing in the meadows, seemingly "blinking" from one spot to another. Yet tonight the fields were dark and empty, ominously so. Gmellin didn't dare ask anyone in the lodge what had happened to the glow dogs, for fear others would suspect him of scavenging to the point of hurting the dogs. He slept uneasily that night.

After prayers and an equally uneasy breakfast, Gmellin searched the edges of the larger meadows for traces of dog hair. Most folks would think it was from foxes or perhaps a ferret or weasel, but Gmellin could tell from the luster that it was from a glow dog. These hairs were much harder to find this year than in the past, and he wondered what had caused the population to decrease so dramatically. Where there used to be large complexes of burrows, there were only scorched remnants of the villages. That didn't make sense, since all the locals loved the meadow dogs or prairie dogs as the folks in the Markasandra delta and beyond called them. They didn't eat many crops and they really were very cute. They even kept away some harmful insect pests. Yet someone (or some mob) had deliberately burned them out. To Gmelin's trained eyes it looked as if the fire had been blast-like or magical in nature. Only an evil group would do that, and Gmellin couldn't imagine why they would bother. From the kind of growth in and around the charred spots, he estimated that it had happened last winter. Master Kresov was the only magic user gone from the guild at that time. He was also the only one whose reputation included the ability to conjure up magical (some said infernal) fire.

After an hour's journey further northwest, Gmellin came to the Fairfield meadowlands. These were areas where pegasi normally visited because of the good landing fields and the nearby orchards. The area was strangely silent. With great difficulty Gmellin found a Pegasus feather – or part of one, again with burn marks on it. It was in a rabbit's nest in a thicket by an orchard near one of the larger meadows. It also had been there since winter, and no more recent traces (or droppings) of the pegasi were evident anywhere. Yet Gmellin noticed that a few of the bones next to a piece of horse hoof were wing bones. Something was strangely wrong.

Unfortunately, Gmellin didn't know any druids or rangers in that part of the valley to ask about what might have happened. Finding one today would not be possible, for none of "those kind" would be willing to even speak to an unknown magic user – especially one that smelled of the duke's city. Perhaps Patrick might have heard something about this too. Then again, even if he did know something about it, he might not be able to talk about it – but he might know people who would be likely to know, and who might be willing to talk to him about it. Gmellin put this out of his mind till later, and contented himself with gathering up the last of the rarer herbs and berries and leaves likely to be needed for Master Philip's exam spells. He hoped he wouldn't find any more troubling evidence of magical vandalism – but feared he might.

The trip down to Dennistown was uneventful, with only a short stop in Springfield in late afternoon for something to drink — for both the horse and himself. After all, how could he let that poor animal drink all alone? He had wanted to stop as well at Silverhorn Tavern to visit with Cutter and Morning Sky who had always been very kind to him. He had heard about their children being wounded in the battle at Runningbear farm and wanted to check on them and offer any comfort he could; but he just didn't have the time to do so. Indeed, by the time he had stabled the horse in D-town, gotten a little something to eat and finally arrived at St. Steven's church, Patrick was already upstairs resting. He was about to leave and come back the next day when Father Roger, the older cleric, told him to go up to his room to visit anyway. He knew Patrick wasn't asleep, just very weak these last several days since the battle at the orphanage. Beyond saying mass and doing his prayers, he did very little but rest each day.

Gmellin bounded up the worn walnut staircase and knocked quickly on Patrick's door – eager to see his classmate. He heard slow, almost painful footsteps make their way across the room and stop at the door. When it opened laboriously, Patrick recognized him at once and reached out to give him the friendly bear hug then try to mess up his hair. Gmellin just stood there, shocked by the sight of his friend's pale and gaunt appearance. It seemed like a portion or dose of life had been drained from his body. Had Gmellin believed the old world tales of vampires, he would have thought he was looking at one of their victims.

Seeing Gmellin's reaction, Patrick added quickly: "I'm OK, just very weak still. Come on in and I'll tell you all about it."

Gmellin did just that, trying to help Patrick over to the small table and chairs. He backed off, however, when Patrick's gestures and demeanor made it very clear he did not want any kind of help. As Gmellin waited for Patrick to lead him across the room, slowly and hesitantly, almost as if he were rationing his energy, Gmellin had a chance to gaze around the room. Though the wood-stave walls had been given an inside coat of lathe and thick plaster, the walls and floor, indeed even the furnishings, were much rougher and more austere than the elegant abodes Master Edgar provided for his students and servants. In one corner of the tidy room was a single bed covered by the strange-looking quilt Patrick had used back in magic school days. Gmellin remembered the sad story: how his adopted halfling mother had taken the only item Patrick had from his real parents, the quilted infant blanket in his crib that had floated with him free of the drowning wagon, and had extended it into a full-sized quilt for him to take to school. He treasured it as much as he did even his chalice. A small, multicolored rag rug next to the bed softened the coldness of the dark-stained floorboards.

Also next to the bed was a drawered-chest made of that same rough-hewn oak. On one side hung a wooden bar with a homespun towel. On the varnished top were several pieces of ordinary grey pottery, such as a candle holder, wash basin & pitcher, and shaving mug. Next to those were Patrick's prayer book and a few other medicines. Across from the bed and under the only window was a small table and two chairs near the tiny fireplace. Except for the portion of the wall holding the crucifix, with a kneeling bench directly in front of it, most of the rest of the walls were covered with properly spaced pegs from which hung Patrick's clothing or equipment, like his buckskins and his belt and his bow saw. Above these various sets of pegs were a number of shelves for his few books and his many pieces of alchemical equipment.

The layout of the room reminded Gmellin of their student days where a room just like that would have housed two (or more) of them. As an ordained clergyman, Patrick was required to have his own room – just as monks or nuns were each required to have their own individual cells. And just like those monastic cells or student quarters, Patrick's was far from luxurious.

As Gmellin sat down across the table and looked more carefully at him, he noticed that Patrick's eyes were still bright green and his smile was still genuine. It was just as if his blood was low. By the time they had traded their stories about the past few months, Gmellin realized that that's exactly what the problem was. He also understood why Patrick's recovery was so slow: for his blood to still carry an antidotal character, it took longer for his body to synthesize each dram of blood.

"Have you tried healing spells?" Gmellin asked. "After all, you're certainly surrounded by clergy who could do them."

"Of course I did," Patrick replied with a trace of annoyance in his voice. "But you know how healing spells work. Short of an actual miracle – which I don't need, thank you – healing spells merely focus the body's energies on healing itself."

"Didn't it help?" asked Gmellin, not put off a bit by Patrick's attitude.

Patrick's indignation dissolved immediately in his class-mate's genuine concern, as he explained further: "No, they can't help."

"Huh?"

"Here's the whole story: That Sunday afternoon at the or-phanage everything was OK at first. Sure the blood-loss was debilitating; but my energy and composure had returned after the battle – especially since the orphans were safe and others were helping restore things there. I was getting ready to head back here for vespers, when suddenly it seemed like a trap door opened inside me and all my energy just drained out. It felt like an interior hemorrhage of blood, but no blood showed up. But it wasn't really blood that flowed; it was the life or power or energy "in" the blood that was suddenly gone. Kind of like the brain still functioning but the mind gone. You've seen that happen, haven't you?"

"Yeah, who hasn't had their thoughts just go blank?" Gmellin commented. "In fact, Meaghan claims my mind goes every time she needs me to remember something. There've even been times when I was so sick that I felt as weak as you describe – and sometimes it came on very suddenly too. Do you think it's some kind of evil influence – or as the Romans called it, 'influenza'?"

"No I don't think it was anything from the outside. I couldn't ask Heather how she felt because we really don't know what happened to her. We've not seen her since she teleported away with the bowl of fire and I'm really worried about her. Mike and Killian and Alex told me they all felt the same kind of thing come over them from the outside, almost an immense fatigue, starting in their weapon's hand. They recovered quicker because their blood is different. With me, it was all the energy in the blood gone – just gone.

"Well, that's why healing spells only did so much," Patrick continued. "Once the few wounds were healed, the strength or energy rebuilding needed the nutrients carried in by the blood supply. But I have less blood, and now it takes longer to reproduce."

"Now I understand," replied Gmellin; "but what about the other ways of repairing your blood? Have you been drinking lots of extra water?"

"Yeah, … sorta, …well, …no, not really."

"Well, are you passing enough water? You can tell by the color, you know."

Looking down at the floor – away from Gmellin – out of embarrassment, Patrick replied quietly, "I got to admit that I'm not." Then he straightened up, looked directly at Gmellin and smiled as he said: "But thanks to you I will."

"Hey, what are lab partners for?" asked Gmellin as Patrick went over to the pitcher and poured them each a big tankard of branch water while they continued visiting. That water, from the upper portions or "branches" of a creek where it springs out from between layers of limestone, was as clean and healthy as one could find – and it accelerated the healing process.

The evening sped by as the conversation went back and forth from old times and studies to how Meaghan and the family (and Edgar who was almost family) were doing to Gmellin's upcoming exams to a discussion and comparison of all the signs and experiences of magical attack Gmellin had found. Patrick remarked that the exams were easier for him because he had only spent one year as an apprentice. He hadn't intended to race through those practical studies so quickly, but his master, James Meaderer, had come down with an incurable disease halfway through the year. Because of Master James' extremely kindly reputation (he had developed a process for extracting sugar from beets – thereby developing a major valley industry) and because of Patrick's diligence, the other members of the guild helped tutor him and got him through that apprenticeship in just one year. From his deathbed Master James was able to bestow the journeyman bag and his "colors."

Gmellin noticed that melancholy look creeping over Patrick's face again, so he redirected the conversation back to the attacks on the pegasi, glow dogs and even the unicorns. From all the evidence, they slowly pieced together a picture of a shadowy conspiracy. Patrick knew first hand the evil Kresov had done and tried to do against the unicorn herd. From Gmellin's notes all fingers pointed to him and his assassin friends as the destroyers of the pegasi and glow dogs. But why? It didn't seem to be a harvesting of magical parts; nor was it chaotic cruelty. Patrick also reported that he remembered having heard about this from Kilian and Heather, but neither of them understood that senseless attack either. Why this deliberate destruction of groups of good magical land animals in each corner of the dukedom? Why would anyone go to that much trouble?

The revelations about George Paddlefoot and how the Fine Goods Company was really a front for selling harmful drugs to children had shocked everyone. When the story got back to D-town, there were rumors about the group who had left the bloodied linens and the broken alchemical equipment and the magic book, which had subsequently been entrusted to George. As Patrick and Gmellin continued relating the notes they each took to each other, a pattern began to emerge which had all the hallmarks of a major operation by the assassins' guild.

"George always seemed so nice. How were we to know it was only an act?" Gmellin wondered aloud. "Even the last time I saw him, when he brought Kresov's spell book for my Master to keep, he was most polite ... until ..."

"Until what?" asked Patrick, noticing a change in Gmellin.

"That's it! Jules & I have been worried about it and it was right under our noses. No wonder he's so troubled!" Gmellin exclaimed to himself, but aloud – like he had always done in school.

So Patrick slipped back into his old "lab partner" routine with him: "OK, now start from the beginning. What did George and Edgar do together?"

And Gmellin, slipping into that same set of memories, described in detail what had transpired on that Easter-week meeting he had unintentionally overheard. This time Patrick could make him describe explicitly the memories Gmellin had overlooked. The reluctance of Edgar to do what George requested yet his eagerness to "hold safely" Kresov's spell book pointed to blackmail. And Gmellin finally remembered that George had threatened to take that spell book to a cleric. The uneasiness Edgar had experienced at reading some of the spells and the horror at one in particular, to the point at dropping the spell book, marked it as evil. It was clear evidence that Kresov had become a sorcerer. George already knew this and was willing to keep quiet about it – for a price: the binding spell.

"Ah, now I understand the dilemma you tried to describe earlier when I had asked about Edgar," replied Patrick. "Weighing on his mind each day is what does he do with this evil spell book now?"

"Exactly!" interjected Gmellin. "Why couldn't we have realized it? He'll be in trouble now no matter what he does. And who can he even talk to about it? He can't give it to Kresov's sister Nadine (they both shuddered involuntarily at the mention of that name), for no one but you and your friends know for sure that Kresov is truly dead. And from Edgar's perspective, from what he knows now, how would he approach Kresov to give it back? Does he choose to join him and become an accomplice in Kersov's evil, or does he resist and become an assassin's target because now he knows too much?"

"But now with George and Kresov at least absent, he's less likely to be linked to either of those two villains, isn't he?" asked Patrick.

"Unless others in the assassins' guild – for whom George was a front man, as we now know – also knew about the severity of the spell book. They could have set Edgar up to be caught with it," Gmellin observed. "Why did he accept it?"

"To protect you and your children."

"How?"

"You just quoted George as threatening to reveal the spell book's contents to the underlings in the city. If word got out that Kresov had become diabolically contaminated, the shadow of suspicion would fall upon all magic users. Since it probably contains directions for the fire-blast potion used in the orphanage attack, how can Edgar explain how such a book got into his possession without implicating himself in at least some kind of complicity in the orphanage attack? Even though you and I know that Edgar is one of the few people in the entire dukedom that, had he known about the attack, would have tried to thwart it personally; a city mob will use any excuse to attack someone like him and plunder his house. Even magic defenses only go so far if the authorities don't back you up."

"You mean he was protecting Meaghan and the kids from a greedy mob by going along with the 'guild of terror' to hide the spell book?"

"You got it," Patrick replied, "and now he's put himself at greater risk."

"No!"

"Yeah, he's beholdin' to the guild, fearful of the authorities, and even afraid that Kresov might return. That's probably half of what's bothering him."

"What do you mean half?" Gmellin asked very apprehensively.

"Can't you see how the danger is now twice as great?" Patrick asked. "Does he turn it in to the magicians' guild to be held for Kresov – and possibly misused or leaked? Does he keep it and risk copying the good stuff in it, not sure that something evil might be hidden in those spells? Does he risk the temptation of wanting to 'examine just a little bit, out of curiosity' of any of those questionable spells? What happens if someone accuses him of something unrelated and it is found in his possession? Alternatively, does he destroy it – the whole book, the bad and the good – acting against every instinct we have of preserving all that is magical for posterity and even adding to it? And what if Kresov should return and want it back after it has been destroyed?"

"Can't we tell him Kresov's dead, so he can destroy it?"

"Yes, but then does he have to give it to Nadine as next of kin? How then does he explain to her what happened to Kresov – or how he knows about it? Right now the book is just sitting in his lab, eating into his conscience," Patrick concluded. "He's got to destroy it, but can he bring himself to do it?"

Just then the chimes in the church tower next door sounded Compline, and Gmellin knew he had to leave right then to get to the inn – lest they give his bedspace to someone else. He gave Patrick their normal "lab hug", right hand onto the other's right shoulder, as they recited the "nunc dimitis" together. Gmellin promised to ponder these issues overnight and visit after mass and breakfast the next morning, and bounded down the stairs. The older cleric gave him that "You know you're late" look as he let him out the rectory door, and Gmellin got to the inn just in time. He really enjoyed a pint of ale in front of the fire and listened to the visiting bard, William Coltan, or "Colt", play and sing some very haunting melodies from other parts of the Dukedom – or perhaps from even beyond its borders. Gmellin thought he remembered seeing him as part of the guild-hall special orchestra the night of the annual meeting, and felt even better. When Colt finished playing Gmellin bought him a stein of beer and they talked a bit. He had also noticed the absence of pegasi during the past year but had no clue as to why they had left. When Colt went into the back room for a supposedly friendly game of cards, Gmellin went upstairs to sleep. Having discovered the problem afflicting Edgar, Gmellin had his first really good night's sleep in a long time – and slept all the way through mass time that next morning.

Chapter 28
REMINISCENCES OF MAGIC RESEARCH

When Gmellin finally awoke, the rest of the bunk house section of the inn, a large upper room with 8 bunk beds, was empty. He eased himself down from a top bunk, stepping on one of the iron-banded cedar chests or footlockers to do so. He went out back and washed up at the pump uphill from the out-house. He regretted missing the left-over and cold porridge that was the inn's breakfast. After paying his bill, he headed back down the block to the red-stained rectory. Just as he got to the whitewashed front door, Fr. Roger who was leaving at that same time let him in with a "you're late again" look. Gmellin didn't say a word as he bounded up the stairs.

When he knocked on Patrick's door, he was greeted with "Come on in, Gmellin; I've got something special for you." As Gmellin let himself into the room and shut the door behind him, he noticed Patrick still sitting at the table – in vestments. Moreover, despite the bright daylight coming in the window, he had a candle burning.

Patrick immediately explained: "Since I didn't see you at mass or afterwards, I prayed for you and your exam Saturday, and for Edgar. I also kept Communion for you – if you haven't eaten anything since midnight."

Gmellin spontaneously raised his hands to heaven and exclaimed: "The Lord is kind and merciful! Not only did I oversleep mass, but I overslept breakfast too. He preserved me from food for His Communion! Thank you, Guardian Angel!"

Patrick immediately began the Communion preparation prayers: Pater Noster, Agnus Dei, and Domine, non sum dignus. Gmellin knelt next to his chair and received without Patrick's ever having to get up. Patrick even gave the final blessing without rising, so Gmellin knew how weak Patrick still was. Alex and Mike were completely recovered by now, and so was Kilian – though he kept milking his wounds for as much sympathy as he could get.

Patrick blew out the candle, folded up the white linen corporal and purificator from the table, stood up and slowly removed his vestments. Gmellin watched him carefully and reminded him about water consumption. Patrick looked up at him and smiled.

"We've got that covered," he said as he walked across the room to hang up his vestments. He set two tankards of water on the table on his way back. Gmellin stood by the extra chair and watched with delight as Patrick next brought over a tray with two mugs and a pot of tea, a couple of slices of home-made stone-ground wheat bread, some butter, cherry preserves, a small hunk of cheese and an apple. Pulling out his pocketknife Patrick explained: "I asked for a whole pot of tea this morning from our housekeeper. Since I had some extra mugs here, I figured I could share a bit o' breakfast with you while we talked."

"I can't eat your breakfast," replied Gmellin, feeling embarrassed and ashamed. "You need it much more than me."

"Says who?" replied Patrick, smiling angelically. "My blood can't process a full meal's worth of nourishment anyway. Besides, how many times have I shared your table? Now you're tellin' me that you're ashamed to share mine? And back when we were lab partners and the whole group of us didn't have a coin among us didn't we share whatever any of us could scrounge? So sit down and help me eat this before the tea gets cold.

Gmellin looked at Patrick, then at the food, and his stomach started growling.

Patrick pounced on the occasion to remark: "See, even your stomach agrees with me. You're outvoted. Come on 'n' sit

220

down and eat something with me," he pleaded. Then he began to say the short blessing.

Gmellin stood there with head bowed for the blessing, then slowly sat down and started to eat. Despite his embarrassment he really enjoyed the slice of bread, half the apple and half the cheese along with his mug of tea. When it was almost all gone, he mentioned: "Before I forget, I've got to ask you what you remember about Master Leo's course five years ago. He's gonna be on my board, and I just can't remember what he taught us."

"Do you realize how long ago that was?"

"Yeah, five years, like I just said," replied Gmellin between bites.

"And how much each of us has worked on since then?"

"Yeah," he replied again. "So?"

"And that we learned all this by memory because parchment or almost anything else to write on was too expensive? All we had were birch bark and these smooth pieces of black slate," said Patrick as he got up and gently pulled one of those slates from the shelf. Gmellin continued to remain unimpressed with Patrick's objections; and Patrick, after looking into Gmellin's trusting face, finally gave in and reached for a smooth wooden box that the monsignor had once kept tobacco in. "I don't remember back that far clearly either, but perhaps between the two of us we can reconstruct it. I still have my four sets of bark notes. I just hope they haven't faded or crumbled," he added as he pulled down the cedar box from the shelf above the window. "I remember when your oldest child shredded yours and even ate some of them."

The box was about a span square and four fingers deep, and would seal rather tightly. He raised the top very carefully and lifted the press (a flat piece of wood with a small wooden handle on it) off very gently. Looking at the contents listed underneath the lid of the box, he decided he needed sheaves near the bottom of the pile. So he pulled very carefully on the two ribbons running under the contents to retrieve the stack of flat, pale brown sheaves of birch bark. This "poor man's parchment" was dangerously fragile and so could not be bound together in any fashion – lest it crumble as one tried to turn a page. Each page was numbered very carefully in the upper right-hand corner by a short code: a letter for the school of magic (Medicine, Influence, Craft, and Appearance) followed by the semester of study (I, II, III, or IV) and a sequential page number. From the index Patrick had determined that Master Leo's class, # MI2-8, was about ten pages from the bottom of the box.

He carefully moved each bark sheaf off the top of the pile until he got to Master Leo's class: "Introduction to the Making of Good Medicines." Patrick read the notes aloud and Gmellin took his own notes on the slate. Slowly they both started to remember Master Leo's thrust and the pathways he used in his methods of reasoning and testing his theories and ideas.

Patrick started looking over the bark-notes and half concluded/half remembered aloud: "The thing that comes back to me most was that Master Leo's goal in his magical research and ongoing practice was a restoration of harmony."

"Yeah, now I'm beginning to remember, too," replied Gmellin almost whimsically. "Music. He was always referring back to the music we studied even way back in the druid schools – and how harmony occurs only when certain tones come together. It's coming back: those glasses filled to different levels with water or the pieces of metal that formed the sets of chimes. Remember when we had to do all those measurements of how many drops of water changed the tones in the glasses into and out of harmony?"

"Yes," replied Patrick, "but do you remember using the math, from our first year in the Cathedral School, to make the calculations to convert the water-glass chimes into just the right sizes of metal for chimes? And how we also had to learn how to purify the metals and (what did he call it?) 'alloy them?'

with special mixtures of metals to prevent corrosion – since corrosion would dull the harmony?"

"OK, OK" continued Gmellin, "yes I do remember. How I hated those math calculations! But I got to admit I liked what they showed us. I remember noticing the more subtle patterns in the harmonies, like overtones – which sometimes made other musical instruments (or even the room itself) vibrate or echo."

"Master Leo called it REVERBERATE" interjected Patrick. "You'd better use his term if you want to pass his test."

"OK, OK" continued Gmellin despite the interruption (which he nevertheless wrote down). "But those echoes – alright, reverberations – kept going even after the original tone had ceased. Didn't we even make special tubes that allowed those echoes – OK, reverberations – to keep going for a long, long time – almost indefinitely?"

"Yes, we did," replied Patrick, "and I just found the page with the calculations on it. Have you got a piece of bark handy to copy it? After all, he can't ask you to purify metal in the time you've got, but he can ask you to do the calculations and choose the best tubes for a chime set. As I remember, part of my exam was also with him. He wanted to see my calculations as well as hear the chime set I had put together for that specific size room. There was a harp at the other end of the room, and part of the test grade was how long the harp continued to resonate after the chimes I had put together had stopped. It was not an easy test!"

Gmellin sat there with his mouth partially open and a worried look on his face.

"Better bring a long measuring cord for the room as well as a few tools to put the set of chimes together," Patrick added. "Oh, and don't forget a file to 'sharpen' or clean the corrosion off any of the chime pieces. And check the density of the metal pieces because some that look the same size are thicker than others and therefore sound different. I even had one that was so corroded that it had some holes in it: looked like a piece of cheese."

"I understand," replied Gmellin with a muffled sigh as he looked up from taking notes. "I think I can do that. Was that the whole test?"

"You're kidding, right?" Patrick replied with a sideways glance, as Gmellin's confidence started to erode again. "That was only the first portion of the test. I also remember a segment on his philosophy and how spell components work to focus our thoughts and instincts together – with specifics on what components work for what spells. The final portion was a test on harmonizing a personal aura."

"Huh?"

"C'mon, you remember," Patrick pleaded. "Let me find it in the notes," he said encouragingly as he very gently moved bark pieces from one pile to another. "It starts with patterns of force at a distance, like magnetism or light – just like the harmony in music. Remember the reverberations. It's the pattern that makes a difference. Ah, here, I've found the three principles:

"Principle #1: There is a God-given structure in the universe, and a natural capacity in all matter for fitting into that structure.

"Principle #2: Humans can detect that structure by noticing the patterns – coordinating their instincts together with their conscious minds to do this.

"Principle #3: We can put parts of creation back into harmony – making it sing – by putting pieces into the right pattern.

"To me, this (putting things back in the right pattern) is the same capacity we have that lets us change a jungle into a garden or random notes into music."

"Does he mean that by simply noticing the patterns in creation we should be able to put order into chaos?"

"The first step is noticing; the second is doing it."

"Can we really do that?" asked Gmellin hesitantly.

"Of course," replied Patrick. "Just look at a pile of flour, some pieces of chocolate and nuts, two eggs, some sugar & a hunk of butter. It's not very appetizing. But when our house-keeper organizes those specific ingredients just right, and heats them just enough, they become chocolate chip cookies. Their aroma can call to people half a block away. They've got the same nutrition value as the ingredients, but there's something magical about those cookies."

"But that's just cooking," Gmellin interjected. "It can be done by anyone."

"Are you sure?" asked Patrick. "Even knowing the recipe or formula, some people are great cooks and others can't boil water."

"Right," murmured Gmellin. "That's why I still say simply finding the ordered pattern is a lot easier than trying to put creation back into that pattern."

"OK, I agree," admitted Patrick. "But that's why we studied all those dexterity skills like basket weaving or knot making. Look at the difference it makes between a random pile of wicker strips and the power of those same strips woven into a basket, or even a chair. It's using the right organization technique that adds immense strength to weak materials – and we have those weaving or connecting techniques. Don't you remember him going on and on about how we impose that order on creation, and so increase efficiency – like making strong rope out of weak strands of hemp. Just adding organization makes the whole greater than the sum of the parts. Humans have been doing this for centuries."

"But that's just craft, not magic," replied Gmellin, somewhat dejectedly.

"It's the same process, just done better – using our natural skills," Patrick argued. "It seems different only because as magicians we can pull more parts together (even non-material parts) and each effect augments the other."

"OK, OK, I remember," admitted Gmellin." I remember having to repeat over and over again that as magicians, we don't just take ordinary things like stones and make them depend on each other to make an archway. We take that special glow we feel about certain things and weave it together to enhance creation. But I'm still not sure I believe that. I always thought there was a magical streak or vein inside certain things, but Master Leo claims it's simply putting them back in the pattern – because all creation has a touch of magic in it. If we find the right spot, the magic in each portion enhances the other."

"Didn't you and he have a discussion about this idea after class once?" Patrick asked.

"Yeah, we argued for quite a while – even continued it at my house over supper despite Meaghan and the baby. You were there, too, remember? We had some rabbit stew – and you brought a carrot and some wild onions for it. Meaghan even made some cornbread."

"Yeah, I remember. The onions added a flavor that permeated the whole stew, but it didn't taste like onions. That's like the way magic works: it permeates and modifies the 'flavor' of all creation.

"That sounds more like God's grace than magic," observed Gmellin.

"You're right," replied Patrick. "Unfortunately when I made that comparison in theology school, that magic is much like God's grace, I was laughed out of the class. Even when I used references to the very first verses in the bible they shouted me down."

"Seminary students did that?" asked Gmellin. "They're supposed to be really nice people."

Patrick rolled his eyes, then replied "Even the professors were uneasy. Tell me if you think this is so bad an idea. You know the passage from Genesis 1:1. 'In the beginning God created the heavens and the earth. But the earth was waste and empty, and darkness covered the abyss.'"

"That abyss I described as chaos, a negative energy that destroys. They were OK with that, so far. Then I continued quoting:

"And the Spirit of God (ruah, which in Hebrew means both wind and spirit) hovered over (or blew over) the waters. And God said: 'Let there be light' and there was light."

"And the light I described as an upbuilding of creative energy coming from the power of the order imposed on the chaos by the 'ruah' or the Holy Spirit."

"Beautiful!" Gmellin exclaimed.

"But they got uneasy when I asked if that very uplifting, creative action of adding order to chaos isn't what magic claims to be. Their reply was that there is a difference between what is miraculous and what is merely magical. I asked them if that was a difference of 'kind' or simply a difference of 'degree'. They weren't real sure, but made it clear they didn't like this kind of discussion. I should have stopped there, but unfortunately I kept going.

"Foolishly, I continued quoting that same chapter in Genesis. Verse 27 asserts we each have a 'ruah' (spirit) made in the image and likeness of God. The second chapter of Genesis, verse seven, as well as the psalms and prophetic books frequently assert that it is breathed into us by God when we are born and returns to God when we die. We have that power of life itself and every aspect of life only because of God's image operating in us. I really see magic as the creative power of God the Holy Spirit working in us – just as miracles are that creative power working directly in Him. Our 'ruah' is the image of His."

"You mean even things like musical or literary inspiration are the action of God the Holy Spirit? Isn't that just our own skills acting in an 'inspired' way?" Gmellin asked. "Are you saying that finding those kinds of patterns with words that some call eloquence is really a magic-like process? Or that music is really just using strange sounds in a magical pattern that others call melody and harmony?"

"I'm saying it's all connected," Patrick replied. "Because our spirits are an image of the divine Spirit, our 'inspiring' creations are like finding wonderful patterns and restoring things into them. He, on the other hand, created the patterns. Magic, in its very essence, is an uplifting or creative energy. I believe it is different in kind from the original act of creation because we are too insignificant to create anything like the original patterns. But I believe our ongoing magical 'actions' differ only in degree from the 'inspiring' that the Holy Spirit does so often and so wonderfully. We put things back into His pattern, and sometimes even create little patterns (like poems) on our own."

Gmellin remained quietly pensive for a while, then he summarized: "So Master Leo sees the magic in the patterns – or really in the putting of things back into their patterns. Like most magicians I see a magical character or vein in matter, much like the veins of precious metals. But you see magic as our limited spirit or ruah, parallel to the unlimited power of God the Holy Spirit, doing creative or restorative things."

Patrick thought for a while, then offered: "Perhaps it's all three … It kinda' makes sense to me. How magic seems like part of us and yet beyond us; how like music it can be practiced to get proficient at it but never is truly under our control; how it can be misused or perverted into evil just as some of the angels were seduced by Lucifer. You've noticed, haven't you, how the more spirited we are the more our gatherings have a good feel or glow. Is that an energy or a force in creation? I think instead that it's our spirits connected with God the Holy Spirit. Matter is the container, which can be part of the pattern. Spirit or aura or ruah is where the magic really dwells. And the idea of 'awe in the presence of God' is a resonance in our soul with the Holy Spirit, the key that opens our 'container' to the magically creative actions of the Holy Spirit"

"But, according to Master Leo," Gmellin added, "even if we are not inspired we can all be trained to discover the patterns. I suspect he would see the re-setting of creation into those patterns as restoring the harmony in creation … making it 'hum' or sing."

"Now you're remembering!"

"Yeah, I also remember him using structures like pyramids to 'put things in order.' And I even remember him comparing 'spell components' to something like pegs that connect the woven spells to a part of the real world outside of the magic user. But I don't ever remember him relating it to God the Holy Spirit – or even mentioning the Holy Spirit."

"You said yourself that that was my suggestion, not his," Patrick admitted. "So you'd better not use that on your test."

"OK," replied Gmellin quietly, almost pensively as he wrote himself a few more notes. Then, after a few moments of silence he asked very tentatively: "Is the aura around humans and other living things the same as that ruah? The way you describe them they sure seem rather similar. And if we pull a connection with those auras into a pattern, then have we woven a creative essence that should function more profoundly in a focused way?"

"That touches the very essence of what magic is," replied Patrick rather softly and deliberately, almost as if he were afraid someone might overhear him. "Just how close aura is to ruah I don't know. I keep pondering and debating it within myself."

"I hear you," replied Gmellin just as quietly. "I'm not sure our kind of research can answer that question. It probably belongs in theology school discussions."

"The faculty didn't think so," Patrick replied dejectedly. "They threatened to expel me just for suggesting that we discuss that question. There was even talk of 'a bonfire in the courtyard' to purify the school from people with 'such ideas'."

"That sounds like a threat, perhaps even inciting an attack."

"No, all I had to do was keep quiet and they left me alone. You're the only other person I've ever told this to. They couldn't drive the idea out of me, though. But I was very careful to obey all the rules and I sincerely did all the prayers and studies and charitable works they required. I just … I just didn't ever find any friends or even acceptance there." With this last sentence Patrick's voice cracked and trailed off into silence. Gmellin looked away.

After a moment Patrick started up again: "Only recently did I realize what a real attack was. Two of them in a fortnight! Kresov and the huntsman and the assassins against the unicorns, George and the huntsman and the assassins against the orphanage and Alex's family's farm … If only we could figure out the connection…."

Patrick's voice trailed off into a whisper, just as it had often done in the lab when he was working on a problem and started calculating things inside himself. He didn't usually realize he was even doing that instead of continuing the direct discussion with Gmellin. Now it was Gmellin's turn to revert back to old tricks and bring Patrick's discussion back into audible terms.

"OK, classmate, reason outside, not inside," Gmellin started. "What did you notice?"

Patrick paused and seemed to grow much paler than earlier. He replied: "Only perhaps a pattern, or two: that the guild was apparently trying to destroy good creatures in all areas of the dukedom. The pegasi were in the Northwest, the glow dogs in the northeast, the unicorns in the southeast – and we stumbled in on it. But the common thread between both recent attacks was our little group: Kilian, Michael, Heather, Alex and me. The orphans and Cutter's family and Alex's family were just extra victims. In this second attack we were the ones marked for death."

"But why would the guild put a contract out on you?" Gmellin asked. "You're not influential or rich; and you're no threat to anyone – except yourself when you try to play wizard ball and trip over the ball."

Patrick shot him a "I didn't need to hear that" glance and then grew even more silent. "Maybe Kresov meant that much to them," he finally replied. "But they threw in Alex's family because the guild hates the clans. And they used the orphans to gather the others to a place where they knew I would be but which I wouldn't suspect as being dangerous. None of us would be watchin' for trouble there. It also wouldn't have any normal protection because it wouldn't need any. Nobody attacks orphans."

"This also means that the guild had ways of insuring that Michael and Kilian and Heather would be sent there," added Gmellin. "Their influence network must be exceptionally strong."

"Yes, but they influenced through good people," Patrick replied; "and some of their naturally good instincts and actions interfered with the guild's evil plans. Even George still had to behave pretty well. He had to work with and through good people. Little did he realize that Cutter & Rips and all the others might put something together & warn us in time, or that Weed would notice the poison or that Heather would teleport away to save others. Evil can corrupt, but it often doesn't corrupt thoroughly enough to make its plans succeed completely."

"But you're telling me also that it keeps trying to corrupt – or at least coerce," Gmellin observed. "With Kresov gone – which you took care of very nicely, classmate, thank you – the assassin's guild had to get magic help somewhere else. So they blackmailed my master into helping them. If he had not, and if the spell book got out, there would have been a riot."

"Of course," Patrick added, "and with disastrous results from mobs of locals. But now what does he do with the spell book?"

"Looks like he's got to destroy it."

"Sounds like you've got your answer to that dilemma," replied Patrick. "Just make sure he destroys it in the right way."

"What do you mean?"

"Well, if magic items have some special portion of the pattern of creation in them, and if it's creator chooses to weave in some evil, the evil in a magic item might make one or another portion of the pattern 'unravel' or break somehow. I remember something about these things, but it may have been in theology school rather than in magic school. Please check it out in the magic library in the guildhall."

"OK, I will."

"I think now you also remember enough of what Master Leo taught that you can discuss it intelligibly."

"The only thing uncertain is how much skill it will take to weave it."

"Partner, you'll be fine!" reassured Patrick. "Remember your success with Sir Wolf? You can understand and you can function with the best of us."

"Thanks. You don't know how much your saying that means to me ..."

Just then the Angelus chimes rang, signaling the prayers that began the lunch hour. Patrick and Gmellin stood for the prayers: "Regina Coeli" rather than "Angelus" during paschal time. When they had finished, Gmellin took his leave with: "I'll let you know the results by courier – and add your Meaderer's colors to Edgar's on my hood if I get the journeyman bag. You just take care of yourself. Remember, the assassin guild's still out there and you're still a target."

Gmellin reached out and messed up Patrick's hair, then gave him a big clan-style bear hug. As he headed for the door Patrick called after him: "Give Meaghan and the kids a hug for me. My prayers will be with you during the exam."

Gmellin raced down the stairs but stopped to ask Fr. Roger's blessing as he left the rectory. The journey home among the flowering dogwoods was just as delightful as the one coming out, and Gmellin was in much better spirits with his two quests complete. Even the horse could sense his more confident attitude. Meaghan and the four kids were very happy to see him, and Jules eagerly helped him secure the special spell components. While doing that, of course, they had the chance to whisper together what he had found out about how to heal Edgar. Here and there on Friday, even though they were just barely able to snatch a moment or two between exam preparations, they began to develop the beginnings of a strategy for healing him.

Chapter 29
THE JOURNEYMAN MAGE JOURNEY

Gmellin breezed through the exams. Master Roy had him make a sand sculpture of a watchtower that appeared to be just a stone outcropping of a nearby hillside. Master Philip wanted a couple of exotic potions, and Gmellin remarkably had all the materials at hand. The discussion with Master Nick left that teacher as frustrated as when he couldn't quite intimidate witnesses who were too naïve to catch the confusion he was trying to sow. Finally, Master Leo was so delighted that Gmellin had remembered so much – and had thought through the calculations to use for chimes and harp harmony – that he only had him lull some toddlers to sleep. It was an easy spell and he finished the test long before the vesper chimes signaled the end of the test period – as well as the end of the workweek and the beginning of the Sabbath rest.

That evening the judges compared exam scores and the overall reputation of each apprentice. They had to decide not only whether they thought each candidate was capable of handling magic, but whether they really wanted them in their guild: could they truly fit in? A few years ago when they debated admitting Patrick Elfkind, his aspiration toward priestly ordination raised a number of concerns about the two kinds of magic contaminating each other. Fortunately, magic user-clerics had some precedent (among those of partial elven stock only), but there had not been one in the valley in over a century. Because so many of the guild masters had helped tutor Patrick so that his master, James Meaderer, could bestow the silks and journeyman bag before he died, those concerns were shelved.

No harm had come of their decision: Patrick had caused no troubles. He kept a respectful distance from other guild members and had generally been very quiet about magic during his seminary years. He rarely visited the guild hall commons and only used the library occasionally. His attitude and demeanor were as humble as the newest apprentice, which seemed fitting for someone who was after all, as they say, "from the valley." The senior guildmasters were pleased that the bishop had "known what was proper to do" by assigning him outside the Duke's city once he was ordained.

Gmellin was a more difficult case because he was decidedly more boisterous. Not only was he from a clan family, he was too vivacious and socially naïve to ever become a master in the guild. However, Edgar, their ducal council member, really wanted him to stay and clearly worked well with him. His test scores were excellent, but his attitude was just not mature (some would say cynical) enough for urban life. He was simply too trusting and friendly. But because of the test scores and Edgar's status, the guildmasters almost had to admit him – though they secretly hoped he'd eventually settle elsewhere. They gave Edgar the good news shortly after sunset, so that he could prepare the journeyman bag and the silks for the investiture ceremony the next day.

After the last mass on Sunday the bishop did not leave the altar area but waited in full white and gold paschal-time vestments with miter and crosier to bless the bags and silks. Three brown leather bags approximately a cubit by a half-cubit in size were carried up to the altar by the masters. Each had the long black magic-user hoods draped over them in such a way that the silk linings were displayed for all to see. One was peacock blue and jonquil yellow and belonged to Dean Whitcomb, the noble lineage apprentice of Master Nicholas Earthenglow. All his aristocratic relatives were there to cheer him on – but most politely, of course. The second was equally elegant in the papal colors of white and gold, but crossed diagonally by a crimson stripe – signifying the Fideles family whose founding ancestor had shed some blood in defense of the pope many generations ago. Their son, Augustine, had been the smartest member of their class and was an honor and delight to that faithful family whose scions were now engaged more in merchandizing than in guarding. The third one was Gmellin's. True to his promise to Patrick, he had added the pale wheat and beet red colors from Master James Meaderer to the Royal blue and Scarlet of Edgar's college colors. But as the two reds were so close in hue, ducal heraldry required merging them into one common stripe. The result was a royal blue stripe and a bright red stripe separated by a beige stripe so pale that it looked almost white from a distance.

The cooperation between the clerics and magic users from their work together on the rings of alignment reflection showed in the obvious joy the bishop expressed in blessing these bags this year. His exuberance and glee in sprinkling the holy water on the bags, the new journeyman mages, and even on their relatives would have been considered overzealous by the nobility there had one of the inductees not been one of their own. After the bestowing of the hoods on the new journeymen mages and the beautiful final blessing to the mass, the bags were carried in festive procession to the guildhall and ceremoniously bestowed by their sponsors.

In the short reception that followed, Nadine tried to pit each new journeyman or junior mage against each other by comparing their families. When she started making subtle insults about Gmellin's clan family, she was cut short by his youngest daughter. That toddler just happened to escape from her mother, stumble into Nadine, and spill milk all down the bottom front of her Duke's council gown. It got all over the black lace and the red velvet trim. Meaghan ran up and apologized so profusely, all while wiping off the milk, that her "moment" was ruined. Edgar suspected that Meaghan had engineered the whole episode and was secretly delighted at her resourcefulness. Both he and Gmellin were very uneasy about the look Nadine gave Meaghan and the kids. They remained alert for trouble on the way home. Edgar even hired an extra outside guard for that whole next week.

That evening Junior Mage Lawrence Gmellin and his wife Meaghan entertained Edgar and Jules for supper. When Meaghan left to put the kids to bed, the three gentlemen immediately discussed her safety. None of them trusted Nadine. They quickly concluded that Gmellin needed to take his family out of the city for good. Returning to the bear-clan lands, or going even further east into the mountains seemed to be the safest of options. They would remain in Edgar's guarded compound and leave as soon as they could pack.

With that issue settled, Gmellin and Jules brought up the spell book. Each described to Edgar how they had noticed its attacks on him and his preoccupation with it. Gmellin then described the results of his trip, and what he knew of Kresov's fate. Knowing that Kresov would never return to claim it, the pathway was open for the book's destruction. Edgar hesitated, but finally agreed to destroy it; and Jules promised to safeguard it until then. He also promised to keep it away from Edgar and help in its destruction if necessary. A brightness, like a breath of relief, seemed to dawn on Edgar. Apparently just having someone else know of his burden – and perhaps the decision as to what to do about it – had removed the weight and gloom hovering over him. Edgar promised most profoundly that he really would destroy the book – without ever opening it again. But when Gmellin mentioned Patrick's warning that something that evil had to be destroyed with certain safeguards, Edgar became a bit indignant, replying appropriately:

"Remember, Junior Mage, that I am a master in the guild. I'm certain you're not questioning my knowledge of how to destroy a magic item or my ability to do it properly, are you?"

"Oh, no, Master," Gmellin replied; "I was simply passing on a message I had promised to deliver."

"Well, you may tell your rustic junior mage friend that I believe I know what I'm doing," Edgar replied as he somewhat gleefully watched both Gmellin and Jules squirm. With that, Edgar's wry smile broadened, and for the first time since Easter week he really, truly relaxed. The three of them lingered over desert and drinks, savoring the bittersweet moment. With the ending of Gmellin's apprenticeship, and with the danger to Meaghan, this joyful time together would be their last.

After a few days of packing in the well-guarded house, Meaghan, Gmellin and all four of the kids bid an extremely fond farewell to Edgar and Jules. Jules very properly shook hands with each of the kids, but Edgar bent down to their size and hugged each like his heart would break. To each of the kids he had been so much like a grandparent that they couldn't imagine leaving him. Still, they had to go.

Edgar and Jules and two guards with crossbows escorted their wagon safely out of the city and promised Gmellin that they would take care of "the burden" soon. The family stopped at Silverhorn Tavern where the kids played with Ricky and Lee and Anna while he and Meaghan visited with Cutter and Sky. They got up very early that next morning, Ascension Thursday, and went to D-town for mass which Patrick said in St. Steven's church. Afterwards Fr. Roger invited them all over for breakfast and let the kids share stories with old Monsignor Kieley. Meanwhile he swapped some recipes with Meaghan and admired with her how well the purple rhododendron were starting to bloom. This gave Gmellin and Patrick time to take a short walk around the church and update each other.

Patrick seemed much stronger, and confided that the extra water intake had helped a lot. Gmellin thanked Patrick in turn for the help with his exam preparations – and for helping him find the key to bringing Edgar back to functional reality.

"Jules will help guard the book and even help him destroy it," he reported.

"What did you discover about the safeguards needed in that destruction process?" Patrick asked. "I'm sorry I couldn't give you clearer references for looking it up in the library."

"Sadly, because of the danger to Meaghan and the kids, I didn't have any chance to research it," Gmellin replied as he looked down at his boots. "But I'm sure a Master Mage like Edgar would know what kind of risk it posed and how to minimize it."

Patrick put his face in his hands as he shook his head, then looked back up at Gmellin and said: "Minimizing a risk won't work. Something that evil needs an absolute guarantee of protection against disrupting the patterns that God set up to safeguard us. At the very least, surrounding it with holy water and blessing the fire that burns it – all while praying fervently for assistance – is absolutely necessary. With something as evil as you describe, having a senior cleric there with a brace of paladins would be a minimum requirement. Do you think Edgar will do this – and more?"

"As elegant and precise as he is, I'm sure he knows what to do," replied Gmellin. "And as cautious and careful as he is, I'm confident he'll get the help he needs to do it."

Patrick seemed only slightly reassured by that assessment. He promised to find out whatever he could about destruction of magical objects and offer his help to Edgar. As the family left for Gmellin's ancestral Bear-paw homestead, just beyond Runningbear farm, for a few days before heading further east, all the clerics there gave them a blessing and asked the angels to watch over them on their trip.

The blessing worked. Nadine decided it was revenge enough to drive a clan family out of the Duke's city and deprive Edgar of both a trusted co-worker and foster grandchildren. And she delighted in the fact that she was able to accomplish this by fear alone; she didn't have to do any action

240

at all to get the results she wanted. Moreover, at this time any outright attack would still be too dangerous for the guild. It was all part of the game she played – in the Duke's Council Chamber, in the city streets, and in the lives of the inhabitants who feared her rather than respected her. She would content herself for the moment with concentrating on protecting her guild and completing the Fishbowl Project. Inside she still seethed and brooded, and waited for her chance. But by the time she came out to spread her verbal poison at the orphanage rededication on Pentecost Sunday, Gmellin and his family were already enroute over the Eastern mountains to begin his new life as a journeyman mage.

....

The groups of clansmen finished repairing the orphanage by Ascension and even helped hoe the sprouting corn and vegetables and potatoes – though the spring rains were spotty and sporadic at best. Yet nature itself seemed to reflect the growing trust and civic pride among the clans. It was symbolized by the billows of wild roses reddening the edges of the roadways in honor of the fast-approaching feast of the Great and Holy Spirit. On that Pentecost the orphanage was crowded with paladins and barbarians, magic users and clerics as the bishop himself solemnly rededicated it with incense and holy water to the cheers of all. He also blessed all who had helped protect the orphans or rebuilt the compound – a special individual blessing for each and every clan, and for their lands. Each clan also got individual words of praise from the Duke, of course. His arts councilor, Nadine, "had" to be there to do the awards part of the ceremony at the reception afterwards, but she seemed less than pleased to have any part in it. Her remarks were much less joy-filled than the rest of the Duke's entourage; and she was decidedly displeased that Patrick and Kilian had skipped her part of the presentation or that the orphans were a noisy distraction.

No one ever heard about the unicorns: they remained a druid's legend, though none of the druidic leadership had ever seen one either. During paschal time Kilian also was rarely seen and didn't even try to repay the owners of the ponies he had rented. The paladins took care of it all – helped by the clans in finding the owners. Kilian spent most of his time away southeast of Gunner Mountain, except for his visits each Saturday morning with Patrick to see how he was recuperating. By the time Pentecost arrived, both were recovered enough to attend the orphanage rededication; but they stayed for only a portion of the ceremony. They went out back and prayed in their own little and quiet way to personally thank the Great Holy Spirit who had kept watching over them. Rather than go back in for the reception party and Nadine's speeches and awards ceremony, they took a walk south at Patrick's still slow and weakened pace. They eventually reached Fogle Creek and followed it a little way down to a quiet glen long before it joins the Markasandra River. There, near a large, very old dogwood tree, a yellow and white rose bush had recently been planted on a new little mound of dirt. They both prayed again and cried a little and said good-by to someone. As they walked home slowly, neither of them noticed how brilliantly the sun set behind them. Those who had looked at the sunset from Dennistown claimed they saw a white speck flying among the purplish clouds into that red-gold sunset. Since it was Pentecost evening, most observers – Christian and druid alike – believed that speck had been a special white dove who had visited them that day, just as He, the Great and Holy Spirit, had done so many centuries earlier and far to the east across the legendary great water. But Kilian and Patrick knew who it was when they heard the account; and they knew they had said their last good-by to Heather. They named the rose bush "angel tears."

Though the weather during that whole paschal season had been wilder than usual, it had still been calm enough to get all the crops planted. At the orphanage rededication the bishop had prayed for a good harvest, and his blessing seemed to off-set the effects of the weather control spell – for a while. Everyone at the rededication hoped that his prayer would be heard: everyone, that is, except the Nightshade – whose tongue kept insinuating veiled insults into even the sentiments of joy at the reception.

The Nightshade hated the paschal season and especially the month of May. Not only were the sentiments of romantic love springing up fresh and new loathsome to her, the devotions to Mary, the mother of Jesus, made her angry. Even though she appreciated her own mother's memory, the idea of a gentle and kind woman, meek and always in the background yet staying to the end even beneath a cross, was the antithesis of what she intended to be. She wanted to be strong and dominant, perhaps even feared – and never loved. May devotions were the exact opposite of everything she tried to push. Now, because of the failure of this second strike force, she had to remain in the background herself. Through this difficult time she hid her true intentions, and her people, well. As the paschal moon gave way to the strawberry moon, she began plotting her revenge – more carefully this time. Inside, like a thunderstorm on a sultry summer afternoon, she still seethed and brooded.

Chapter 30
DIABOLICAL INTERLUDE

Not far, and yet very far below them, other things had been happening. These events had started much further away, in the realm of eternal pain: the silent, empty, burning, angry darkness. In that tormented realm where confusion holds sway over the eddies in the never-ending stream of hatred, this paschal time had been worse than any other. One of their scouts was missing. Over the years, over the uncounted centuries they knew it could happen; but it never had, until now. Normally the ups and downs of human events were viewed simply as the antics of their grazing herd: intelligent and free-willed cattle to be fattened on indulgence, yielding a harvest of regret and recrimination to be savored at the tables of hell.

The local herd had been doing well. One of their magic users had been seduced into sorcery and been rewarded by being given a diabolical friend. These are called by many names in various cultures: imps, gremlins, poltergeists, haunts, shadows, etc. Magic users call them quarterghosts. They are parasites, former magicians caught earlier in the same trap, who season their hosts by spreading the addiction of sloth and self indulgence both within their hosts and into their guild. With magic users (and more rarely with clerics, though the flavor is better) portion after portion of the conscience is darkened, its moral sensitivity and outrage against each type of evil traded for physical power. Through deliberate procurement of more and more horrid spell components, the magic user begins weaving his own evil net around himself.

The only concern the masters would have was the untimely death of their magic user before total depravity could be achieved. It was much like removing a succulent dish from the oven too soon. The net of evil would be incomplete: the more broken spaces, the greater the risk of repentance. True, there was always some risk of it short of the final battle that the mortals call the final or general judgment at the end of the world; but once a being as powerful and proud as a sorcerer became a part of hell, hatred would make each of them want to recruit others – and their human experience made them very good at it.

Whenever a quarterghost was sent forth from the icy inferno to be the familiar companion of a magic user who had been lured into such a diabolical bargain, it had always been trackable from below by the point of emptiness in the hurting world. The song of harmony in all matter, painful to those in hell, was squelched wherever the quarterghost touched its evil foot. But now that point of blight had been erased, neutralized, almost (dare they admit it) healed. The sorcerer and two groups of assassins were among them, but they had been harvested much too soon: mere ordinary dishes for the tables of Satan's court banquet. Their infection hadn't spread sufficiently.

Their entire department was outraged. This had to be stopped! Not only was the spread of infection blocked; but a scout had been taken from them and neutralized, possibly even given a chance to start over and choose again to turn away. Though Satan's crops in the rest of the world were harvesting nicely as the Black Death ravaged Europe and devastated in particular the clergy who were attending the dying, this setback in the corruption of magic was not something they could tolerate. Lilith, the dark mother, would look into it herself – lest Satan replace her with one of his other lieutenants.

But getting there to investigate was the problem. She knew her chances of getting through were small in spite of – in fact, because of – her great power. Quarterghosts, because they had once been human, could come and go between earth and hell – with some difficulty. It depended on the permeability of the area and the atmosphere. The dark of the moon and its being called by certain spells or anti-prayers made passage possible.

But human attempts at direct summoning and their deluded sense of enslaving a true devil only brought onto earth a projection or a tiny portion of a diabolic essence. For true entrance, because of the thoroughly disrupting effect so intense an evil would have on the freedom of moral creatures, direct divine permission was needed – or a human rupture of the divine protection of His earth.

That rupture involved the deliberate destruction of some powerful magic item (evil, of course) without a (prayer) blockage by the humans involved, and at a time and place where the earth itself and the collective moral fabric of those on it was weak. Rarely could this happen, for anyone destroying an evil item, sending it back to their realm, and thereby opening a passageway in one direction, usually blocked their coming through in the other direction by the intention of removing an evil from the earth. Conversely, someone wanting to encourage evil would be unlikely to be destroying an evil object; he would use it to increase his own power.

Moreover, the earth itself and the community inhabiting that portion near a rupture needed to have their unconscious guard down: be distracted by petty sins and corruptions of their own. For whatever reasons He may have, the Almighty and Good One, whom Satan and Lilith and all his minions fear, would abide by His own designs and not keep out what His stupid and negligent creatures let in. Still, it was highly unlikely that the dark mother would find an opening to ooze through – even in the battles around Constantinople. Yet, with a perseverance fueled by hate and the pervasiveness of immateriality, she spread herself under the likely points where she hoped the protection fabric of surface dwellers might rupture. There she waited.

Made in the USA
Columbia, SC
18 September 2022

67425292R00135